'Take off your clothes,' he said.

As he watched, she squirmed before his unflinching gaze, and began to peel off her clothing. First she kicked off her shoes, and then pulled up under her skirt and unhooked her nylons. She pulled the sheer hosiery down her long legs, revealing full thighs and rounded calves. First one leg and then the other until they were naked, open to his eyes, young, firm, fresh and inviting.

'Keep going, little editor,' he rasped. 'Take off all your clothes and show your boss what a hot little number you are.'

Also available from Headline

Hot Type

Anonymous

HEADLINE

First published in Great Britain in 1992
by HEADLINE BOOK PUBLISHING PLC

10 9 8 7 6 5 4 3 2 1

ISBN 0 7472 3768 9

Typeset by Medcalf Type Ltd, Bicester, Oxon

Printed and bound in Great Britain by
HarperCollins Manufacturing, Glasgow

HEADLINE BOOK PUBLISHING PLC
Headline House
79 Great Titchfield Street
London W1P 7FN

To
Betty
Beverly
Frances
Linda
Margo
Pat
Sheryl
Uta
. . . for helping to create the legend

‘Men and women are not different genders of the same species, but the same gender of different species.’

Mark Eisenstein

ONE

The conference was staggering on into its third hour. Joan was bored. Almost unable to stifle her yawns, she screamed inside herself as the voices droned on. As always, when meetings reached this point, she began to look around for a sympathetic eye, a reassuring smile, to tell her that all hope for humanity had not been abandoned to the necessities of the business machine. But most of the people there were men she barely knew, salesmen who had travelled to New York City for a week of gatherings just like this one.

She glanced over the faces. Lou Morris, president of Centaur Publishing, was listening to a complicated report from the midwest representative. He was leaning back in his chair, his hands folded over his chest, and staring at the ceiling. She would find no support there. Jack, Centaur's top salesman, and one of the few of that breed that Joan could relate to, was drawing elaborate doodles on his scratch pad. Joan continued to scan the room, and was brought up short when she found herself staring into the eyes of Margaret Hayes, Lou's executive secretary, a tall, cool career woman who rarely spoke except by way of giving orders. Now, surprisingly, she narrowed her eyes and insinuated her gaze into Joan's, indicating not only that she knew what Joan had been feeling, but that she empathized with her.

Joan looked away hurriedly. It was perhaps the sixth or seventh time within the past month that she had been captured by the other's awareness. Something about the experience frightened her, although Margaret had not done or said a thing which could in any way be considered threatening. Rather, it was some sense within herself that responded peculiarly to Margaret's attentions. She had thought about it, but had not been able to come to any conclusions about the matter.

She raised her eyes from the table top, and glanced back in Margaret's direction. The eyes were still there, looking back at her. This time they held a glint of amusement, as though the two of them were partners in some naughty secret. As Joan felt herself pulled into Margaret's gaze, getting lost in the other's grey-green eyes, fascinated by the highlights in her golden hair which was swept back severely and wrapped in a tight bun, Margaret slowly and deliberately ran the tip of her tongue along the entire length of her full lower lip, moistening the soft maroon flesh in such a way that it glowed. Then, to Joan's astonishment, she wrinkled her nose impishly and smiled.

It was one of those moments of exquisite uncertainty. On one level, Joan took the gesture as an extension of the comment on the sterility of the proceedings; but on another it seemed to contain a provocation that had Joan's breath sticking in her chest. Joan let her gaze fall from Margaret's face to her body. Margaret was dressed in a black knit turtleneck shirt that gripped every square inch of her torso. Her high, aggressive breasts bulged shamelessly forward, climaxing in half-dollar nipples that seemed blatant on such a sophisticated woman. Seeing Joan examining her breasts, Margaret twisted in her seat so that the twin mounds shifted dramatically, jiggling slightly with the movement. The movement was an unmistakable sexual signal, but for a few seconds, Joan couldn't understand why it was being sent to her. And when it did become clear, she looked away in confusion.

'And that's it, Lou,' the representative from Chicago was saying. 'We're doing so badly that we wouldn't be operating now if we didn't have support from Zenith.'

The company had been in a decline for over a year. For a long time prior to that, it had succeeded as one of the few sources of literature pornography in the nation. But with the sudden upsurge of smut since the late nineteen-sixties, it was being squeezed out on two ends. On one side were the West Coast sex factories, run mostly by young people who knew how to circumvent the guilt-and-dirt syndrome which had permeated all erotic writing in America since the first copies of *Fanny Hill* had been secretly printed a century earlier. The California atmosphere provided a natural base for orgiastic attitudes, and books, magazines, and movies had been pouring out from Los Angeles in tidal-wave proportions. On the other side was the constant pressure from federal and state authorities, forcing Centaur to tone down its output. Since Lou didn't have the volume or exuberance or the shoe-string overheads of his California competitors, he had been pushed out of the market until now his back was to the wall and Zenith, the distributing company which owned Centaur, among a score of other properties, was demanding a radical change.

Lou shifted his weight and his chair came back to the upright; he leaned forward with his elbows on the table. His face was drawn. It was obvious he would have preferred being anywhere else but at that spot at that time. Joan, who was fond of him, looked away; she could see the mortality in his eyes and it disturbed her. She glanced at Margaret again, but the other woman was staring out the window, at the thin, grey New York sky. Across the street, in a building almost exactly like the one they sat in, a hundred windows exhibited scenes not unlike the one now going on at Centaur.

'It's extraordinary,' Joan thought, 'there must be a million meetings like this going on in the city alone. And millions more in the nation, and all over the world. What an enormous waste of time.'

'Joan.' It was Lou's voice. She turned back to him. Her presence at the meeting was purely formal. As a copy editor she had nothing to do with policy, but Lou had wanted her there. 'Maybe you can add something from a fresh perspective,' he had told her.

'Would you get us some coffee?' he asked.

She suppressed the impulse to make a face at him. She resented doing what she considered maid duty, but there was no gracious way to refuse. Besides, her relationship with Lou was more complex than a simple employer-employee bond. Almost a year earlier, ragged and unhappy, her savings gone, working as a night-waitress in Bickford's, her dream of becoming an actress mocked by the realities of the theatre scene in the city, she had decided to find a regular office job and pull her life together. She couldn't even consider going back to Arkansas, which she had left, a diploma in hand certifying that she had graduated college as a drama major, to conquer Broadway. She grimaced now when she thought of how naive she had been. Two years of workshops and making the rounds had taught her much about life and what went on behind the productions. She had done the customary things, getting odd jobs, having an affair, dabbling in promiscuity, seeing a therapist, and gradually come to love New York. Then, sadly aware that she would not make her way on the stage, she was forced to consider ways of earning a living. Through a friend of a friend, she got an interview with Lou, who was looking for a copy editor.

She remembered the afternoon clearly, one of those false spring days in March when the city seems in the throes of rebirth. She was then almost twenty-four and had forgotten how attractive she was, since she had had her ego badly bruised by the refusals at off-Broadway and Broadway tryouts. She was five-and-a-half feet tall, thin, and with a look of intensity that sometimes flared into rich beauty. Her features were standard American, that is to say, she was pretty enough to have served as a model in a Pepsi ad, with a long straight nose, a wide generous mouth, and deep black eyes. Her auburn hair, with glints of red, came down almost to her hips in a shimmering shower of silky invitation. Ordinarily, she wore it in a pony tail, and let it hang loose only when she went to bed. Her legs were slightly longer than was strictly proportional, two tapering stems that were lost beneath the short, loose skirts she generally wore. Unable to make the full step into clothing ease, she still kept her breasts encased in a brassiere, complementing the panty-girdle she sometimes wore as a shield over her arched buttocks.

Lou had been gracious and demanding, confronting her with complete honesty and yet not trying to force her. It hadn't taken more than five minutes for him to understand exactly what Joan's situation was. And after a quarter of an hour of formal interview, he had leaned forward over his desk and said, 'Look, without experience, you really aren't qualified for this job. But you seem intelligent and quick, and I'm sure you can learn as you go, and within a month should be doing fine. It's a pretty good job, not bad pay, and nice people to work with.'

Her mouth went dry. From one standpoint, the job wasn't much, but from another, it was like salvation. She could get out of the hectic restaurant where she rushed about for eight hours each night, find a decent apartment, start to involve herself in studying again. In her state of confusion and fatigue, the job seemed heaven-sent, and Lou like an angel. He watched her carefully.

'Frankly,' he went on, 'at this point it's a buyer's market.' That was a lie; he was desperate for help. 'And if you want to sell your talent and time, you must be aware I'm interested in more than your literary skills.' He had paused for a long moment and then added, 'Perhaps we can continue this interview at my apartment later.'

Her face flushed. Not only because of the openness of his request, but because she felt a strange tingle of excitement at the idea of prostituting herself in that way. She had slept with men several times in the off-chance they might be able to help her, but she had never given her body in direct exchange for a solid offer. A slow warmth filled her breasts and made her nipples sweat, and her thighs squirmed ever so slightly on the chair.

Now Lou looked around the table. 'Coffee for everyone?' he asked.

Joan stood up, pad and pencil in hand, to write down their preferences. To her amazement, Margaret got up also, and walked around behind her and went to the door.

'I'll give you a hand,' the other woman said. 'I'll start the water boiling.'

'Shouldn't you be in on this?' Lou called out to her, a ring of harshness in his voice.

'You know my feelings about all of this,' she told him.

The two of them had been arguing policy for six months. Margaret insisted that the only way for Centaur to get out of the hole was to inaugurate a radically new line of books. She had evolved a theory of pornography which Lou refused to take seriously. His contention was that people who bought 'dirty books' cared for nothing except their excitation value, and the thing to do was to increase the percentage of explicit sex per chapter and to run hotter covers and more suggestive titles. Margaret argued that pornography was a valid genre, like science fiction or gothic novels, and that its real audience was among the college crowd, and the generally literate public. She wanted to scrap the entire Centaur approach and work from a concept which would be revolutionary among publishers of pornography: to put out no more than twelve titles a year, and to invest all their money and distribution talent and advertising potential to sell those dozen to respectable bookstores and chains.

'Before anything else,' she said, 'pornography is literature.'

'Before anything else,' Lou countered, 'pornography is a way to get your cock hard.'

'And what if you don't have a cock?' she had replied.

'Then go find one,' he had yelled, ending their discussion as their talks usually ended, in a flare of anger.

Finally, Margaret had taken matters into her own hands. She had been given the sales figures now being discussed a few weeks earlier by Jack, and fortified with the knowledge that Centaur could do no worse than it was doing, no matter how else they approached the problem, she had decided to see Al Leeds, the president of Zenith, the parent company. Thus, her attitude toward the present meeting was one of disdain.

She left the conference room, and Joan, after listing who wanted cream and who wanted sugar, followed. But as she turned to leave, she was seized with a bizarre psychic convulsion. Perhaps it was the fact that the eyes of every man in the room were riveted on the cleft of her ass, boring holes through the cloth and into the damp darkness beneath. She could feel the pressure of their gazes tugging at her panties which had worked their way up until they were jammed tightly in her crotch, causing her cunt to twitch. For an instant she imagined what it would be like if the conventions of civilization were suddenly suspended. She could feel the mass of male bodies rising behind her, surging over her, bearing her to the floor. She could feel the hot breath in her ears, the frantic lips seeking hers, the tongues over her face, in her mouth.

Quick hands peel the clothing from her body, from a body that is, despite herself, beginning to respond to the terrible excitement. Fingers probing, pulling, pushing.

She, half-naked, her stark white thighs flailing about, half-protesting, half-desiring, as her legs are spread, and urgent flesh is thrust against her skin. Then, a hand reaches the curled lips of her cunt, pries apart the fragile defenders, and thrusts rudely in, to find a cavern that is already hot and wet and throbbing. Wanting. Needing. She opens her mouth to make a sound, and she is filled with a large anonymous cock, ingratiating itself with her tongue and invading her throat. She gags and her legs come up, her knees rising to her chest, exposing the long curves of her tender ass. Her bra is yanked off, and more hands and mouths descend on the tossing breasts. There is a long moment of indecision, and suddenly she is opening herself up, letting the channels into her body fall loose and inviting. The cocks in her mouth and ass and cunt multiply and interchange, there is the smell of sweat, of sperm, the sound of deep grunting, and before she is lost entirely she gets a glance at herself from the ceiling, a naked lustful woman sucking into herself a roomful of insatiable men.

A low whistle caressed the backs of her knees as she went through the door, and was followed by the sound of low laughter. The whole fantasy had gone through her in a split second. Her chest heaved with heavy breathing.

'Can they possibly know what I've just been thinking?' she wondered as the hallway tilted before her eyes.

But the moment passed, and ordinary reality returned. She went off toward the office kitchen, tailored, prim, and there was no trace of the drooling lapping animal that lurked just beneath the surface.

'I must be schizophrenic,' she thought, musing again on the fact that she was capable of diametrically opposed types of feeling and behavior within practically the same record. The idea returned her to her first meeting with Lou, in which that quality of her personality was most sharply underlined.

She had gone to his apartment, caught up in the slight sense of degradation involved. She was going to take her clothes off, lie on her back, and let a complete stranger fuck her as he wanted. And she would enjoy it, not only the sensations, but the experience of giving herself like a whore. 'I wonder what it is inside me,' she thought, 'that gives me pleasure in this kind of scene? Or is it that I am in touch with something that exists in all women and only I have the honesty to admit it?' It was a far cry from her teenage years when sex was considered a function of what was called love; a girl was supposed to like a boy before she let him touch her. It took many years before she understood that liking him was synonymous with wanting him to touch her. And that was the thing about Lou. She actually liked him, from the first moment she saw him, and wanted him to touch her. He was almost fifty, heavy-set, with thick features, but his physical appearance was not important.

He mixed very strong martinis, and made a great show of the splendors of his apartment. She was impressed with his obvious wealth – by the opulent Moorish furniture, by the expensive rugs, by the nine rooms and balcony which overlooked Central Park. The entire place was wired like a single electrical gadget, with stereos, radios, videotape recorders, vibrating beds and even a movie projector. To her chagrin, as he took her coat and had her sit on his seventeen-foot kangaroo-hide couch, her knees wobbled and she felt that unmistakable quickening between her thighs which told her that her cunt was beginning to secrete.

He brought out a pile of manuscripts and while they worked their way through a third drink apiece, he talked about his concept of pornography. 'It is a valid function,' he said. 'Sex is at the core of the human condition. After all, what are we but the result of a meeting of cock and cunt? Sex is our origin, and our continuing fascination with it is perfectly understandable. I publish over three hundred books a year. There must be thousands of titles coming out yearly in this country alone. And considering that there are a very limited number of things that can be done with the human body, and that most sex books are a repetition of the same behavior, it is amazing that millions of people keep buying them and reading them. It proves conclusively that sex is the most important of our involvements, and pornography is perhaps the most vital of all the arts. Of course, given the nature of our civilization, it is considered the lowest.'

She ran her eyes over one of the manuscripts. It was titled *Sentimental Swinger*, and she opened it at random. '*Marcia knew that she had lost him*,' it read, '*her own sweet Jim. As he pressed his cock between the undulating cheeks of the other woman's ass, he closed his eyes and moaned, and Marcia knew that he no longer cared who it was that gave him so much pleasure. "Is this how it all ends?" she asked herself, "the so-called sexual freedom, the experimentation? Wasn't it better when a man and woman had sex because they loved each other, and not because they were hungry for excitement?" But even as she watched the thoughts go through her mind, one of the men at the orgy they had come to had moved up behind her and was running his finger up and down the crack of her cunt, teasing the outer lips, pushing slightly into the moist center. And as her heart broke, her thighs moved; as her dream of romance faded, her scream of lust welled in her throat. "Fuck me," she moaned, "you big-cocked stranger who doesn't even want to know my name. Shove your hard prick up my cunt and make me come like crazy." He pushed her to the ground. "First suck it," he said. And then with tears in her eyes, listening to her husband's groans of passion, she curled her tongue to lick the underbelly of the thick cock that descended to her face.*'

Joan looked up from the manuscript to see Lou smiling down at her. 'What do you think?' he asked.

'It's like a soap opera with sex,' she said.

He clucked his tongue against his palate. 'That's right,' he said. 'And that's the sort of thing we want. You catch on fast.' He squinted and stared at her. 'Don't you?' he added. And after a pause, 'Well, do you want the job?' he went on and glanced down at his crotch.

She leaned forward. 'If I take the job,' she said, 'how often do I have to be available for these private consultations?' Her breath was hot against his thighs and he swayed where he stood. Her mouth was slightly open and her tongue was a pink shadow in its depths.

'I'm a busy man,' he told her, 'and my main interest is money. I love sex, but not if it distracts me from my most important direction. And quite frankly, once I satisfy my initial curiosity about a woman, she doesn't hold too many charms for me. I don't know. I may want you again a month from now, or six months from now, or never again. No, what I'll enjoy is knowing that you are available to me. I'll enjoy watching you walk around the office, all corseted and clean, knowing that whenever I want I can have you rolling naked on my rug, spreading your pussy wide for me, licking my balls, letting me fuck you up that pretty little ass of yours.'

He sat down next to her, and like an actor switching costumes he said in a gentle voice, 'I hope you don't mind my being direct. I mean, I think you're an intelligent woman and you understand the way the world works. If you're looking for romance, do it on your own time; if you're looking for freedom, go live in the woods. In the office, you belong to me. I'm an old-fashioned kind of capitalist. I don't hold with euphemisms. People who work for me are wage-slaves. I pay the wage; they are my slaves. When I buy you I buy your skills and your body. Because I don't beat about the bush, you always know where you stand, or . . .' he smiled, 'where you kneel.'

'Well,' she said, emboldened by his honesty, 'then I might as well be a whore on the street.'

He chuckled. 'No,' he said, 'that kind of life is too rough for a nice middle-class girl like you. The competition would kill you, or the cops would get you, or you'd wind up working for a pimp. I'm offering you a respectable job, with good pay, and regular hours. It's not asking you to do anything that will permanently fuck up your life.'

'Except to act as your sexual plaything.'

He laughed, a deep, resounding baritone laugh, much like that used by men who play Santa Claus in department stores at Christmas. 'No,' he said, 'we're doing that because you enjoy it. And because I don't like to run an office rife with sexual hypocrisy. If you worked there and I didn't try to fuck you, I would be lying to myself and to you, and the tension would mount. This way, we stay clear with one another.' He put one hand on her breasts, and the sudden warmth made her lean back against the arm of the couch. 'Besides, it's just perverse enough to titillate you.'

She lay back and her lids lowered as she watched him through the prism of her oddly mounting desire. He loomed over her, huge and indistinct. Her eyes went to where his right hand moved, and she could see his erection already outlining itself against the fabric of his pants. He stroked his cock slowly, and she watched like one hypnotized. Her breathing became shallow and, to her amazement, she could smell the secretions from her cunt as her ass dug into the leather couch. A strange lassitude crept over her and her mouth dropped open even wider than it had been. Her tongue wet her lips, leaving a thin glistening of saliva over the red lipstick she still wore, against the advice she received about its being out of style. He laughed again.

'Yes, I know all that,' he said. 'You respectable girls are the ones who want it most badly. You're the dirtiest ones. Growing up in those small towns with those picture-postcard families, with nothing to do but dream about it, and no one to relieve you except dumb high school kids. You build it up, year after year, until you're eating and drinking and breathing sex. I can see you, night after night in your bed, rubbing your clitoris sore, pushing candles up your cunt, harder and deeper, never able to get enough. And the next day dressing up all neat and proper and pretending you're a nice little girl, just like momma wants you to be. And the real you is naked and writhing, begging for cock, licking the air with your tongue and wanting desperately for there to be a man standing over you, a man who will look at you and see what you are and who you are.'

He reached forward and in one motion slid his hand under her skirt and up to her cunt. He grabbed her fiercely, pinching the sensitive flesh between his thumb and forefinger. She gasped and her knees flew apart, tossing her skirt higher on her thighs. He had her at her most vulnerable point, and they both knew it.

'And then one day you read a book,' he went on, 'or see a magazine, and there they are, real people doing things you didn't dare to dream about. And that's what you really want, isn't it, to do those things, those things you think deep down are dirty and nasty and depraved? Well, all right. With me you can do them all, because I understand all about it. And when we're finished, maybe you won't be so serious anymore, and think what a great big sin you're committing, and maybe you'll get over the melodrama and enjoy it for its own sake.' His hand squeezed her cunt harder and she moaned. 'Now take off your clothes, and then roll over on your belly and let me see your ass while you put my cock in your mouth and suck it until you go wild.'

The effect of his words was like that of an earthquake. All the codes and inhibitions by which she attempted to define herself melted and a deep blackness overcame her. All her intelligence went into her belly, where a deep warmth began to throb and spread down into her thighs and up into her breasts. Her nipples were on fire, and her cunt was like the mouth of a volcano, hot and red and shooting fire. She itched as though she were covered with biting ants and she began to toss and writhe on the couch.

'Take off your clothes,' he reminded her.

And as he watched, she squirmed before his unflinching gaze, and began to peel her clothing off. First she kicked off her shoes, and then reached up under her skirt and unhooked her nylons. She pulled the sheer hosiery down her long legs, revealing full thighs and rounded calves. First one leg and then the other until they were naked, open to his eyes, young firm, fresh and inviting. He couldn't resist and leaned forward to run his hands up and down her legs, stroking and massaging, feeling the soft flesh under his greedy fingers. His cock was aching in his pants and he wanted desperately to pull it out and sink it into her flesh, but he knew that his patience would be rewarded.

'Keep going,' he rasped. 'Little copy editor, take off all your clothes and show your boss what a hot little bitch you are.'

She unhooked her skirt and yanked it down her legs and over her ankles in one motion, so that now she was bare to the crotch. Slowly, she started to undo her garter belt, but he stopped her. 'Leave that on,' he said. And she hooked her thumbs into the elastic of her yellow panties and began to push them down. He watched hungrily as the small triangle of silk was worked down her legs. She brought her knees to her chest so she could slip the panties over her feet, and the globes of her ass poked out from under, opening as a succulent frame for the patch of hair between. Before he could look at her cunt, however, she brought her legs down again, and he had to be momentarily content to stare at the bristling bush which covered it. Without stopping in her dance, she pulled her blouse up, and now was naked except for bra and garter belt.

'Classic,' he said. He reached down beside the couch and took out a Polaroid camera. 'This may interest you,' he said in an oddly professional voice. Before she could protest, the flash had gone off, and the timer on the back of the camera was buzzing off fifteen seconds.

'Here we go,' he told her, and peeled off the wrapping to reveal a picture of herself, looking like the cover of one of the books sold by his publishing house. She blinked. 'Is that me?' she asked. The woman she looked at appeared so sexy, so voluptuous, so willing for any experience, that Joan could not relate the image to herself.

' "Life imitates art," ' Lou Morris said and smiled to himself.

He took the picture from her hands and put it on the table next to the couch. 'Get on your belly,' he told her. 'We'll take more pictures later.'

'Yes,' she said, her voice trembling.

She rolled over and pressed the front of her body against the couch. She began to pump her pelvis against the leather, feeling the mounting heat and tension as her cunt pushed into the soft hardness. The picture she had just looked at would not leave her consciousness, and she began to be aware of herself as she looked from the outside. Her young lithe body framed in a frilly bra and belt. Her ass exposed and circled by the elastic straps. Her hair falling down her naked back. And her cunt pressing frantically into the couch, silently begging to be touched, to be fucked. Lou moved next to her. 'So nice,' he said, 'it's so good to let it all hang out, isn't it?' And to punctuate his remark he put one hand on the cleft between her buttocks, lightly, his middle finger dipping down to touch the unguarded hole at the core. She clenched her ass tightly and trapped his finger, and then let loose, arching her pelvis so that her ass rose high in the air. And then clenched again, so that it became like a mouth rising and falling to pull in the desired food.

She lifted her head and found herself staring at the giant bulge in his pants. She made a low sound that was unlike anything she had ever heard come from herself before, and checked it. Lou grabbed her ass more firmly and began to move even lower, toward the already yearning cunt that opened each time she raised her hips. 'Let it go,' he said. 'You can do anything you want with me. I've had thousands of women where you are now. And you all do the same thing. It's all one cunt, one ass, one pair of tits, one mouth, wanting the same thing. Don't be ashamed or think you're any different. Let it happen and let me watch. It's all I really want from you, you know, to see you when you're really naked, and really beautiful.'

She sobbed again. 'Lick it through the cloth,' he said.

She pressed her face into him. Her tongue found a life of its own and curled around the tube, finding the ridges around the head of his cock. She licked up and down the entire length, sensing the difference between the rough fabric and the swelling softness underneath. Added to the sensations was the picture of herself, her young innocent face buried in the crotch of this old man, this stranger for whom sex was an amusement that had to do with aesthetics only, and didn't care who the personalities involved happened to be. She thrashed more wildly against the couch, her need growing, her ass a sea of convulsive movement, as she forced herself more deeply into his thighs.

'Oh please,' she moaned.

'Please what?' he asked.

'Please give it to me,' she whispered.

'Where do you want it?' he went on, teasing her.

'Put it in my mouth, in my ass. Stick it in my cunt. Just give it to me.' It seemed that she was the vacuum that nature is reported to abhor, and she cried out to be filled. She didn't care what form the fulfillment took, or how it looked, or what it meant. She was ready to accept that she had to have something inside her to complete her emptiness or go raving down the corridors of her want.

But, at that very moment, he stepped back. She was left frozen in her posture, raw and ragged at the edge of her willingness to submit to anything he wanted to do with her, amazed that he was able so quickly to find just the exact switch to unleash the energies that had been so long suppressed in her. But then, he was one of the few great pornographers of the twentieth century.

'Would you like some coffee?' he asked in a conversational tone.

'Coffee?' she repeated stupidly.

He smiled gently. 'You're beginning to get a bit carried away,' he said. He sat down next to her. 'I must confess something to you. I've already had one heart attack, and

I've been told that if I don't watch myself, I could collapse at any time. According to my doctor, I shouldn't even look at women, much less engage in these scenes, but if I have to give up sex altogether, I might as well be dead. So, I compromise. I indulge, but I pace myself.' Seeing the look of chagrin on her face he went on, 'Forgive me. I didn't mean to frighten or disappoint you, but these are the facts of life.'

She looked at him with concern. He went instantaneously from a horrid but fascinating lecher into a tired old man with a bad heart. Mixed with his rank sensuality and his pictorial grasp of sex was his actual humanity, the fact that he was only a mortal. She felt a pang of empathy with him, and from that flowed the compassion which was to bring them together in friendship.

She went into the kitchen to put coffee up to boil. He disappeared into his bedroom, and when he came out he was dressed in a satin dressing gown. They sat and sipped the hot brew in silence, each enjoying the relaxation of the moment. And after a while she spoke. 'Does that mean we're not going to . . . have sex any more tonight?'

He laughed again, a sound that she was beginning to find heartwarming. 'Not at all, young lady, we will almost certainly have sex for the next three or four hours. It's just that when the fires burst from inside you, I'll have to stand back from time to time and let you, as they say, do your thing. I won't be able to meet you at the peaks of your ecstasy. But then, I will be here, quite sober, should you plunge from those peaks into valleys of despair and self-disgust.'

She gave him a questioning, appraising glance.

'Don't try to figure me out yet,' he said. 'Look upon me as a teacher, perhaps,' he went on, launching himself into his favorite image of himself, a kind of sexual guru to the nation, both in the books he published and in the private scenes he mounted.

'It's hard to switch from such wild letting-go to such rational conversation,' she said. 'I don't know if I can get back into sex again.'

He put his coffee cup down. 'Come with me,' he said, and taking her by the hand led her into a small room that he had specially constructed himself. She felt like a child being led by her father into a garden of delights. The room was covered with photographs and drawings, and it contained a water bed in one corner, a leather massage table in another, and row upon row of gadgets, the use of which she was unable to discern without a studied look.

'Lie down there,' he said, pointing to the water bed. And when she did, she found herself staring into a mirror which had been cemented onto the ceiling. She had forgotten how she looked and was now rudely reminded as her long legs kicked idly about on the undulating surface, and her cunt winked lewdly from around the edges of the garter belt. He knelt next to her.

'Now let's take this off,' he said, expertly unhooking her bra, allowing her breasts to fall out, thick, creamy, lush, tipped with purple nipples. His head fell forward and in a moment she felt his hot tongue laving the soft mounds, while his fingers tenderly tweaked the tender tips. A gasp escaped her lips and her thighs parted of their own accord. As though his hands had eyes of their own, his fingers found their way down her flat belly, past the humped hairy mound of venus, and into the sticky hole beneath. Her cunt, hot and pulsing with a life of its own, sucked three of his fingers into its depths.

'Oh God,' she sighed as his hand slid back and forth, in and out of her tingling pussy, his fingers twirling against the slimy walls.

He let out a single surprised breath. 'I'll bet you can take my whole fist in your cunt already.'

In response, she opened her legs wider, spreading her ass on the warm support of plastic and water. 'Do it,' she murmured. 'Put your fist up my cunt, Lou, shove it in all the way to the elbow.'

She closed her eyes and let him do what he wanted with her, and even when she could sense a bright light go on, and knew that from somewhere a camera was recording her every moan, her every thrust, she didn't care. She had wanted for her entire life to let go and put herself in the hands of a man who understood what she wanted, when she wanted to be passive. And now that she had found one who was not only expert, but kind, nothing in the world would have prevented her from draining the experience of its last drop.

'I'll get to your cunt,' he said in a low, firm voice, 'but first I want your mouth.' And he knelt above her, his bulk hovering over her head, as she opened her lips and curled her tongue out to receive him.

'That's good,' he said, 'that's what I want to see. Show it to me, show me your cocksucking mouth.' And again, the phrase pressed a certain button inside her, and she began to whip her head from side to side, her lips opening and stretching as wide as they could, while her tongue danced in a frenzy of lust. She twisted her pelvis, humping her cunt into the air. He seized one of her breasts and kneaded it like dough.

'Oh, give it to me,' she moaned. 'Please, put it in my mouth.'

'Yes,' he said quietly. 'I'm going to put something in your mouth, and as soon as you feel it, I want you to swallow it. Do you understand? Now, reach your lips up toward me.'

Frowning, she made sucking noises as his body descended toward her face.

That had been almost a year earlier, and since that night, Lou had taken her to his apartment a dozen times, with each visit finding her stretching the limits of the spectrum of sexual expressiveness, until one time he invited two of his friends to visit and spent the evening working her up to greater and greater peaks of desire, and then giving her to the other men to use as they wished. 'It's easier for me this way,' he had explained. 'Not so much strain on the heart when a younger man finishes what I begin.'

Finally, he had let her know, gently, over dinner, that he did not think there would be any further meetings. He had pleaded increased business, schedules, but she put her hand on his arm.

'You're bored with me Lou, isn't that it? There's nothing more I can show you.'

He nodded. 'I didn't want to put it that way,' he said, 'and maybe hurt your feelings.'

'What do we have together if we don't have honesty?' she asked him.

'But I want you to keep working for me,' he told her. 'I'm even going to give you a raise.'

She laughed. 'I'll bet that's the first time a boss has given an employee a raise because he *didn't* want to fuck her,' she said.

'Well, I'm glad you understand,' he replied. 'You're a nice girl, with a lovely ass and an educated cunt, and you have a good mind. But you know, you're one of thousands, millions. Me, I'm interested in pictures. And as a model, you've shown me everything you have to show.'

'And what happens to those movies you've been taking?' she asked.

'Don't worry,' he told her, 'they'll never be seen in Arkansas.'

She now walked with habitualized rhythm down the corridor, glad to be away from the interminable drone of male voices, and wondered about Margaret, who was already in the small kitchen at the other end of the suite of offices, waiting for her. Joan sensed that the other woman was about to lift matters to a new level of relationship, and while she did not dwell on the particulars of what might be involved, she was charged with a slight expectant randiness that primed her for whatever might take place.

TWO

'Are you nervous?' Margaret stared intently at her visitor. Joan shifted her weight, uncertain as to how to answer.

'I don't know,' she replied. 'I'm perspiring, if that's any indication.'

'Where are you perspiring?' Margaret asked with a wry smile.

Joan shifted her weight again. 'Under my arms, along the inside of my thighs.'

Margaret licked her lips in that way she had, falling somewhere between amusement and invitation. There was a long pause.

'Well, why did you invite me here?' Joan asked.

While the two of them had been making coffee that morning and agreeing that men-at-meetings were the most tedious things in creation, Margaret had asked Joan to dinner at her apartment. Not sure of what was being offered besides food, Joan had felt a tingle of anticipation that something exciting might happen, and after three hours of the conference, she was ready to take anything that offered an antidote to the deadly boredom of business.

In her Chelsea apartment, a single huge room painted Mandarin red with all black furniture and furnishings, except for the bone-white curtains on the windows, Margaret had greeted her, dressed in a transparent canary-yellow dressing gown through which could be seen her legs, the vermilion gash of the panties she wore, and the white fullness of bare breasts tipped with tantalizing glimpses of brown nipples. They had had drinks and a light dinner of broiled whitefish and a tossed salad and garlic bread, followed by strong Turkish coffee and Sherman cigarettes. Now, at ease on a thick rug in front of the fireplace, they were moving into that space of encounter in which the souls of two human beings become naked before one another.

'I asked you here to talk business,' Margaret said.

'That's a disappointment,' Joan said, stretching out to her full length, her tight slacks folding and creasing behind her knees and at her crotch. Margaret stared for a long moment at the bulge between Joan's thighs, picturing the soft mound, the swamp of hair, the tangled lips beneath, the succulent aromatic hole beneath them. Joan, aware of the other's gaze, at first went to cross her legs in a reflex movement, then checked herself, and let her thighs fall open. She had promised herself that she would go with the total flow this evening, and while she was unable to initiate anything, she could certainly cooperate with Margaret's desires.

'I think you have a one-dimensional understanding of business,' Margaret said. 'I should have thought that after your relationship with Lou, you might have understood it differently.'

At once, Joan was on the alert. 'What do you know of my relationship with Lou?' she asked.

'I've seen the movies he made of you,' Margaret told

her. And before Joan could say another word, went on, 'I've seen you with legs spread wide, a dildo in your cunt and a dildo in your ass, squirming at his feet, begging him to fuck you in the mouth. I've seen the one where he gives you to his friends, and after being fucked for four hours, with every hole red and raw, still unsatisfied, you stuffed your fingers in your cunt and rubbed yourself until you were wracked with shuddering orgasms, and spent, weak, crawled up to the men and pleaded with them to fuck you again. Until they had to pick you up and throw you in a bathtub of ice-cold water to snap you out of your delirium.'

Margaret lit a cigarette, let out a cloud of smoke, and continued, 'I know all about the fire inside you, Joan, and I'm not shocked. I'm a woman too, and I have felt the same things. All women do, who are at all honest with themselves. But that's only one face of the phenomenon. Sex is one part.'

Half horrified, half captivated by the knowledge that Margaret had seen her in her most exposed moments, she asked, 'And what's the other part?'

Margaret smiled. 'Why, power, of course.'

Joan shook her head. 'You're just like Lou,' she said.

'In a sense,' Margaret told her. She ran her free hand over her breasts and down to her crotch. 'Except that Lou doesn't have this lovely body, and he doesn't have the knowledge of what it is to be a woman, although I must admit he's made a more thorough study of it than anyone I've ever met, even though his perspective is rather limited. No, the one thing we have in common is clarity. We both know exactly what we want.'

'I knew what I wanted once,' Joan said. 'More than anything, I wanted to be an actress.'

Margaret leaned forward and put her head on Joan's calf, the pressure of her fingers just enough to capture her attention. 'I know,' Margaret said. 'And that's the business I want to talk about. The only trouble with your wanting to be an actress was the scope of the stage and role you allowed yourself. The old form of theatre is dead and ridiculous. All life is a drama, all the world is a stage. Trite words, but powerful meaning. Why limit yourself to a few bare boards and a painted set and someone else's lines, when you can be starring in your own play all the time, twenty-four hours a day?'

Margaret's hand had moved, as though of its own volition, up past Joan's knee to her thigh. Margaret was lying much closer now, her face at a level with Joan's breasts, her hand gently stroking the cloth which clung to Joan's full thighs. Its movements were in rhythm with her speech, and as she spelled out her vision and plan, her hand made insistent and persistent forays further up Joan's leg toward the tempting, taut triangle made by the folds of fabric around her cunt.

'It's time to wake up,' she went on. 'This movement is the only moment we shall ever have. There is always only now, even though the content of now continually changes. The thing to ask is, "Who is in control? Who is writing your script? Who is deciding your role? Who is designing your set?" '

'I think I understand you,' Joan replied, 'but your words have implications I don't really grasp.'

'Don't worry about the implications,' Margaret said,

'they will become clear in time But for now, I want to know whether you are ready.'

'Ready for what?' Joan asked.

'Ready to help me take Lou Morris' publishing empire away from him.'

The words rang like a gong in Joan's mind. It was the single most enormous proposition she had ever heard which fell within the realm of her possibility, and yet lay beyond the limits of what she thought she could accomplish.

'How can . . .?' she began.

But Margaret silenced her sentence with her hand, putting her fingers over Joan's mouth. 'No details now,' she said. 'You've already got more than enough than you can assimilate. Just let that thought rest inside you, and in a few days, we can talk again.'

Joan let her head fall back onto the floor. Her mind was spinning around and all she could focus on were the shadows made by the flames in the fireplace as they danced across the ceiling. Although she was making no future motion to speak, Margaret did not remove her fingers, and after a few moments, Joan could feel their heat and texture on her lips. Slowly, her mouth fell slightly open, and Margaret's fingers slid inwards, first touching her teeth, and then, moving past, rested on her tongue.

Joan lay passive for a second, and then began to lick Margaret's fingers gently. The two of them barely moved, and the only sounds in the room were of the fire spitting and the two women breathing heavily. Joan had never been with a woman before, although she had thought about it often.

'It's going to happen,' she thought, 'it's going to happen now.' She checked her body and found herself tense with anticipation. Her thighs locked together, her belly flat and taut, her toes curled. Margaret's hand went deeper into her mouth, until she had four fingers between Joan's stretched lips.

'Why don't we get our clothes off?' said Margaret after what seemed like an eternity.

Joan opened her eyes and found herself looking full into Margaret's face. It had the precision beauty of an ancient Greek mask, except for the eyes, which were like snakes slithering in a pit of smoke.

'You're so beautiful and so frightening,' Joan whispered.

Margaret pulled her hand back slowly and replaced it with her mouth, covering Joan's lips with her own. Joan stiffened against the contact, for despite all her tendencies toward libertinism, she had the conventional conditioning against intimate contact with a member of her own sex. But Margaret's lips were so soft, so knowing, so warm, that she soon melted under their insistence. Again her mouth opened, and this time, instead of rigid fingers, she was greeted with a hot sinuous tongue that instantly greeted her own with an invitation to dance. Joan responded with a gasp, her mouth surging upward, crushing her lips against Margaret's in a grinding kiss. Her hands curved around the other woman's neck and pulled her head down to her own. Margaret snuggled in closer, and their bodies flew together, breasts crushing breasts, thighs touching thighs. With the expertise born of experience, Margaret tilted her pelvis forward in just such a way that her cunt slipped in against Joan's crotch, and with the contact made, she began slowly to grind her pussy between the other woman's thighs, teasing the lips folded beneath panties and slacks, inflaming the clitoris that started to clamor for nakedness. Margaret sucked the breath from Joan's lungs and then abruptly pulled back, leaving the stunned copy editor gasping.

'No clothes,' she rasped. 'I want you naked.'

They parted reluctantly, and Margaret shrugged herself out of her dressing gown at once. She lay back and bent her legs at the hips, bringing her knees to her exposed breasts, which fell in flattened mounds on her chest, sagging to either side of her torso, the huge nipples already wrinkled and erect. She slipped her fingers in the elastic of her panties and with a single motion pulled them down her legs and over her feet, uncovering the patch of yellow hair that modestly guarded the full sensual cunt lips that now burst from between the naked thighs and buttocks. Joan's eyes went directly to the furry mound, and Margaret saw where her glance went. She brought her hands down to her cunt and rubbed the outer lips languorously.

'Yes, my love,' she said, 'now you see my cunt. Men have gone mad to get to where you are now. And I give it to you so easily. Does that make you happy?'

Joan couldn't answer. Her mouth was dry and her lips felt drawn. Margaret slipped one finger between the outer lips of her pussy and stirred it around inside, then pulled it out again, now glistening wet. She moved up and brought her hand up to Joan's face. 'This is how I smell,' she said, and put her finger under Joan's nose. 'Take a deep breath,' she ordered gently.

Joan inhaled, and the fragrance that assailed her made

her heart pound. It was so like her own, and yet not her own at all. It was the smell of cunt, but not her cunt. It was another woman's cunt, and she was at the edge of feeling and tasting that cunt herself. She grew dizzy at the realization that she was at the verge of committing what she had always referred to as 'a lesbian act', and the very words only served to inflame her further.

'And now, taste it,' Margaret urged. 'See what this perfumed slime tastes like.' She put her finger at Joan's lips, and trembling, Joan opened her mouth. Margaret's finger slid inside, and with a groan Joan closed her lips over it and sucked it clean in a single motion, then gulped as though she had swallowed an entire cupful of water. The taste was indescribable, but more than the sensation of what she swallowed, the meaning of her doing it assailed her reason.

'Lou was right,' Margaret chuckled. 'Most of your pleasure still comes from your idea that all this is dirty. Well, so be it. It doesn't matter to me right now what's in your head. We each use our own devices to get us off.' A stern note crept into her voice and she said, 'Take off your clothes, Joan. I want to see you in the flesh.'

With a sense of unreality, Joan began to remove her clothing. First the blouse, button by button, and then the bra, freeing her captive breasts. Margaret reached forward and cupped Joan's large tits in her hands. They fell from her chest like pears, possessed of that same ripe fragility that makes one want to bite into a fruit. Her nipples were very small, but because of that were doubly sensitive, so that the slightest touch sent ripples through her entire body. Now, as Margaret appraised and teased, Joan began to feel the generalized tingling that heralded an onslaught of sexual eruption. It began to be unimportant that the hands that turned her on were a woman's hands. All she could feel was the softness, the firmness, the gentle indifference of the touch. She knew that, as with Lou, she was in the presence of a master of the craft of sensuality.

'I don't know what it is about you,' Margaret said in a low voice, 'that makes me want to give you pleasure. But it makes me almost cum to see you getting hot, watching your lips purse, seeing your cunt drool, feeling your nipples get hard. It's as though everything you feel gets projected outward, so that the more you enjoy, the more I can enjoy through you.'

She guided Joan to a standing position by increasing the upward pressure on her breasts. Margaret knelt in front of her and began to unzipper Joan's slacks. 'Soon, soon,' she crooned, 'I am going to have that succulent cunt on my mouth and I'll suck the juices right out of you and drive you crazy.' As she spoke she tugged the pants down Joan's long curved legs, revealing the private flesh, until they had been brought to the floor, and Joan stepped easily out of them. She now wore only her panties, the crotch of which was already soaked with secretion. Margaret pressed her face into the sopping mound and ran her tongue along the groove where the silk had stuck in the crack of her cunt. Joan let out a soft grunt and her knees buckled.

'Keep standing,' Margaret ordered.

She bent even lower until she was completely between Joan's spread legs, and then brought her face up to the exact center of Joan's thighs, pressing her lips into the hot musky-sweaty space between cunt and asshole, smelling the deep body aroma and licking the moisture from hair and panties and flesh. She brought her hands up and worked her fingers around the edge of the elastic, feeling at last the vulnerable folds of flesh that had only one last shred of protection.

From the outside, they made an extraordinary picture – the young soft Joan, swaying and moaning, her hair cascading down her back and over her shoulders, while the stunningly beautiful Margaret, naked, crouching, her hair still pulled back in its severe bun, burrowed in the most central space between the other woman's legs, her tongue lapping indiscriminately, her fingers probing, pushing into the now overflowing hot cunt and the throbbing asshole.

'Oh God, I'm falling,' Joan cried, as she felt her legs give from under her.

She let herself sink to the floor and as she fell, Margaret pulled the panties from her legs. when she lay at last on the rug before the fire, she was rapturously naked, one leg bent at the knee and the other extended at full length, leaving the treasure that Margaret so urgently desired, the deep luscious cunt, totally exposed and craving penetration. Joan's eyes were closed, and her mouth was open, as her arms spread out to either side of her, putting her in a posture of complete submission.

'Now,' Margaret whispered to herself, and moved slowly over until she was kneeling over Joan's head, one knee on either side of her face. 'Now,' she said again, and very slowly lowered her body down until her cunt hairs were tickling the very tip of Joan's mouth. Joan blinked. 'What . . .?' she started to say, and opened her eyes to see Margaret's body descend upon her. From her vantage point she could see Margaret's mouth curved in what seemed a sinister smile, and beneath that the swaying tits, looming large; and below that the full belly, like a cliff of sheer shale; and then the single black gash that went from cunt to the black cleft between Margaret's full, wide and classical rounded buttocks. She was able to let out a single gasp as the expressionistic torso descended totally upon her, smothering her in flesh and heat and wet.

'Suck it up, little girl,' Margaret said, 'suck it dry.'

Joan tried to move her face to the side but the pressure from Margaret's thighs was too strong. All she succeeded in doing was to throw her body about in a panic, which only added to Margaret's excitement, and oddly, to her own. 'That's right,' Margaret said, 'it's even better if you fight against it, isn't it? Do it your way, but do it!' And with that she let her full weight fall on Joan's face. Her nose covered and unable to breathe, Joan was forced to suck air in through her mouth, but as she did so, Margaret's cunt seemed to yawn in width and covered the full extent of Joan's lips, so that what she sucked in was the total smell and secretion of the other woman's cunt. Her mouth and nostrils filled with it, and she momentarily gagged.

'Swallow,' Margaret demanded.

And with a shudder of distaste and relief, Joan gulped down the entire mixture of cunt juice and musty air that had been mouldering in the recesses of Margaret's pussy. The entire experience verged on the vile, and it was that very feeling which, perversely, drove a bolt of excitement through Joan's body. Her hands came up and grasped Margaret's thighs, pulling them down even harder on her own face. Once again, she sucked in with all her strength, and this time avidly lapped up the juices that ran down her tongue. Hungry, beginning to verge on sexual hysteria, she probed her tongue up into the crevices of Margaret's cunt, causing the other woman to writhe with pleasure.

'Oh yes,' Margaret moaned. 'From cocksucker to cuntlapper in one easy step. Now get down to it. Lick my sticky cunt. Come on, suck it until your jaw aches.'

The outrageous beauty of Margaret's body mixed with the base physicality of that body's functions drove Joan into a frenzy of excitement. The image and the actuality vied for supremacy, and all the while she was lost in the anonymity of the sensations involved, her mind was running over the fact that the cunt she was licking and sucking belonged to Margaret, Margaret the cool executive secretary that she saw five days a week in the civilized confines of office routine. This was the same woman, now naked and bearing down on her, pressing her hot convulsive pussy into her mouth, writhing with her own orgasms, and pushing provocative words into her ears.

'Feel me cum on your mouth,' she urged. And indeed more than half her pleasure seemed to come from the dramatics of the situation rather than from her inner experiences. For Margaret, as with Lou, the sensations of sex had long since ceased to be the primary motivation. Like him, she was a pornographer, and the essence of her pleasure lay in the configurations of bodies, motivations, and attitudes. She knew that Joan was playing a game with her resistance to her own enjoyment, and while she wished that the younger woman would soon drop that posture, she realized that such matters couldn't be rushed. So she was allowing herself to take the role of sadistic fucker, forcing a revolting activity literally down the throat of a half-unwilling recipient.

She reached down and put one hand on Joan's cunt, feeling the soppy gush of viscous cum that spilled from the parted lips. Her finger went inside and tickled the ribbed walls, then withdrew to concentrate on the sensitive clitoris. As she rubbed the small nerve ending, Joan began to pump her hips up to receive more of Margaret's touch. Simultaneously, her mouth opened with the pleasure of her own erupting orgasm, and as she began to spend, she took in more and more of Margaret's cunt into her mouth until she was sucking at it as though it were a peach she had just bitten into, and was inhaling the pulp and juices through her teeth, down her tongue, and into her throat.

'Oh yes,' Margaret hissed, and flung herself down so that her own mouth now covered Joan's surging pussy. Her lips reached the cunt lips at precisely the instant that Joan began to climax, and so she received the full gush of tangy juice and the total vibration of her undulating pelvis. Margaret dug her tongue and teeth deep into the center of smell and secretion, taking in the sweat and tang from the cleft of Joan's ass, and licked the entire crack from one end to the other again and again, until, with the sensation, Joan wrapped her thighs around Margaret's head and rocked back and forth, fucking the other woman's face with the total involvement of her cunt and hips. They dug into and wrapped around one another in a pose of sixty-nine, their hands now roaming freely, enjoying the lush fullness of one another's breasts, exploring the arcane crevices between cunt and asshole with their tongues. They were lost in a shower of sound and rhythm, lost to time and place, rocketing into the inward reality of complete sexual connection.

They sucked one another's pussies for over an hour before they fell apart and lay there, exhausted and temporarily fulfilled.

After what seemed an eternity of silence, Margaret was the first to speak. 'You say that's the first time with a woman?' she asked in a wondering tone.

'Oh Margaret,' Joan said, 'You don't know how long I've waited to let go like that, to do and be done to. To make the circle complete. With men I've always had to hold back because I knew they couldn't follow me all the way. I don't know how I've gone so long without it.'

'A lot of women ask themselves that once they've tried it,' Margaret said. 'And quite a few never go back to making it with men again.'

'Do you?' Joan asked her.

'Sure,' Margaret said, lighting a cigarette. 'I'm very democratic. I think everyone has something to offer. I mean, after all, there is nothing in the world like a cock. Even a dildo won't do it, not really.' She offered a smoke to Joan and the two of them sat there, quiet and lost in thought and the afterglow of the intense experience.

After a few minutes Margaret got up to go to the kitchen to heat more coffee. As she went, Joan watched the globular cheeks of her ass shift as she walked. How often had she seen that walk during the day, when both were dressed, and how little she had suspected that so much fury was to be found beneath a skirt and panties. She felt the deep ache in her cunt from the continued friction it had received. And that was only the beginning.

As though reading her thoughts, Margaret turned at the door and said, 'We can go in late tomorrow. I doubt we'll get too much sleep tonight.'

Later, they sipped coffee and smoked cigarettes, leaning against each other in front of the fire, listening to Scriabin's *Poem of Ecstasy*. Margaret let down her hair and it glowed like a halo around her head. They were enmeshed in the red light of dancing shadows from the flames. Joan could not seem to get enough of holding Margaret's breasts in her hands, and kept cupping them, feeling their weight and texture, putting the nipples in her mouth.

'You know, I used to do this to myself for hours. But even though I don't get the pleasure in my breasts, giving that pleasure to your breasts is somehow even more gratifying.'

In response, Margaret reached over and stroked Joan's nipples. 'You know you'll always get as much as you give with me,' she said.

'I know,' Joan said, 'somehow, instinctively, I know that . . . I trust you.' And she tilted her head back as Margaret covered her mouth and with a long kiss, the taste of tobacco and coffee mingling on their breaths.

'You do remember what I said about business?' Margaret asked.

Joan nodded. 'I remember.' She looked up, her eyes filled with confusion. 'I like Lou,' she said. 'He's been good to me.'

'I like him too,' Margaret told her. 'But his time is over.' She began to go on but Joan silenced her in the most direct manner possible, by cupping her hand over Margaret's cunt, while slipping a finger into her own.

'No use trying to talk to you now,' the older woman said.

Joan slid down again until she was lying between Margaret's legs. She held her cunt lips open with both hands and began to lick the moist lips like a deer at a salt block, gently and insistently. Margaret looked down at the lithe body, the extended curved spine, the flaring ass, the full white legs, which opened and closed again and again like a scissor, indicating the fact of Joan's pushing her cunt against the rug.

'How lovely,' she thought.

She held Joan's head between her hands as she slid down and also turned over on her belly, until Joan's face lay across her buttocks. 'I want you to do my ass,' she said. 'Lick the whole crack and then get your tongue as far in as you can. I want you to ream me until your tongue feels like it's being pulled out by the roots.'

And she stretched full out, her hips rotating, her breasts crushed against the floor. Joan parted her succulent cheeks with both hands, exposing the pinched serrated hole at the core, and then, with a flick of her tongue across her lips, she buried her face completely in Margaret's ass, swimming in the mass of hot flesh. Her tongue found the target and she burrowed in at once, sending the other woman off into a cascade of squeals.

Margaret raised her hips, arching her exquisite ass off the ground, and Joan burrowed into it even more deeply, now licking the hole and then sucking it, now biting it gently and then kissing it passionately. With her full wet mouth she made love to Margaret's lovely ass, pouring into it the total passion she was capable of, until her mouth and tongue were sore with the activity. And then she reached under and put her bunched fingers at the opening of Margaret's cunt.

Margaret gasped as she felt the pressure against the other opening, and tried to push down to get the hand inside her. But as she did so, Joan licked her asshole again, causing her to lift her pelvis. She teased her for five minutes, as Margaret was torn between lifting up to get Joan's tongue in her ass and dropping down to get the fist in her cunt. She tossed back and forth, her excitement mounting into frenzy, until Joan relented and brought the two together, and as her mouth pressed hotly into the now wet crack, her hand insinuated itself up into the widening cunt, which gaped to receive it. Joan and Margaret pushed together, until Margaret's yawning pussy swallowed the whole hand and it was lodged inside her up to Joan's wrist.

The blonde woman made a wide circle with her lips but no sound emerged from her mouth. She was impaled on the thick rod of flesh and bone, and it felt as though her very soul had been stuffed. Joan pushed in even further, and Margaret screamed with pleasure and suddenly began to churn up and down, plunging her cunt with rapid hard strokes onto Joan's arm, until the young woman had to brace her elbow on the floor to sustain the force of Margaret's thrashing blows. Up and down her pelvis pumped, gorging itself on the fingers that were lodged in her entrails.

'Oh my God, fuck it to me, fuck it to me,' she cried.

Taken by the force of Margaret's response, Joan began to move her arm back and forth like a piston, until

Margaret felt the movement and stopped her own pumping. She came to her knees, her thighs spread wide part, her hands reaching around her ass cheeks and pulling the lips of her cunt apart. 'There,' she gasped, 'it's open, it's wide open. Now, give it to me.' And Joan's fingers churned in and out of the frothing hole with unrestrained fury.

Carried away by the noise and the smell and the sight of the gorgeous crack that ran from the brown cleft between the buttocks to the dripping red cunt, Joan plunged her fingers again and again into the gaping hole.

'Oh God,' Margaret screamed and then clamped her thighs shut, imprisoning Joan's hand deep inside her cunt. Joan pulled out with all her strength, and with a swishing pop, her hand flew free from its trap.

At that, Margaret let loose a scream so piercing Joan thought it would crack the glass in all the windows, and then, like a fish just landed, Margaret hurled herself forward, and thrashed about the floor, knocking over furniture, pounding her cunt with her fist, screaming and wailing, her ass contracting and letting go, her breasts flailing about, until she underwent one final convulsion and then fell still, and lay there, completely spent, covered with sweat and secretions, panting, mouth agape, open, fulfilled.

Neither of them moved or spoke for a very long time. From a great distance, street noises could be heard. Cars, voices, the sounds of normal life. Like two people who had just had their car hit a patch of ice at high speeds and spun wildly about, death lurking in every split second, and had finally slid to a long halt at the edge of a high cliff, they clung to their lives with extraordinary awareness. Perhaps twenty minutes passed, and then Joan let her head drop to her chest. A few moments later, Margaret rolled over and came to her knees. Joan looked up, and the two women stared at one another. A slow smile grew on Joan's face.

'Well, do you still want to talk business now?' she said.

To the surprise of both of them, Margaret began to weep, without making a sound.

Joan went over to her, and held her until the crying stopped. Margaret pushed the hair away from her face, reached over for a cigarette and lit it.

'What would we do without tobacco?' she asked. And answering her own rhetorical question, went on, 'We might have to face some awkward moments.'

Joan shook her head in puzzlement. She was confused, but did not want to intrude. After three deep drags, Margaret looked up at her. 'It's extraordinary how much is repressed inside us, isn't it?' she said. 'I sometimes wonder what we would be like if we blew it all out, once and for all. What kind of creatures would we be if our motivation was something other than the release of tension?'

Joan listened to the words and heard their meaning. But the other woman had left something out.

'That's not what made you cry,' she said.

Margaret glanced away, pursed her lips, looked like she was deciding whether or not to reveal herself further, and then looked back. 'You're right,' she said. 'What made me cry was something else altogether.'

'What was it?' Joan asked her.

'Just the realization that I could really love you,' Margaret said.

The words hung on the air between them. They were to have two more rounds of sex before they fell asleep in one another's arms, but the word love was not used again. It was too frightening to both of them, who were used to handling sex and power, and who would want to think a good while before taking the shields off their hearts.

THREE

The rest of the staff had left. It was the way Joan liked the office best, empty and still. Having arrived late that morning, a half hour before Margaret, she had some catching up to do. The two women had decided to come in separately, for at parting they were unable to keep their hands or their eyes off one another, and couldn't go into work in that condition. Sitting at her desk, Joan sagged inwardly at the thought of having to finish the manuscript in front of her. It was one of those moments when life seems nothing more than a progression from one wearisome task to another, and existence appears as a broad path leading directly to the grave with no interesting distractions along the way.

'How odd it is,' she thought, 'that each mood is so total, even when it is wildly different from the one that preceded it.' She was not conscious that this quality she possessed, of becoming fully the immediate vibration, was her most powerful faculty. She did not yet perceive that very few people had the instinct of living in the present still intact.

Her attention drifted away from the task at hand to reviewing what had happened with Margaret. Joan ran her tongue over her lips in a conscious imitation of

Margaret's habitual gesture, and remembered their goodbye.

Kissing her softly, Margaret had said. 'I've done things with my body that were like what happened last night, but I've only felt that much with one other person before. I don't know if you realize how deeply you've touched me.'

Joan had been at a loss. 'It's still all so confusing,' she said. 'You're the first woman I have ever had sex with, and I'm still reverberating from the novelty. But I feel that I could give myself to you totally, easily.'

'I know,' Margaret said. 'And I wasn't prepared for this. I wanted to bring you in with me on the change-over, if I can push Lou out and step into his place. And I also wanted to make love to you. And now, it's all mixed up, and I'm not sure what's happening with us.'

'Will our being lovers make it awkward at the office?' Joan asked.

'It doesn't have to,' Margaret told her. 'Especially if I take over. Then if people find out, we won't have to be coy about it.'

'It's all going so fast,' Joan said.

'Right now, the only way I can count time is in waiting to hold you in my arms again,' Margaret said. And right after, Joan had left for work.

Now she tried to shake the memory out of her head and concentrate on the book in front of her. It was a two-hundred-and-thirty-eight-page manuscript that had to be gone over with an editorial fine-tooth comb, its spelling corrected, its punctuation made uniform, and any discrepancies in internal consistency straightened out. The real trouble with that kind of work was that if the story was interesting, she became so engrossed in it that she forgot to pay attention to the mechanics; and if it was dull, then there was no pleasure perusing it so closely. This was one of the latter, a rather pedestrian tale about a good girl gone bad, 'destroyed,' as the author put it, 'by the insatiable fires of lust.'

'Insatiable fires,' Joan thought. 'What can one do with a phrase like that?'

She forced her eyes to the page. '*Laura was in trouble*,' it read. Joan wrinkled her nose. 'Considering that she's tied naked to a cot with seventeen motorcycle nazis closing in on her,' she thought, 'I'd say that's a reasonable description of her situation.' She read on. '*Laura tried to scream, but realized there was no one within miles of the deserted shack she had been brought to.*' Joan applied the tip of her pencil, and in a moment 'brought' was changed to 'taken'. She let out a low growl. 'I'll never finish if I keep going at this pace.' She lit a cigarette, took a deep drag, stretched and read on.

'*The men feasted their eyes on the succulent flesh in front of them. Laura was totally defenceless. Her arms were tied at the wrists and fastened to the wall behind her. She tried to twist her lower body to hide from the relentless eyes that bored into her, but no matter how she moved she exposed another area of succulent flesh to their view.*' Joan sighed. 'That's two 'succulent fleshes' in the same paragraph,' she said to herself. 'Rick is getting sloppy.' Rick Fantusi was one of Centaur's regular contributors, and he could always be counted on to turn in minimally acceptable works. Usually his novels were, if not literary exercises, at least well-crafted. But he had been turning them out at the rate of one a month for the past six months and he was getting slophappy.

'Well, fuck it,' Joan thought. 'Who's going to notice the excess of "succulent flesh" usage besides me?' She continued to read, '*Tears sprang to Laura's eyes,*' the story continued. '*She could hide nothing. Her sweet lush breasts, her round belly, the delicate thighs, all these were now being brutally ravished by the hot eyes of the heavy grizzled men who were beginning to take their clothes off, peeling off the grease-stained shirts and leather chaps, revealing huge muscular arms and immense hairy thighs . . . and cocks that hung huge and menacing even in their relaxed state. Laura let out a sob at the thought that their rough hands and sinister mouths would soon be probing and sucking at her soft white skin. She pressed her legs together in an insane attempt at modesty, but the men only laughed.*

'Roll her over,' said one, 'I want to see her ass.'

'She was seized and turned onto her belly, her legs were pulled apart, and she cringed in shame as she realized that they were peering at the center of her intimacy . . .'

Joan jumped up and slammed the manuscript down. 'Center of her intimacy!' she yelled. 'By God, that's going too far.' She enjoyed, when she was alone, mimicking the stories she read and acting them out. She was able to understand a bit of the excitement in pornography that gets lost from too much sophistication and exposure. She was able to rediscover the *humor* in sex, the fact that it is possible to be aroused and laugh at the same time.

Joan sat down again and read on. '*Anonymous hands pulled her ass cheeks apart, other hands lifted her hips, still more hands ran up and down the lips of her cunt.*

Hands went to her breasts, hands stroked the backs of her legs. Despite her resistance to anything but terror, she felt herself melt, as she had only been able to do with Ron, the man she had been saving herself for. A finger slid into her cunt and stopped at the still intact maidenhead.

' *"Hey," a voice said, "she's still a virgin."*

'Laura began to cry, and as her mouth fell open, she felt her lips being nudged, and she opened her eyes to see a large, thick, unwashed cock burying itself in her face. She tried to protest, but the immense engine only forced itself farther back in her throat. She thrashed about, attempting to escape, but each movement only brought another part of her to exposure. She was turned over on her back again, her legs pressed to her chest, leaving her cunt gaping. She wanted terribly to cover herself, but there was nothing she could do, except to gasp as the first cock she had ever known in her life fucked her mouth, and the second began to press against the never-before-penetrated pussy lips.

'To her undying amazement, Laura began to enjoy herself.'

'Well, far out,' Joan said out loud. She leaned back in her chair and lit another cigarette. 'It's amazing the fantasies people have,' she thought. She closed her eyes and tried to picture the scene she had just been reading about, only instead of Laura tied to the cot, she placed herself. All at once, the ambience changed. Far from being an absurd exercise in sexual hyperbole, the thing became feasible and desirable. Joan let out a mouthful of smoke and let herself sink into the scene. To be tied, to be overwhelmed with brute male energy, to know the smell of it, the power of it, the deep penetrating sensations. Yes, she could understand the logic of that kind of rape. To be nothing but a hole, a hot wet pussy, a lapping mouth, a twitching ass. She had known what that was like being with just one man, and not being bound by ropes. To make the leap to a gang-bang concept was just to project the reality a bit further.

She let her free hand fall to her thighs, and smiling to herself, she let her fingers walk to her crotch. Then, as though her hand were a man jumping off a cliff, she leaped from her leg to her cunt, landing with a long slow glide. The pressure felt good through the cloth of her dress, and she lazily rubbed herself up and down. Little jolts of electricity shot from her clitoris deeper into her vagina, and she pressed her thighs together with pleasure. She could smell the first secretions, and she tightened her ass to heighten the sensations. She put her cigarette out and with her other hand she began to play with her breasts, reaching down the top of her dress and slipping under her brassiere, to caress the thick flesh and tweak the taut nipples. Joan's eyes closed and her mouth fell open. She began to work in earnest, going from a light masturbation to a steady effort to bring herself off. All the while she stroked and pinched her tits and dug her fingers into the soft heat of her cunt, she maintained the fantasy of the chapter she had just been reading. Her pussy was mushy under the fabric, and she was hungry for it to be bare and spread, open to the eyes of the men surrounding her.

'*She lay on the dirty cot and the men began to climb over her. Her tight asshole was nudged by a thick cock, and she groaned out loud as she pictured her buttocks spreading, and the tiny hole grasping the giant engine as it slid haltingly into her. Another man straddled her shoulders and masturbated over her. She opened her mouth wide, yearning upward, waiting for the thick creamy sperm to come splashing down on her tongue and into her throat.*' Joan's toes curled as the Hell's Angels of her dream world fucked her again and again, making her cunt sloppy and sore, and she rotated her fingers faster and faster, pumping toward climax.

'Oh fuck me,' she cried out, 'you big thick cock, fuck me, fuck me, fuck me.'

The sentences spilled out from her as she clenched her ass, bunched one breast in one hand, and humped the air. She rolled from side to side in an anguish of expectation. And in her mind she thought, ' "an anguish of expectation," that's not a bad phrase.' And she laughed as she came, the deep sound breaking from her chest, and the juices seeping from her pulsating pussy into her panties, through her dress, making her fingers damp and fragrant.

'Oh, yes,' she moaned as her climax sang through her. She arched her back one last time and fell quiet into the deep chair, breathing heavily. She lay there for several minutes, letting herself return to normal, and very slowly opened her eyes. And when she found herself looking up into the serious gaze of Manuel, her heart almost stopped with fright.

He worked in the mail room, and because of his low-status position, and because he was Puerto Rican, Joan had rarely even thought of him as a person. But he was over six feet tall, and wore his two-hundred pounds with the muscular ease of an athlete. He was thirty years old, and lived in a totally self-involved world, saying little, thinking much. He was keenly aware of the caste system that operated through and around him, but his goals were in a different realm. His only ambition was to save enough money to buy land in Puerto Rico, and work it as a farmer. Although his formal education was slight, he had a deep understanding of the nature of social reality through having seen it from the vantage point of always having been low man on the totem pole. As far as he was concerned, a simple life of growing one's own food in a land that was warm and clean, next to clear beaches, was all that one could aspire to in life, and surpassed the artificial pleasures of the tycoon and politician and urban hustler of any level.

Joan tried to sit up, to pull herself back into the accustomed role she assumed with Manuel, to assert her white skin and college education and importance as editor. But one glance at him showed how utterly senseless all that was now. There was no way to know how long he had been watching her, listening to her. A blush crept up her throat and into her face. He had seen her completely exposed, her face in its orgasmic contortions, her body thrashing wildly about. He had seen her masturbating and was now gloating over her. 'It's like Lou says,' she thought to herself, 'life imitates art. Only instead of a roomful of motorcycle freaks, I have one horny mail boy.' The last word stuck in her mind. 'But he's not a boy, she said to herself, 'he's a man.'

Without a word, Manuel reached down and grabbed her arms. Effortlessly he lifted her from the chair, turned her around, and bent her over the desk. She flushed even more deeply at being put in this frank posture. He pulled her skirt up and tossed it over her back, covering her head. She was in semi-darkness now, her legs bare, her ass jutting up under the thin fabric of her red panties. Her knees trembled as she waited for him to pull her panties down. She considered screaming, but there was no point in making a mess.

'He's caught me fair and square,' she reasoned, 'and it's foolish to be a bad sport. What on earth is he waiting for?'

Manuel did nothing but look at her, letting the beauty of the moment sink in. He had been consumed with desire for Joan from the very first day she walked into the office. With his looks, and his strength, and his inner resolve concerning what he wanted to do with his life, there were thousands of women he could have had, of any race or nationality. Sex was easy for him, as was winning women's hearts. But when Joan came into his life, he was like a man possessed by a demon spirit. He knew at once that he had to have her, and not just to fuck her, but to own her, to make her his cunt.

Of course, he had very old-fashioned ideas about women. When a woman gave herself to a man, she became *his*. And if he loved her, he treated her with concern, and care, and tenderness; and when she needed it, he beat her. But through everything, she belonged to him, and found her deepest identity in knowing that. Given all this, he was tormented by Joan. He could see that she didn't even see him clearly enough to despise him. To her, he was a cipher, a nothing. Fucking her was going to be next to impossible; possessing her was beyond his hopes.

So, he tried hating her, comparing her to other women, seeing that this one had a nicer ass, that one had bigger breasts, the other one was prettier, and yet another one exuded a hotter sexuality. But he was branded in his soul, and no matter how much he fucked other women, he knew no real satisfaction. Because it was Joan he wanted, and he could not get her out of his skin.

And now, here she was, bent over the desk before his eyes, her legs shaking, her cunt sopping wet from having just fingered herself into orgasm, and she was waiting, waiting with bated breath for him to fuck her. It was so sudden, so overwhelming, that he was practically paralyzed with wonder. He had come back to the office to pick up a book he had forgotten, and when he passed her room he glanced in and almost fainted at what he saw. She was stretched out across the chair, her legs wide, one hand rubbing her breasts, the other digging at her cunt, her mouth stretched wide, her tongue curling in the air, and a stream of pornographic prose coming from her lips. He entered quietly and stood there until she came, his cock growing rock-hard in his pants, hurting with desire to break loose from the cloth and sink into her hot box.

Joan straightened her knees, lifting her ass higher into the air. She slid her feet apart, allowing her thighs to open. The situation was extraordinarily erotic, with the combination of having read the book, and having made herself cum, and now pitched face forward over her desk while the taciturn dark Manuel ravished her legs and ass with his hot eyes.

'What is he waiting for?' she thought to herself again.

Manuel stepped forward. He was weak with desire. He

wanted to do everything at once. To fall to his knees and worship her cunt with his tongue. To spin her around and cover her mouth with his. To feel her firm soft breasts in his hands. To force his way between her cheeks and up her puckered asshole. To have her suck his cock. To hold her, to stroke her, to slap her. To merge with her completely.

'My God,' he said to himself, 'It's more than a man should be asked to bear. How much beauty can a person stand?'

He was now standing less than an inch from her body. His hands went forward tentatively and his knuckles grazed the insides of her thighs, gently, going from the backs of her knees to the fold of her buttocks. He stroked her a number of times, deliberately, fleetingly. She felt it like butterflies fluttering up and down her legs. she pushed her ass back an inch, wanting him to do more, to go deeper. But as she approached, he retreated. It would do little good to take her. He knew that instinctively, in a way he could never have articulated. He would not be satisfied until she wanted him as badly as he wanted her. And he had waited almost a year to come to this point, so he could wait longer until it was just right.

He knelt down and brought his face up to the valley made by her panties stretching over the cleft of her ass, and did nothing but to breathe into it, letting the hot breath out with long slow exhalations. She felt nothing at first, and then slowly she began to be enveloped by the warmth, the golden warmth that spread across her buttocks, and into the crack between and finally to her cunt. His hot steady breath penetrated to her waiting pussy, and caressed it with the most delicate of touches. She almost screamed with the need it began to spark in her. She pushed back again, wanting to cover his mouth with her crotch, to have his lick her cunt, to suck it, to touch it with his fingers. She wanted him to fuck her cunt.

But he pulled back again, leaving her trembling on the edge of frustration.

'Manuel,' she moaned, 'please.'

His mind reeled. There she was, his 'little Protestant lady,' as he called her to himself, the prim proper copy editor, the white goddess of his most persistent dreams, who had always passed by him on a cloud of untouchability, corseted and distant. And now she was ready to go on her knees to beg him for his cock. But it was more than his cock he wanted her to want. He wanted her to want him completely – his whole body, and his mind.

He stood up and stepped forward. His hard cock bulged against his pants, and he pressed it up against her quivering ass. Cloth met cloth as his rough jeans rubbed against her silk panties. He leaned his weight into her, and began to rotate his hips slowly, pumping his throbbing crotch into the crack between her legs. For her it was a sensation she had not known for years. When she was a teenager, and all that she could conceive of was petting, if she really liked a boy after an evening of heavy necking, she would let him rub against her until he came in his pants. With a rush of poignant memory, her entire teenage came back to her, the hopes, the frustrations, the yearnings, the boys she thought she loved, with that tender vulnerable love that rarely survives adolescence in this brutal world.

Joan became unutterably sad, for she suddenly saw a circle in her life. From bright-eyed girl being dry-humped in the back seat of a car to supposedly sophisticated pornographer's assistant being humped over the edge of her desk . . . it all closed in upon itself, and all the years in between vanished like a dream.

'It's as though I never lived them,' she thought.

For Manuel, the situation was critical. Having at last come to the point of sex with Joan, he found that his heart was breaking because it was so harsh and impersonal. He had been carried away by his lust, and had thrown her over the desk without thinking. Now, his cock screaming for release, he felt he couldn't fuck her without destroying all chance for something deeper to happen between them. And yet, he couldn't stop himself. The sight of her upturned ass, the aroma that rose from her cunt, the exquisite sensations of his cock rubbing up and down the length of her bottom, brought him closer and closer to cuming.

He dug his fingers into her hips and pulled her buttocks toward him. His hands crept around her front and went to her cunt. When he touched the springy mound he stopped short. Her panties were literally dripping. What a woman of passion she was. If only he could make love to her properly, to feel her thighs around his back, to feel her ass in his hands, her hands digging into his back, her mouth on his. He wanted to turn her around, to grasp her to him, but he was afraid that the abruptness would break the mood. He could not forget that on one level he was the mail boy and she was the copy editor, and she might suddenly turn on him with scorn and rejection. And then he would either destroy her in a rage of anger, or be destroyed himself by her loathing.

The heat began to mount in his loins and he knew he would cum soon. Joan lost all sense of time and place. Massive realizations tumbled down her mind like landslides, to strongly and rapidly that she could not even perceive their content. She was in utter turmoil, and all she could hold onto was the solidity of the desk beneath her.

'This is my desk,' she said to herself again and again. 'This is my desk, and this is my office,' she chanted, until the words lost meaning. 'Oh, what is happening to me?'

Her legs stiffened and she pressed her ass back, pushing it harder into Manuel's body. She could not differentiate between the immediate sensations and the sensations of memory, and it was no longer important to her. The two of them were moving to a climax, she could feel that. And even though she wasn't cumming herself, that wasn't important. It was like her teenage boyfriends. She found her pleasure in a process that was not entirely physiological. She was giving him immense enjoyment, and through his excitement, she found her own happiness.

'Yes,' she whispered, too low for him to hear, more to herself than to anyone else in the world, perhaps to the self she had been ten years earlier, to the girl that had become a woman only to find that the girl was still alive in her. 'Yes,' she said, 'rub it against me, rub your cock against my ass. Feel how hot and soft my ass is for you. Rub it against my cunt, feel how wet I am. Make your cock get hotter and hotter. Let me feel how stiff it is, how terrible it is.'

She brought her hands around and spread her cheeks for him, letting him push deeper into the cleft, closer to the cunt that was the real object of his sexual desire. He almost cried out with the outrageous wonder of seeing her that way, of having her do these things for him.

'But it is not for me,' he thought. 'She does not even know who I am. She would do this for anyone who found her the way I did. It is true. Under that mask she is just a hot pussy, a whore who will do anything if it gives her the thrill she seeks.'

Paradoxically, as his sense of moral distance grew, so did the heat in his groin. His balls were now aching with the need to release the boiling juices inside him. There was no motion now; their bodies were perfectly still. And in that stillness came a strange realization. Without the panting and the thrusting. Joan suddenly felt more naked than she could remember feeling. There was something terribly embarrassing about the stillness. She wanted to be lost in a frenzy, for only in that excitement could she feel free.

'No,' he told her. 'I don't want it that way. I don't want to be just any cock. When I come inside you, I want you to know who it is that splashes your pussy with his sperm. I want you to know whose flesh it is that drives you wild. This is not one of your dirty stories that you read all day. This is real life.'

She did not want him to talk, to ruin the magic of the moment with some drab declaration of integrity. She knew that she was running away from facing something real, but she didn't care at that moment. She wanted completion. She answered him without speaking, by rolling her ass gently around on the hard outline of his cock. She clenched the cheeks together, pulling the throbbing rod into her.

'Fuck me,' she whispered. 'Put that big spic cock inside me. Come on, I've been watching you eat me with your eyes all these months. Are you a man or aren't you? What do you want me to do? Do you want me to suck it? Do you want me to sit on it? Do you want to slide that juicy cock up my tight ass? Come on, Manuel, take my panties off, and fuck me right.'

Her words were like lashes along the backs of his legs. He began to move again, his pelvis pumping with short chaotic pulses. His breath came in short, harsh bursts. His eyes narrowed to slits as he prepared to let himself go. Her ass loomed before him like an iceberg in thick fog. His hands reached around in front of her and pulled her thighs apart. Her feet came off the floor and her body took to the horizontal so that now he was squarely between her legs, his encased cock pressed in the hot crevice between cunt and asshole. She bent her legs at the knees and felt her breasts squashed against the desk top. She felt her excitement mount and wondered whether she could cum again.

Manuel was unable to prolong it another second. Knowing that this might be the last as well as the first chance he would ever have to get this close to Joan, he closed his eyes and let out a yell which reverberated throughout the entire suite of offices. He pumped furiously, faster, and faster, and faster, his cock tingling until he thought it would burst. And then, with a gush of scalding heat up the entire tube, it did burst, sending wave after wave of sperm into the blue cloth of his jeans. It ran down his leg, soaking the material. His entire body jerked sideways, for the ejaculation was as painful as it was pleasurable, since his cock was pinned at an awkward angle inside his pants. They hung together like that for a full minute until the spasm passed and his cock started to shrink, retreating from its cramped extension.

Slowly, he let Joan down, and she slid to her knees, her back still toward him. She knew he had cum, and didn't know what his mood might be. Would he want to take her again, or would he be momentarily disgusted, as many men are after ejaculation? She turned timidly, shuffling on her knees, until her face was level with his crotch. She could see the broad stain in his pants leg, and she pressed her mouth onto it, to savor its flavor and smell. She was screamingly horny, and would have licked the jism off his thigh if he would let her. Her cunt ached for penetration, and her ass was on fire from friction.

Manuel didn't say a word. He was split in two-happy because he had confirmed his strongest prejudice, that Joan was like all women, a blind hungry hole once the deep part of her was reached – and sad. And despite all that, she was still Joan, herself, and not all women, or any other women, but *this* woman. And he had lusted for her from a distance, and now had her kneeling at his feet, sucking his cum through the fabric of his pants, her soft tender lips making little suction kisses on his thigh.

What could he do now? Could he fuck her? And then? he would still need to talk to her. And what could he say to this strange lady? 'Come with me to Puerto Rico and we will raise chickens and corn.' She would laugh. She would try to be kind, but she would despise him. No, his dream was finished. There was no way for him to really have this woman. He saw now that the past year had been a way for him to distract himself. He would go home now, and get drunk, and go see some whore and they would fuck like dogs until dawn. And he would return to his own level.

Abruptly, he turned and walked out of the office, leaving Joan swaying on her knees, her mouth wet with her exertions to lick him dry. His movement startled her, and for a moment she didn't know what he was up to. When she heard the front door slam, however, she realized he had gone for the night. Her thoughts were momentarily disrupted by her feelings of surprise mixed with shame.

'He used me and then he left me,' she said to herself. 'He must think I'm a slut.' And she began to give herself to a chant of self-loathing when she remembered the things he had said when they had fallen silent. He wanted more from her than a piece of ass; he had been trying to tell her something about himself. She shook her head. And she had replied by flinging herself more violently onto his cock.

For the first time in many years she was confused after a sexual encounter. 'And we didn't even really have sex,' she said to herself. 'Just some dry-humping over a desk.'

She reached for her sense of cynicism to rescue her. 'Hold on to yourself,' she said out loud. 'You've been frigged by the Puerto Rican mail boy, and it's spun you around a few times. Now just calm down and don't go reading mysteries into it. He came, he saw, he conquered, and he came; and then he went. And left you hanging. It was probably his Catholic guilt,' she concluded, explaining his rapid departure to her satisfaction.

But on her knees, her lips moist, her eyes on the edge

of tears and her cunt feeling its emptiness, aching for Manuel to fill it, she couldn't quite believe her own story. She stood up, ran a hand through her hair, lit a cigarette, and sat down in her editor's chair. A sharp sob pierced her pussy, and she caught her breath. For five minutes she just smoked and stared into space, her mind empty. All she could do was jump from level to level, realizing that in one context what had happened was utterly trivial, and in another context, that it had shaken her to her very roots.

'He made me feel,' she said out loud, 'more than just sensation, he gave me real feelings,' she added, echoing what Margaret had said about her that morning.

She put out the cigarette and lit another. She glanced at her wristwatch. It was seven-fifteen. She decided that the best thing she could do was to get back to work, to do something routine to put her back on a track she felt comfortable with. 'I'll soak for an hour and then go have dinner,' she thought. 'And then go home and have a hot bath, and watch television, and do all the inane things that will help put my head back in shape.'

The manuscript had been scattered over the desk top and she began to put it in order. Some of the sheets were wet from where her mouth, lying open, had dripped saliva. Once again she began to tremble. The impact of the experience assailed her once more. In terms of sexual detail, it was nothing, especially in comparison to things she had done with Lou, and just last night with Margaret. But there was a quality of contact, of emotion, that she didn't get when in throes of orgasm with someone else.

'I felt more with Manuel's cock rubbing against my panties than I have with cocks shoved all the way inside my cunt,' she concluded – and wondered precisely what that would entail when she saw him the next morning.

She stacked the sheets of the novel together, and she began to read.

'Laura knelt in front of the row of men. Naked, spent, she begged them with her eyes to leave her alone. They had been at her for twenty-four hours now, and she couldn't count how many had been inside her how many times. Her cunt was a raw gash, and her ass was bleeding. But they were implacable. "Start sucking," one of them said. She closed her eyes and opened her mouth. Seventeen cocks. How would she be able to suck seventeen cocks after what she had just been through?'

Joan stood up abruptly.

'I don't know, Laura girl,' she said out loud. 'But I've got my own problems to deal with.'

And without bothering to put out the light, she picked up her coat, nodded her approval of her decision to do no more work that night, and walked out of the empty office, leaving the characters of fiction to their own perils and devices.

FOUR

On the street, Manuel was a different man. It was as though some fierce and nameless animal suddenly came awake, and the same body which behaved in its civilized routine at the office downtown, now smouldered with an intensity that bespoke its true energy.

Manuel prowled the streets of East Harlem, walking without seeing or hearing, down the stone canyons that overflowed with teeming life, with men and women who had left the hot climate of their native island to find a life of bitter competition and grainy poverty that was more degrading than the hunger they had fled. The buildings seemed to ooze children and dogs and flies and unending mounds of garbage. It was almost midnight, and he had been on the move for over four hours, going from bar to bar, trying to get drunk, but becoming instead more and more sober, his thoughts lacerating him like icy rain.

He went down streets which would have caused apprehension even in a brace of armed policemen, and certainly to any of the average hard-working church-going members of the neighborhood. They held a sinister atmosphere that could almost be smelled, for in the shadowed hallways lurked junkies almost literally dying for a bit, ready to take a life for the necessary money; muggers who enjoyed the fear they caused as much as the property they stole; rapists who waited with sharp-eyed monomania; groups of psychopathic teenagers with switchblades at the ready; and random derelicts who sometimes carried guns.

But Manuel was impervious to harm, for he was shielded by his total introversion. From time to time he brought his fingers to his nostrils to sniff the rapidly facing aroma of Joan's cunt.

'Oh, if only I had fucked her,' he thought again and again. 'If I had just got my cock inside her, I would have made her mine.'

He replaced each second of the incident, starting from the moment he saw her masturbating to watching her kneeling in front of him, licking his rough sperm-soaked jeans with her tender pink tongue. And at any one of a thousand places, he told himself, he should have done something different. But she was so open, so fragile, so lovely, that he was unmanned. He drank and he walked and he thought, and he grew cold inside, the result of the repression of a fury and despair that echoed the thirty years of frustration within himself and oppression from without.

'I got to get her out of my mind,' he said to himself. And as the thought struck him, he saw the phone booth on the corner.

'I'll call Alma,' he thought, the notion taking him by surprise, for he had not spoken to her for a year, since he had gone to work for Centaur Publications, and become enamored of dating white women.

The phone rang six times before she answered.

'Whoever this is it better be important it's after midnight,' she said all in one breath.

He hesitated. 'Alma,' he said, and paused. He knew she recognized his voice because he could hear her gasp. 'It's Manuel,' he said, unnecessarily.

'Manuel,' she repeated. There was a long silence, and then she asked, 'Are you in trouble?'

Manuel's eyes misted over. He had forgotten how good-hearted and practical she was. He smiled to himself. 'No, not with the police or anything. Just inside myself.'

'Must be a woman,' she said, and the bitterness in her voice almost seared the wire. 'One of your fancy ladies from downtown.'

He hung his head. He had forgotten this too; that the other side of Alma's enormous warmth and acceptance was a hardness that cut like razor blades. He almost hung up on the spot. Sensing his response, she relented. She could picture him as she always did, a little boy in a man's body, someone she wanted to hold to her breasts, to comfort, and then to give herself to in an explosion of passion, totally, without reserve, with love and desire.

'Manuel,' she whispered. 'Do you need to see me?'

'Yes,' he said, noting how she had said 'need', not 'want.'

'Well, come on,' she said, 'you know the address.'

'All right,' he said, 'all right, thank you.'

'Knock off that "thank you" shit,' she told him. 'We been too close for that kind of stuff now.'

He hung up and his hand was sweating from holding the receiver so tightly. After what he and Alma had known together, he knew that calling her was more than going to see an old friend for comfort, or an old lover for a pleasant lay. She had loved him so fiercely that it had bent his heart; and deep within him he knew that she fulfilled everything he might want in a woman, except that she didn't flood him with the terrible excitement he got from just looking at Joan. He and Alma had fucked, and it had been good, but it did not make him swoon. And when they split up she had said, 'Don't ever call me unless you're serious. I don't want to play this game again.'

And his steps went in the direction of her apartment, he kept saying to himself, 'It's not too late; you don't have to show up. Just go home. Go to a whorehouse and get laid. Forget it.' But he was like a man in the grip of a hypnotic force, and he walked mechanically the eight blocks to her place, and climbed the four flights of the ancient tenement. Up the narrow staircase with its polished wooden banisters, and a smell that had not changed for over sixty years. The building had been a home for waves of Jews, Irish, Italians, and now housed Puerto Ricans with the same gentle indifference, its water and steam pipes complaining a bit more loudly, the cracks in its walls a bit wider, but still sturdy with the craftsmanship of an earlier century.

She answered his first knock.

And when the door opened, he could not believe his eyes.

The girl he had known a year earlier was an entirely different creature. The plump, pleasant woman who wore print cotton dresses was now thin, her hair piled high on her head, wearing a black silk robe. She had no makeup except for a swatch of violet eye shadow on each eyebrow, and sported a single silver earring in her right ear. From behind her came the faint aroma of marijuana.

He stood there stupidly, blinking, until, laughing, Alma grabbed his arms and said, 'Come in, you lunk, I can't say hello properly in the hallway.'

She pulled him into the apartment and slammed the police lock closed behind him. If her personal appearance had startled him, the decor of the pad was equally surprising. The interior walls had all been knocked out, and the plaster removed from the supporting walls, leaving exposed brick which had been washed with acid and shellacked. In the process, a fireplace had been uncovered, and it now held a low glowing fire. Originally a railroad flat, the place was now a single loft, perhaps a hundred feet long and twenty feet wide, and all the furniture was in keeping with the sense of spaciousness, including a white net hammock that spanned one entire corner. From a stereo he could not yet see, Cat Stevens sang his need for a hard-headed woman.

He could not catch up with the rush of sensations that flooded him. But Alma made up for his astonishment by putting her arms around his neck, pressing the full length of her body against his, and covering his mouth with her own. The effect was eerie, for it was the same woman he had made love to many times, and yet it was someone different. He ran his hands down her back, remembering the curve of her spine, and then he cupped her ass in his palms and pulled her pelvis toward him. Her buttocks were large and wide, but now they stood out in contrast to the rest of her, which was some forty pounds lighter than it had been. Even her breasts improved with the contrast, for whereas they had been part of her general softness, they now stood out against her slim ribcage, two hot mounds of yielding flesh that pressed into his chest. His mouth opened and her tongue immediately snaked inside, licking his teeth, his palate, and then pushing far back toward his throat, a thick pulsing organ with a wild sensual intelligence.

They held each other for a long, long time and then separated.

'Whew,' was all he could say.

It did not take long for them to get comfortable, lying by the fire with shoes and socks off, hot coffee in front of them, cigarettes sending off curls of yellow smoke. And they told each other their stories, encapsulating time with language.

Manuel told her about his job, about his plan to buy land, and finally, about his infatuation for Joan. He didn't go into the details of what had happened, but only told her that it had been totally frustrating, and he was so confused he didn't know whether he wanted to go back. 'You see,' he said, 'it is hard for me to keep my manhood in the white man's world. They treat me like a pet monkey. But in the back of my head, I know what I am there for, so I can keep my dignity. But when something happens, like with this woman, then the bottom is pulled out.'

'I know what it is like,' she agreed. 'After you left, I decided I had to find out more about this new country. You know, we came here when we were children, but all the years we spent in the barrio might well have been spent in Puerto Rico. The rest of the city was a mystery to me. So, every night after work, I went to different places. And finally, I discovered Greenwich Village.' She smiled to herself, remembering something she didn't articulate. 'I met a musician, and he introduced me to grass, and to fancy parties, and to very sophisticated people. Well, I started to change fast. I lost weight, I learned how to dress to please myself and not my mother, I began to think about how I wanted my pad to look. And then I got lucky. Someone approached me about bringing certain packages in from Puerto Rico. Since I'm a woman and since I have family both here and there, it was likely I wouldn't be searched. So I made a half-dozen trips within three months, and all of a sudden I was twenty-thousand dollars richer. I quit that miserable job in the bank, and I've been hanging out ever since.'

Manuel looked at her with awe and embarrassment. He had called her thinking she would be the timid overweight girl he had loved but could not take seriously as a mate, and that she would be overjoyed to see him. Instead he found a sharp beautiful woman who treated him with a certain warmth, but definitely with deference. He felt clumsy and oafish in front of this woman of the world.

He didn't realize he had fallen so silent and was staring moodily into the flames until she rubbed the back of his neck with her hand.

'Hey,' she said, 'where you off to in your head?'

He could find no words. Depressed by what had happened with Joan, he was almost paralyzed at finding Alma as far, if not farther, beyond his grasp than the sexy editor at the office. But almost without his being aware at first of what was happening, Alma slipped her hand inside his shirt and was slowly and gently rubbing the firm pectoral muscles, tickling his hair, and grazing his nipples. He got aroused before he was conscious of his growing erection. He turned to look at her.

'What are you doing?' he asked tenderly.

'Remembering how good you feel,' she told him. 'Remembering what a strong handsome, fierce lover you are.'

'Don't pity me, Alma,' he said.

She pinched his skin hard enough to make him wince and grab her wrist. 'The only pity here is coming from you, and it's all for yourself. What's the matter with you? You have a little run-in with a chick where you work and it destroys you? In the old days you used to eat women like that for breakfast. When you were with me you used to go downtown and pluck them off the streets and fuck them in the back seats of their cars, those little white girls with their itchy asses.'

'I know,' he agreed. 'I guess I'm just getting old enough to feel lonely, that's all.'

'That's why you came to see me, isn't it?' she asked with a quaver in her voice.

'Sure,' he said. 'And I'm really glad to see you doing so well.'

She shook him roughly. 'Why are you talking to me like I was a stranger?'

'Well,' he told her, 'you're in a different world now. You got money, you got new ways, you got fancy lovers.' He looked at her sadly, 'It's nice of you to take me in off the street for a night, but there is nothing for me here.'

She pulled away from him, lay back on the rug, and looked up at him through half-closed eyes. 'I loved you so much,' she began, 'that when you went away I just wanted to die for a long time. But I lived, and I changed.

And I've been making my way. And now you're back, and you're pissed off because I'm not the way I was when you left. And you're feeling sorry for yourself. Well, I'll tell you something. All this while I've been going through changes, I've been thinking, "If Manuel comes back, I'll be a real woman for him, a beautiful woman who can stand on her own two feet." But I didn't think you would come back, I just kept loving you anyway, way in the back of my heart, thinking I would never see you again. And now you are here. And if you want me again, you can have me. I'm not going to play games with you about that. I still want you. And I have money, yes, and I have new ways, yes, and they are all yours if you want them. And I have lovers, yes, because I am a woman and not a child. And if you come back into my life, I'll make every other man I know disappear, like that!' She snapped her fingers. 'But you got to show me something. You got to show me that you want me. You got to win me. You got to fuck me so I forget every other cock that's been inside me. And if you want to do that, here I am baby. And if you don't, you can go out the same door you came in.'

Manuel rocked back and forth as she delivered her speech, words that jumped lie sparks from her mouth. At the same time that they intimidated him, they turned him on, making him at once afraid and desirous of the strange and familiar woman who was stretched out in front of him.

'Manuel,' she urged. 'Don't have such a stiff neck. Just take me in your arms, and find out what is here. Don't try to think about it. You can't know if the meat is good until you taste it.'

His heart skipped a beat. She was ravishingly beautiful,

her dark lustrous skin picking up the highlights from the fire, her eyes liquid with yearning, her body arched toward him, her mouth slightly open and moist.

She traced her fingers across the top of his thigh and then sat up abruptly, bringing her face to his ear, biting the outer ridge and running her tongue into the sensitive center, breathing lightly. 'Do you think I've forgotten how your mouth feels on my nipples, how your fingers feel in my cunt, how your cock tastes on my tongue? Do you think I could forget how I cried each time you entered me? Do you know how deeply I loved you? And now, after a lot of men and a lot of experience, I am not the naive girl I was. I am a woman who has tasted a few things, and I tell you, nothing is as sweet as feeling you cum inside me, and squeezing my thighs together, and sucking the juice from your cock. It's only to you that I have ever opened in that way, because it's only with you that I want to make a baby.'

She kissed his cheeks and lips and she smiled. 'I'm still the old-fashioned woman under this chic dress,' she said. 'I still want to have a man make me his. I still want to feel his seed grow inside me.' She ran her hand down his broad chest, over his belly, and onto his crotch, where his cock stirred lazily under her touch.

'My cunt is hungry for you Manuel. Feed my cunt. Give it what it wants.'

He wanted her with growing lust mixed with astonishment. 'Can it be that she still feels this way for me after all this time?' he thought.

As though reading his thought, she whispered, 'Do you imagine your feeling for me is dead?'

Manuel let go of his doubts, his hesitation, and with

a single gesture took Alma in his arms and pressed his lips to hers. At once, they merged into a single sensation, losing all sense of separateness as two beings. Manuel remembered how often they had verged on this, and how desperately he had wanted this, not to remain outside the woman, fucking her, but for both of them to enter the space of fucking together, so there was no one fucking and no one being fucked, but rather a fucking which happened of its own accord, in which they were both taken up and transported to a state of bliss.

Her mouth opened and sucked his tongue inside. The breath was pulled from his chest, and she breathed the air from his lungs, filling herself, and then emptying herself back into him, so that the same air went from body to body, without being dispersed. Her tongue pushed his way, hot and wet, forcing itself into his mouth, sending vibrations of pleasure down in to his belly. He crushed her to him, his powerful arms enveloping her entirely, and she stretched out her legs so as to lie more easily against him. The two of them sank slowly to the floor, until they lay side by side, thighs touching thighs, his cock bulging out and into the hollow between her legs, her lush breasts flattened against his firm chest, their mouths hungrily eating at one another, trying to overcome a year's fast with a single meal.

Alma pulled back, reeling from his kiss. Manuel's face was a hollow mask of lust. His eyes were turgid with smoldering sex. Something deeper than he had planned on had been triggered in him, and his response had taken him far past the mildly erotic experience he had been expecting.

'My God, you can still do it to me like that,' she

gasped. 'I was so afraid that after all this, maybe I wouldn't find you enough for me. That maybe I had become too sophisticated for you. But not down deep where it counts; down there, I'm still your woman.'

He looked at the woman in front of him. She had become undone, her hair falling out of its knot and starting to pile down her shoulders, her black robe slipping down her arms.

'I want to see you,' he said, 'I want to see your cunt. I want to see that giant bush of black hair.'

She took his hand and guided it slowly under the robe, letting his fingers slide up her smooth thighs, and toward the moist center of her body. He could feel the warmth increasing as he approached her pussy, and then the first tickling of the pubic hair, the lustrous bush that went from halfway up her belly, down over her cunt, and into the cleft of her ass.

'I didn't realize how much I'd missed you until now,' he said.

'This is what you missed,' she said, and led his fingers into the wet crack itself, past the crinkled outer lips, past the slippery inner lips, through the serrated hole at the core, and then into the hot wide cavern inside.

'This is what you missed,' she repeated, 'this hot cunt that's been waiting for you, that's been aching to feel you inside.' She licked his throat as his hand went inside her. 'Feel me now, Manuel; put your strong hands inside my creamy pussy. Make me moan the way you used to.'

Manuel needed little more urging, and he crooked his fingers into her cunt, reacquainting himself with its ridges and contours, and then pulled out to caress the tiny button at the top of the opening, the small clitoris that contained more capacity for sensation than any other organ of the body. As he touched her there, she groaned and her knees rose up toward her chest. He slid his hand down, the middle finger curving over the crack between her buttocks, and the rest of his hand rubbing the inward curve of the two cheeks on either side. He moved up and down, up and down, until she was crowing with pleasure. He stopped from time to time to tickle the small puckered hole that lay at the heart of his explorations, and then slipped up to finger her cunt again, returning at last to her clitoris, taking it between his fingers and rolling it around until she kicked with excitement. She was open and wet for him, letting him play with her however he wanted.

'Is it different with me than with other men?' he asked.

'You fool,' she replied. 'Is it different with me than with other women? Is it like this with your Joan?'

He thought about it a moment. Yes, it was different with Alma. The false excitation was not there. There was no pretence, no sense of outrage or rape or seduction. It was not dirty. It was simply the full energy of a man and a woman going out to mingle and rejoice in the sheer joy of existence. He thought of Joan, and his brow furrowed. No, it could never be with Alma like it had been in the office. For what he had experienced with Joan was the pleasure of eating the forbidden fruit. It was in the realm of the mind, not of the body. It was something that was at the same time more and less than sex. But this, with Alma, was sex itself. It was healthy and right. And he could give himself without reserve, without tension, without considering anything with his brain.

He brought his hand up and began to slide her robe

off the rest of her body. She wriggled and helped him with the task, and in a moment she was naked. He bit his lip between his teeth, for he had not been ready for the sheer luxury of her beauty. she saw him looking at her in that way, and her heart leapt with joy that he was so taken with her. It occurred to Manuel that nothing in the world, not a sunset, not a storm at sea, not a universe filled with galaxies, could begin to compare with the naked body of a beautiful woman for absolute splendor. It was the summation of all creation.

'I am all for you,' she said. 'Please, take me, however you want.'

He bent forward and covered one breast with his lips. The flesh was firm and smooth on his tongue, and the pear-shaped tit slid easily between his teeth and filled his mouth. He licked the nipple, forcing his face into her chest. She put her hands on the back of his head and drew him to her even more closely. He licked the underside of her breast again and again, ending always at the very tip of her nipple, while with his left hand he squeezed and caressed her other breast, and with his right hand he continued to stroke her between her legs, getting her wetter and hotter with each moment. Her head rolled from side to side, her buttocks squeezed and relaxed, and her legs kicked lazily from side to side as he covered her with kisses.

'You too,' she said, 'take your clothes off too.'

He started to undress, but she pushed him back. 'Stand up,' she said. 'I want to see you naked standing over me. I want to lie at your feet.'

Manuel stood up. He peeled off his shirt quickly, his muscular arms bulging with the movement, his broad chest jutting forward. Then he undid his belt, the top button, the zipper, and was pulling his pants down his legs. His cock, three-quarters erect, bobbed lazily forward, swinging in the air. It was thick, succulent, long. The head was purplish and ribbed around the edge. The staff itself was thickly veined like fine marble, while beneath the juice phallus hung the two sacs, like hairy eggs sculpted by a mad surrealist. At the very tip of his cock glistened a drop of pre-seminal fluid. Alma curled her tongue out.

'Let me taste you,' she said. 'Let me hold you in my mouth.'

He knelt slowly and brought his throbbing cock to her lips. She did not lift her head from the floor, but let him come all the way down. His cock slid into her mouth softly, and she did not suck him at once, but just let herself feel the heft and texture of his huge organ. Her tongue flicked the drop of fluid from the tip of his cock, and she swallowed it with relish, enjoying the tangy flavor, the symbolic pleasure of the act.

She mouthed his cock gently, and gradually it became completely stiff, and with that change, transformed its character. Now a nine-inch engine with a single purpose, it seemed to take on a life of its own. Manuel looked down at Alma. Her legs were spread apart, her cunt wet between them, her breasts flattened on her chest, her arms at her side with her hands curled; she was totally open and inviting, waiting for him to fuck her in the mouth. He put one hand on her pussy, slid a finger into the hot slimy slit, and watched as she convulsed with yearning. Her lips pursed and reached up to kiss his cock.

And with that, he shoved the immense rod into her

mouth. He moved slowly at first, sliding up and down her tongue, and then going from side to side, bulging out her cheeks. He pulled out and grabbed his cock with one hand, and rubbed the head of it all over her face. She licked his balls. He pulled his cock as though he were masturbating, and she sucked the head of it between her lips, licking furiously, hungry for sperm. Finally, he thrust deep down into her throat, until the whole thing was buried in her face, and she was glued to his body, her lips lost in his curling pubic hair. She held herself like that for a long moment, and then began to gag. Her legs kicked up and her stomach clenched, and he pulled his cock out of her, leaving her gasping, her face flecked with spit.

'Don't stop,' she whispered. 'Fuck my mouth hard. Don't stop even if I gag. I want to choke on your cock.'

Instead he grabbed her arms and rolled her over on her stomach. With all the weight she had lost, her waist was now slender and shapely between the curve of her shoulders and the sudden sweep of her ass. Her legs, perfectly shaped, seemed vulnerable from behind. He towered over her, his huge bulk dwarfing her feminine fragility, his giant cock throbbing with need. But he put its desire aside and slid down the length of her body until he was resting with his head on her buttocks.

'Come up on your knees, Alma,' he said. 'I want to see you with your ass in the air, and your cunt spread apart underneath it. Come on, show me everything you have.'

Trembling, she came to her knees. She placed her body the way she knew he liked it, with her head and shoulders on the floor, her spine curved in a parabolic sweep, and her ass flaring wide and open. He got down behind her, and brought his hands up to spread her cunt apart. It was already dripping with the secretions of excitement, and he moved up near her to lick the pearly drops from her thighs. She twitched at his touch.

'So beautiful, so beautiful,' he murmured, and moved his mouth to cover the infolded center. His eyes closed, he entered a space which could not be understood from outside. Alma's cunt became the world for him, and when his tongue slithered into the complex gash, he was transported into a totally different sense of scale. At that point, the inside of her cunt might have been the entire universe, for it was all that existed for him.

For her, she could feel his concentration and complete involvement, and she too closed her eyes against the tears she felt rising in them. It had been so long since she had felt this. Other men had been more skillful than Manuel, or more experienced in technique, but no one else had ever given himself so fully to her. It was a gift he had, and she was certain that he had not known it with any other woman, for if he had, he would not have come back to her. She let her cunt be as wide as the ocean, and lost herself with him in the deep clinging kiss of his mouth against her lower mouth.

'Manuel, my sweet sweet lover,' she moaned, 'make a feast of my cunt. Take my delicious pussy and suck it until there is nothing left.'

He drew her juices onto his tongue and let them slide down his throat. His hands went to her buttocks and spread the cheeks apart, his fingers digging into the thick curved flesh. She pushed her ass back further so he could penetrate more deeply into her. He sucked at her cunt until it was dry, and then he licked it with the flat of his tongue, flicking the clitoris and caressing the spongy lips. Then, moving up, he curled his tongue between her cheeks, and slid it into her puckered asshole, forcing his way in as she squirmed with the unorthodox sensations. He tossed his head to and fro, his hair piling about like a lion's mane, corkscrewing his tongue around in the tiny opening.

Alma curved her spine until it seemed it must snap. She had begun a spiral of pleasure with Manuel that couldn't end short of an explosion. As she opened her ass wider and wider, he dug his tongue deeper and deeper, causing her to spread even farther, which caused him to probe even more strongly. Her hands came up underneath her and found her cunt, one going inside the neglected hole and the other beginning to twirl her clitoris with ever more rapid strokes. She finger-fucked herself with mounting excitement as Manuel lavished all his attention on her ass, now biting the cheeks and the crack and the hole itself.

'Oh baby, I'm cuming,' she cried. 'With your mouth all over my ass, I'm cuming on my fingers.' And pumping harder and harder, thrusting her hands into her pussy, she climbed the curve of excitement until the tremors began in her thighs, and the warmth began in her belly, and she let herself go, soaring and tumbling into the chaotic cataclysm of feeling that defined her orgasm.

As she came, Manuel wrapped his arms around her legs and pulled her tightly into him so that he felt every tremor in her body as she reached her climax, and just as she was spending her juices, he brought his mouth down to suck them, hot and tangy from her pulsating cunt.

Afterwards, they lay quietly for a long time, listening to the fire pop, and letting waves of tingling fatigue wash over them, drifting in and out at the edges of sleep.

Finally, Manuel lifted himself off her body. His cock was soft, but bursting with sensation. It felt so tender that just to brush it against her leg was enough to make him feel like cuming. Alma knew that he was going to fuck her now, and she tried to pull herself together to assimilate what had happened. She wanted him to wait a few minutes so she could be ready to receive him, but he was already arched over her, supporting his weight on his hands and feet, his arms and legs stiff. The only part of him that touched her was his cock, and he trailed it back and forth along the crack of her ass. She could feel it responding and slowly beginning to get hard.

Alma turned over and lay on her back under him. She looked up into his eyes.

'Manuel,' she said, 'You are going to fuck me.'

He smiled. 'Yes, *querida*,' he told her, 'I am going to hoist my thick cock into your hole and fuck you until you are screaming.'

'Not like that,' she said. 'Not for the first time.'

She put her hands around his back and drew him down so that he lay on top of her, their bodies touching entirely. His cock slid between her thighs. The heat from her cunt was extraordinary.

'Fuck me gently,' she said, 'I want to feel all of you, not just your cock.'

Her legs parted slightly, and he moved his body up until his cock was at the opening of her pussy. The wet cunt let him in easily. And his cock entered her for a long time, each inch opening her hole wider, each inch touching a deeper part of her, until he was completely embedded in her body. Her cunt quivered and kissed the length of the cock inside of it.

'You are really here,' she said, her voice filled with wonder.

'I feel here, and then I don't,' he told her.

'Don't worry about it, she said. 'It takes time to get over the strangeness.'

'Time,' he repeated.

'We have all our lives,' she told him.

'You mean, to try again?' he asked.

Alma tightened the muscles of her cunt and grasped him tightly. Manuel shivered with pleasure.

'I'm not going to want to let you go,' she said. 'You know that. You can fuck me now, and leave me in the morning. But I'm not going to want to let you go.'

Manuel began to rotate his hips, his pelvis thrusting forward. His cock swelled to its full hardness and length, and he dug it deep into her cunt. Alma groaned and opened her legs wider. Manuel pumped his cock into her a dozen times, each time changing the angle, each time penetrating more deeply. Alma began to moan continuously, and her legs opened still wider, and bent at the knees. Manuel lowered his pelvis and brought his cock into her from below so that it hit upwards into her cervix.

'Holy Mother of God,' she exclaimed. 'Oh Manuel, I am all yours. My cunt is yours, my ass is yours, my tits are yours, my mouth is yours, my heart is yours. Take me, take me, my beloved.'

Manuel slid his hands down until they cupped the cheeks of her ass and he pulled her into him.

'Give it to me, baby,' he said, 'give me that juicy hot cunt of yours. Make it open, make it loose. Just hold it there and let me fuck it. Let me fuck your cunt.'

And they entered that strange litany of lust, that baroque dialogue of sex, in which the words and the actions are complements to each other, serving no purpose but to bring the people involved to higher and higher levels of pleasure.

Alma lifted her legs high in the air, making her cunt and ass an open crack for Manuel's cock to dive in and out with total abandon. His fingers dug into her buttocks and her breasts were flat against his chest. Her hands raked his shoulders, and her mouth sought his until their lips met, and their souls flew together in the breath of their kiss. Manuel rode her with the ease born of surrender, and Alma wrapped her legs around his back, clasping him in the ultimate embrace, as her hips began to rotate, and she pumped her cunt back into the thrusts of his cock, until their rhythms matched, and they were lost in the far reaches of unselfish fucking, in which there was no longer a self and an other, but a single joint movement toward climax.

With the hot juices spilling out of her cunt as his cock sloshed in and out, Alma thought over and over again, 'Oh Lord, please let him stay this time, please let him know what he means to me,' and with her spiralling joy at having him in her arms, there came a chord of despair that he might not understand how deeply he had touched her.

And as he felt his orgasm approach, the rich writhing body of the luscious woman grinding into him, he said to himself, 'I don't know if this is enough. It is the best thing I will ever know with a woman, but I don't know if I will be able to resist if Joan calls me to her.'

They fucked all night long, and when they fell asleep, it seemed that they would never leave one another's arms again. Only the following day would tell if that were true.

FIVE

Joan rang the bell with apprehension. It was the front door to a brownstone in the Park Slope section of Brooklyn. When Jack had invited her he slipped her a ten dollar bill that morning, saying simply, 'For cab fare.'

Manuel had not been to work for two days, and Joan toyed for a while with the idea of calling him at his apartment, and then dismissed the notion as foolish. Falling into a stereotypic understanding of Manuel, she assumed that her running after him would be met by scorn on his part, and she would have to play out an elaborate drama of submission before he would deign to touch her. She conveniently forgot all aspects of their encounter which pointed to something deeper in the man, since she was not ready to confront him seriously.

'It was great fun but it was just one of those things,' she hummed a number of times during the day.

It was while she was humming the tune that Jack poked his head in through the door of her cubicle. An eternally jolly man of about forty, so nondescript in appearance that she could not tell whether he was goodlooking or not, he stood perhaps five feet eight inches, had loose sandy hair, and no one could remember ever seeing him without a smile.

'How's my favorite smut sorter?' he called out to her.

Joan turned in her chair, smiling reflexively. After the inordinate heaviness of the previous several days, she was relieved to relate in a less than cataclysmic fashion. She put down the manuscript she was reading, threw her feet up on the desk, and asked Jack to come in.

He paused a moment at the doorway to look at the way her skirt slid back past her knees to reveal the first glimpses of her full thighs disappearing into the exotic shadows beyond. Joan looked at him quizzically, for he had never seemed to exhibit any sexual interest in her before.

He walked into the tiny office and sat down on a pile of manuscripts. The room was littered with paper, giving it the appearance of a used book shop or a mathematician's study. He lit a cigarette, and took several drags before speaking.

'Been to any good orgies lately?' he asked.

Joan sighed. 'The only orgies I ever get to never have more than two people.'

Jack grinned, shook his head. 'I know what you mean,' he said. And he turned his head sideways to look frankly up her dress. Her ochre panties glowed dully in the dark space between her thighs, and he imagined he could feel the hot moist mound in the palm of his hand. His cock twitched once, but he did not change his cheerful and lighthearted approach.

'I'm going to one tonight that'll have maybe seventy-five or a hundred people,' he said offhandedly.

Thinking he was joking, Joan said, 'Wow, that sounds like a ball. why don't you invite me?'

Jack narrowed his eyes, ran his gaze up her legs and

over her breasts, his face a curious split between humor and lust. 'OK,' he told her, 'you're invited.'

'What do you do at your orgies?' she asked.

Talking with Jack was usually a matter of staying at the edge between seriousness and whims, between fact and fancy. He was Centaur's most successful salesman, and once, when she had an opportunity to glance at the company's pay sheets, she was astounded to learn that he had grossed over forty-thousand dollars in commissions in a single year. 'And that's nothing,' the accountant had told her, 'in comparison to what he gets under the table.'

'Under the table?' Joan had repeated naively.

'That's right,' the accountant said, and had slipped his hand up Joan's skirt and bunched his fingers in her crotch. She had jumped up in surprise, only to land on his hand again, and this time his fingers were waiting to squeeze her cunt. She wriggled away, and he had laughed as though the thing had been a prank. But she retained the feeling of his hand on her pussy for hours afterwards. It was like that in a pornographer's publishing company; people were always on the alert for sexual encounter.

Joan remembered the incident as Jack smoked with studied precision. 'No one does anything unless he or she wants to at the orgies. The only rule is: no watching. Everyone has to do something, even if it's only to masturbate. Having an audience creates self-consciousness. But you know that. You used to be in theatre, didn't you? That's the trouble with theatre – the audience.'

He looked at her so knowingly, so piercingly, that she wondered for a moment whether he too had been made privy to Lou's movies of her. Concurrently, a flash of anger and a spasm of erotic tension went through her. She was torn in two, as always, between her dislike of being a commodity that Lou passed around via his movie projector, and her excitement at thinking of the strange eyes that watched her perform in the dramas of degradation that Lou had staged with her. 'Has Jack seen me with Lou's cock in my mouth, with the sperm dripping down my chin, spilling over my lips and tongue? Has he seen me with two men sandwiching me between them, one fucking me in the cunt and the other fucking me in the ass, while I went wild squirming and humping myself on their cocks? Has he seen me with my legs spread, pulling my cunt lips apart?'

'Well?' Jack asked.

'Well what?' she replied.

'Would you like to come to the orgy?' he said.

She smiled. 'You mean, there really *is* an orgy?'

'Of course,' he told her. 'There are orgies all the time, all over the place. We are living in the shadow of the fall of two thousand years of western civilization. The witches are taking to the woods again. But this time there are hardly any woods left, so we must perform our rites in apartment houses.'

'And what happens there?'

'You take off your clothes, and sooner or later you get involved in something or other. There are no rules.' He ran his eyes down her body, pausing again at her breasts, and seeming to penetrate all her clothing to perceive that her cunt was becoming interested in the image. She had to check an impulse to put her hand between her legs.

Jack had written an address and a time on a piece of paper, and put it on her desk. Then he took ten dollars from his pocket and put it next to the information. 'It's in Brooklyn,' he said. 'If you come, take a cab.'

And now she stood there, waiting for the massive wooden door to be opened. The day had grown progressively duller since Jack left, and she buried herself in detail. She went home, found herself taking a shower and putting on her most inviting skirt and not wearing a bra under the gauzy blouse she chose. Without thinking about it, she was making her decision. And when she went into the street, she began at once to look for a taxi. 'Of course, I'm going,' she said to herself as she gave the driver the address, and had to promise him a large tip for the trouble of taking her all the way to Brooklyn.

A pleasant, plump middle-aged woman opened the door and looked at her inquiringly. Behind her, there seemed to be no activity of any sort.

'I'm Joan,' she said. 'I'm a friend of Jack's.'

'Oh yes,' the woman said, and Joan realized that she might have said, 'I'm Suzy and I'm a friend of Henry's,' and been met with the same response.

'Well,' she thought, 'one doesn't come to an orgy to be intimate. Its just a matter of bodies.'

'The bodies are downstairs,' the woman said, and Joan rocked back on her heels with imagining that her thought had been read. 'I'm Helene,' the woman went on, 'and this is my house. Come in.'

Joan stepped into the foyer. 'I'm sure Jack told you the rules,' Helene said. 'You must be naked and you must not remain a mere spectator. Aside from that, you may do whatever you like with whomever is willing to do it with you. And if you feel that someone is imposing upon you, you need simply to say "No," firmly, and he or she will stop. That is the final rule.'

Helene walked with her to the end of the hallway. 'Please remove your clothing here,' she said, 'and hang it in that closet.'

Joan spun around. 'But this is really all so cold!' she exclaimed.

'Not really,' the woman said. 'Just efficient. We've had it the other way, and had the most terrible imbroglios looking for lost pocket books and skirts and wallets. Also, there is something necessarily symbolic about entering the orgy room naked. It puts everyone on an equal footing at once. There is no way to maintain social identity when you don't have any clothes on.'

Joan began to remove her blouse, letting her large breasts fall out. They jiggled as she bent over to remove her shoes. She let her skirt drop to her ankles. Helene watched her the way a matron might watch a student preparing for a long-delayed shower. 'This is weird,' Joan said as she slid her panties down her legs. Finally, she stood naked.

'Very nice body,' the woman said. 'I wonder how many cocks will cum in that prim pussy of yours, how many fingers will make that delicious ass wriggle with delight, how many cunts will smother those wide lips, how many mouths will feast on those tiny sensitive nipples and those lush full breasts?' Joan looked up with a flash of horror. The woman was stone-faced. 'You are an infant,' she said, 'and you have the advantage of having a young body. But remember, there are those of us who have been reborn in a different dimension. Think of that when you begin to judge us as being cold or unfeeling, or if you begin to condescend to me because I am old enough to be a grandmother, because I am running to fat, because I am no longer desirable. Just remember, when one is no longer desirable, it sometimes means that that person has freed herself from the chains of desire itself, chains which still are coiled tightly about your mind, and make you a slave to the promptings of your cunt.'

She reached forward abruptly and slipped her hand between Joan's legs, and just as suddenly pulled it back. The tips of her fingers were moist. The woman smiled grimly. 'Go on, Jack's little friend, go down into the sea of flesh, and see if you can satisfy yourself.'

A fear began to creep up Joan's spine and she was almost panicked into putting on her clothes again and leaving, but the woman took her by the arm and led her to another doorway. Opening it on a hubbub of sound, she propelled Joan inside, and closed the door behind her. Joan found herself standing on the top step of a circular stairway, and, taking a deep breath, she began to descend.

The scene that greeted her eyes made her reach for the most immediate time and space perimeters she could find. 'It's ten-thirty and I'm in Brooklyn,' she said to herself, but the words were of little meaning in the face of the timeless drama in front of her. There was the race of humanity, in the throes of its ultimate dance, the final attempt to shed all the millennia of inhibitions and conventionally defined reality that had accrued in their twentieth-century mentalities. Gone were the badges of sartorial definition, the social roles, the moral structures which imposed themselves upon the free perception of the real. It was not that they had attained any higher understanding in the essentially bourgeois expression of release they had convened to share, but that in the very attempt to become other than what their civilization would have them be, they found an odd dignity of purpose that laced the superficially riotous affair with veins of seriousness.

'Ah, Joan,' a voice cried out.

Joan looked out over the room to see Jack coming toward her. He made his way gingerly across the erotic battlefield, sidestepping couples fucking, groups of threes and fours and fives in various pretzel forms, and individuals who looked like people out for a stroll in Washington Square Park on a Sunday afternoon, somewhat self-involved and idly cruising. She could not make out any distinguishing characteristic among the people; there were old and young, the age range seeming to go from about eighteen to sixty; there were fat and thin, black and white, ugly and beautiful. The only thing they all had in common was that they seemed well-fed and healthy, products of the cream of the affluent portion of the world's richest nation. The room did not have a focus.

Jack took her hand and led her away from the staircase to a corner of the huge basement, which was now a bare den, covered with a rug, huge pillows, and containing as its only real furniture a fifteen-foot bar that stood against one wall and was stocked with a full range of liquor. The occasional sharp smell of marijuana smoke cut through the haze of tobacco, which further obscured the dim lighting. Now and ten there was a snap and a sweet aroma which Joan recognized as amyl nitrate. The space was a melange of conversational tones and moans of excitement.

'Nice place, isn't it?' said Jack, jovial as ever.

'I suppose,' Joan started to say. But she was interrupted. Without further ado Jack grabbed her wrists and pushed her to her knees. She found herself staring at his immense sceptered cock, an organ out of all proportion to the rest of his body. He continued the pressure and pushed her to her back.

'I want to get you first, before you get too crazy,' he said. 'And then I'll fuck you later, so I can have you at both ends of the spectrum.'

Joan started to protest but such an action struck her as silly. All around her naked people were fucking and sucking and exploring their bodies with fingers and tongues. Not more than five feet away a thin blonde girl lay on her side, her eyes closed, as a large burly man covered with black hair fucked her face with an angry cock. Joan could see the tip of it slide in and out past her lips, and a thin trickle of spittle spilled out of the corner of her mouth as his cock emerged and entered again and again. Her jaw was slack, and from time to time Joan could see her tongue curled inside her mouth, acting as a cushion for his cock to hit against as he thrust into her. Little moans escaped her, sounds that fell somewhere between a sigh and a slurp. He was looking down at her with unbending purpose, seeming to drink in the sight of her defenseless face accepting the ravaging cock. Her only motion was the tiniest movement of one finger against her clitoris as she brought herself to the edge of climax over and over, keeping herself there to use the energy generated in her cunt to enjoy the sensations in her mouth. Her mouth was the complete receptacle, the thing that wanted to be ravished, to be filled, while her cunt was the source of excitement which made her cocksucking so juicy and perfect.

As Jack pushed Joan on her back and spread her thighs apart with his fingers, the blonde girl rolled over on her back. The man's cock slipped out and he immediately grabbed it with one hand and began to pull it frantically. It was clear that he was close to orgasm. Joan felt Jack's tongue on her belly, tracing its course downward and into her springy bush that covered her cunt. She flexed her pelvis, opening her cunt to his mouth, and he took advantage of her willingness by thrusting three fingers into the wet crack while covering her clitoris with his lips. Joan let out a grunt and began to let the heat move her, as her legs kicked wide and closed again, and her hands went to her breasts as she rubbed her nipples into erection.

'Well, so far it's no different than most other sex I've had,' she said to herself as Jack slipped another finger into her anus, causing her to clench her ass cheeks to drain the intruder of sensation.

'I'm going to cum in your mouth,' the hairy man was saying, 'I'm going to cum all over your face. And you love it, don't you, you hot little bitch. Come on, get that finger up your cunt and fuck yourself wild. Let me see you cum while I fill your mouth with hot sperm.'

Through half-lidded eyes, and half-involved with Jack's ministrations between her legs, Joan watched the hairy man begin to shudder. Ripples went up and down his spine and his hips pumped faster and faster. He seemed to fight a battle between keeping his eyes open to watch his cum spurt all over the girl's face, and letting his eyes close to better enjoy his own feelings. Voyeurism won out over sensationalism and he stared down at his cock as it let loose jet after jet of globular jism. It splashed on her closed eyes, on her cheeks, on her lips. He guided his cock down until the opening was between her open lips, and he let the rest of his ejaculation drop on her tongue. The girl squeezed her thighs together, brought her knees up, and jabbed her finger one last time into her cunt. She was clearly in the throes of a silent inner orgasm, and as she came she rolled the sperm around on her tongue, making her mouth white and sticky, and then with a huge gulp, swallowed the entire mouthful of spunk. She curled her tongue out and licked her lips clean. She took her free hand and wiped the sperm off her face and sucked her fingers dry. The man fell back into a sitting position, and did not move for a few minutes. The girl got up slowly and began to look around the room, searching for the next cock to suck.

Joan came on Jack's tongue. She had become so involved with the drama next to her that her climax had built without her being aware of it, and as soon as she realized that the girl she had just seen was ready, willing, and able to have every man in the room cum in her mouth and still be ready for more, Joan's body responded with its own volition, and caught her up in a fluttering orgasm which had her kicking her legs up in the air and pushing Jack's head into her pussy, letting him lick and suck at the most intimate part of her.

Jack pulled back and sat between her thighs, his mouth wet with her secretions. He winked at her with his unchanging good humor. 'Nice,' he said. 'You tasted just like I thought you would.' And he moved back away from her. 'See you later,' he said.

'But, is that all?' she asked him.

'This is an orgy, Joan,' he said gently. 'There are hundreds of experiences to be had. You'll learn after a while not to get too involved with any single one of them. That defeats the purpose of the gathering. If there's someone you especially like, arrange to meet him afterwards.'

Then, swiftly, he leaned forward and kissed her on the mouth. Her tongue touched his for an instant, tasting her own cunt juices. He held her head in his hands, looked into her eyes, and went on, 'Stay light, Joan,' he told her. 'That's why I invited you here. You're really a lovely person and I like you a lot. But you have to learn to lighten up. Sex is like eating fruit. It's delicious and fresh. Don't make a melodrama out of it.'

Abruptly, he turned and crept off. She watched his body until it was lost in the general crush of bodies. And suddenly, in the middle of the orgy, she was alone.

'What do I do now?' she wondered.

The answer was not long in coming, and it arrived in the form of two men who were looking at her as lasciviously as flesh-and-blood reflections of the Tweedledum and Tweedledee archetypes. Both in their late twenties or so, with short auburn hair, they were each almost six feet tall and looked enough alike to be first cousins.

'I'm Marty,' said one.

'And I'm Dave,' said the other.

'This is your first time here, isn't it?' said Marty.

Joan nodded, fascinated by their brisk approach. She was still lying on her back, supported by her elbows as she raised her torso to a thirty-degree angle from the floor. Her breasts lolled to either side of her chest, and her legs were still spread apart from having Jack eat her cunt.

'I can tell what you're thinking,' Dave said. 'Jack told us you work for a dirty book publisher. And you wonder whether we're fags or not.'

'Does everyone around here read minds?' Joan asked.

'Oh,' Marty remarked sitting down next to her, 'it's just that when the repressions are thrown off, people get more psychic, that's all, which is not any different than being more sensitive. You can sort of tell what people are thinking by the expressions on their faces.'

Dave sat down on the other side of her. 'We used to be homosexuals,' he said, 'but then we discovered that what we really wanted to be was partners in a hunting party.'

'A hunting party?' Joan repeated.

'That's right,' Marty continued, taking up where Dave left off. 'We go out hunting women, and when we get them, we give them an indescribable treat: being fucked by two men who are so attuned that they act as one.'

Joan began to reply but her mouth was covered by Dave's lips, and the breath caught in her throat. He pressed his mouth against hers, and his hands went to her breasts. And then, his hands still on her breasts, his hands went to her thighs. Four hands! She opened her eyes in astonishment. Dave pulled back. 'There are two of us, remember?' he said, and licked her lips with his tongue, causing her mouth to open. He kissed her once more and she let herself fall back on the floor. It was getting a little difficult to sort things out. Someone's fingers were pinching her nipples, and as she felt the tremors shoot down through her belly and into her crotch, other fingers trailed up and down the crack of her ass and into her pussy. She closed her eyes and gave herself up to the experience. There was something distant about the excitement she felt and she tried to pinpoint the precise feeling. Physically, she was getting highly aroused. She could tell just by the external manifestations. Her body was writhing on the floor, her ass was hot and itchy, waiting to be touched; her cunt was extremely wet, and her nipples were screaming with tender heat, as though a thousand tiny pinpricks were turning them on. Her mouth had a life of its own as she pressed her tongue into Dave's mouth, giving him a performance of passion. But she was also somehow removed from it all. As though from a great distance she could hear the other people in their exercises, and even her own body felt as though it belonged to someone else. Somehow her awareness was not in herself alone but drifted somewhere near the ceiling, and mingled with the consciousness of everyone else there. She did not articulate it as such, but her experience ceased being private and became one with all the others in the room, as though they were all members of a single body.

All she could think was, 'Ah, so this is what the orgy is about.'

And then she was overwhelmed. For when she opened her eyes she saw that the man kissing her was neither Dave nor Marty, but a total stranger. 'A stranger!' she thought, 'but what makes him more of a stranger than Dave or Marty? The fact that the others at least exchanged a few words with me? Is that all it takes to establish human contact? A few words?'

The man working on her mouth was insistent, probing

with his tongue and lips, wanting to suck something out of her. She tried to resist and wanted to say no, for all at once she felt as though she were being seen and treated as something dirty. But at just that instant, a cock nudged itself against her cunt lips.

'A cock,' she thought. 'Not a person, not a man, but a cock.'

The organ slid ponderously into her. It was very large, and her cunt stretched wide to accommodate it. Her legs opened almost automatically, and her hands went up to embrace the torso that went with the penis. The man fucking her began to move in earnest, swinging his cock from side to side, pulling out, pausing, and then penetrating deeply, giving her a thorough fucking. She found herself moving in response, cupping her ass so that it shifted more fully under him, and pushing her pelvis up, pumping her pussy into his thrusts. A hand swept over her belly and began playing with her clitoris. She moaned and the man kissing her whispered, 'That's it baby, give me your mouth.'

That was what she resented. Somehow it was easier to give her cunt anonymously than it was to give her mouth, and the man kissing her seemed to know that he was reaping a more precious harvest than the man fucking her. She tried to say the magic word 'No' but his lips prevented her, and then, there was the mounting excitement between her legs as her cunt started to squeeze and pump the cock that throbbed and jerked inside her. She could hear the sloshing of the organ in her hole and the heat of her clitoris drove all thoughts from her mind. She was going to cum, and nothing could stop that, and as she got hotter and wilder, the man kissing her sucked harder, pulling in her lips and tongue and breath and spittle.

'Come on,' he urged, 'push that little pussy hard all over that cock. Yes, you hot little piece of ass, go down and get wild.' And his words worked as an anti-aphrodisiac, delaying her orgasm, so that he had an even longer time to ravish her mouth. The two tensions built higher and higher until she could contain herself no longer and she began to wail, the sound filling the strange man's throat, and he kissed her harder and harder as her climax sent her body writhing into contortions of release.

And then, suddenly, she was all alone again. She shook her head, like a person waking from a dream, and there was no one around her, as though the entire thing hadn't happened. And yet, her cunt was dripping and vibrating, and her lips were sore, and her breasts still had red rash marks from where fingers grabbed her hard. She came to a half sitting position, supported herself on one arm, and looked around the room.

Now there were fewer people standing by themselves, and even fewer couples. The number of groups had increased and the numbers of people in each group had grown greater. It was clear, even to her untutored perception, that the orgy was gathering steam.

'It's crazy,' she thought. 'For a minute it's all so intense and personal and wild, and then I'm on the outside again, and just another body in this incredible room. Either there was more smoke or the lights had been dimmed, but it seemed to Joan that it was more difficult to make out details. She desperately wanted a cigarette and something to drink, so she set off in the direction of the bar. She began to stand, but decided it would be more polite to crawl. On her hands and knees, her tits hanging down from her chest, swaying with each movement, her ass jutting behind her, her cunt winking out from between the shifting cheeks, her hair hanging down to the floor, she looked like some mythological beast.

She didn't get more than ten feet before she felt a pair of arms encircle her waist. 'Get her,' a voice whispered, and she was pulled back, the cleft between her buttocks hitting hard on a stiff cock. she tried to turn around to see who was assaulting her, but another pair of hands grabbed her head and pulled her face up. Her half open mouth hit the tip of another cock, and as the one slid slowly into her cunt, causing her to gasp, the other slid between her lips, causing her to gag.

She was worked that way for a long time. The man behind her plunged his cock into her sopping pussy, and when she began to moan with pleasure, the man in front of her thrust his cock into her throat, making her gag. When she gagged, her entire body convulsed, and her cunt bucked up and down on the unknown cock lodged between her thighs.

'Oh yes,' she heard the voice behind her say, 'ride it, ride my cock.' And she would squirm and wiggle her ass around, impaling herself on his cock, beginning to feel herself climb to another climax, when the cock in her mouth would start to insist on receiving its share of attention, and begin to slide back and forth over her wet tongue, until it lodged itself once more in her throat, starting a new cycle. Someone slid under her and began to play with her hanging breasts, slapping them and pulling them, sucking the nipples into a hot mouth, biting them gently. Joan lost all discrimination. the entire thing was reduced to the sensations produced in her. 'It's no use trying to figure it out as it happens,' she thought. 'There's obviously too much going on too fast. The thing to do is just accept it and enjoy it and think about it later.'

The men at her rear and front started to move in more closely connected unison, so that her body was moved with complementary waves. From her mouth to her cunt she was a single wave of excitation. The thick cock in her pussy grew harder and hotter, and the long cock in her mouth thrust deeper and deeper. She gagged and moaned and spit and coughed and rolled her ass cheeks and contracted the muscles of her cunt and was driven crazy by the tongues on her nipples – until the breaking point was passed, and she let herself dive off the edge of all control, and the next thing she knew she was thrashing about the floor, kicking and yelling, spilling out all her inhibitions, while gobs of thick sperm spilled onto her tongue, and strong hands clenched her thighs tight, pulling them back onto a pumping cock that was reaching its own climax deep in her belly.

She rode the orgasm until its final curve, and then fell face downward on the floor. But this time she was not let alone. Hands rolled her over, and before she could open her eyes, her face was smothered in flesh. Huge buttocks covered her cheeks, and her mouth was pressed against a puckered asshole. She tried to wrench herself free, for in a quick flash she saw herself buried in this pile of strange bodies, performing the most intimate services on people whose faces she did not even see, and it sent her freaking down the corridors of her rational mind.

But she could not move far. Her legs were lifted, pulled

apart, and held open. She felt movement between her thighs, and then a finger went into her cunt, slid out, and lubricated her asshole with the vaginal secretions. She tried to squirm away, but the hands held her tightly, and the finger continued its patient task. She wanted to scream, but in opening her mouth, she only invited the relentless buttocks to press more heavily onto her face. She was on the verge of tears.

'I want it to stop,' she cried to herself, 'just please let it stop.' And even as the plea went through her mind, she knew that she was getting a taste of something she might not be able to put out of her life. Now she was being drawn into the orgiastic mood, finding in the enormous energy a vehicle for experience she had hungered for a long time. She thought of Helene who had greeted her at the doorway, and the woman's quiet scorn of Joan's youth.

'Will I become like that?' she thought. 'Or worse?' The alternative sprang before her mind's eye, and she pictured herself as a ragged stinking syphilitic debauchee who could entice only very drunken sailors from Tenth Avenue bars. In her slightly deranged state, fantasy was indistinguishable from reality, and she could project her current situation, lying spreadeagled on a rug with someone's ass in her face and someone else's cock sliding up her own ass, into the prolonged future.

'What foul degradations am I not capable of?' she asked herself. 'How far down this road will I travel?'

But she did not have too much time to luxuriate in her thoughts, for her buttocks were being pulled apart, and a heavy cock was sliding between the cheeks and pressing at the tiny hole at the center. She tried to relax, knowing that he would enter no matter what she did, and if she resisted it would only be painful. More hands grabbed her breasts, and she could feel someone rubbing the head of his cock against one of her nipples.

'Oh God,' she moaned, her words muffled, as the cock lunged into her ass. She pushed out with her sphincter muscles, giving the intruder easier access. She was forced to cooperate with her own ravishing, although, given the fact that she had gone there of her own will, and that she was already bunching her buttocks up to receive the cock more deeply, the act could hardly be described as such.

The man began to pump into her before he was totally in, so that she opened gradually. Her nipples being pinched, her ass beginning to taste the sweet pleasure of deep penetration, her cunt being fingered by at least two people, she let her tongue curl out and into the puckered asshole that bore down upon her, demanding contact.

It was not something she had not done before, but only in special circumstances with someone she knew. Now she began to slavishly lick the crack of the anonymous ass, stopping at each stroke to bury it deeper into the ever-loosening anus. She moved forward, her lower body spreading to accept the heavy cock which was not thrusting furiously into her ass, burying itself to the hilt, pulling out to the tip until Joan was left quivering with relief, and then crashing in again. Her mouth searched for the cock she thought would extend from the crack she was so voraciously licking.

And instead she found a cunt. The body above hers was a woman's. Joan stopped her tonguing, partially out of confusion. But the woman above her tilted her pelvis back, bringing her cunt over Joan's lips. The swampy tangle of hair filled her mouth, and the woman's juices trickled onto her tongue.

'Now eat my pussy, little pilgrim,' a voice said, and she recognized Helene's tones. She was eating Helene's cunt! She struggled furiously against that, and before she knew what she was doing, she cried out, 'No,' the magic word that would save her from any further intrusion.

And it did. As though by a miracle, the hands went off her breasts, let go of her ankles, the cock slid out from her ass, and Helene's cunt rose into the air, away from her mouth, and disappeared.

Joan lay on her back, alone and trembling. Her body twitched of its own volition. And a sense of social disgrace, deeper than any personal feelings of disgust, crept up from her chest to her face and, blushing she rolled over on her belly, and wept silently.

'Was that the wrong thing to do?' she thought to herself. 'Have I insulted them? Have I spoiled the orgy?' And all the little-girl fears that were carried intact in her psyche beneath the layer of surface sophistication, appeared to haunt her. She lost sight of her age, of her dignity as an individual, of her ego-rights. She forgot that her freedom to say no was granted to her not only by the rules of the orgy but also by the dictates of human life. More than all of this, she lost sight of the fact that in that context she was simply another body, another source of sensation and a focus for sexual drama, and was really no more important than any other body in the room, and that the people who had pulled away from her had set-to immediately with another group, in another configuration.

A man lay next to her. She could tell it was a man because his cock pressed up against one thigh. It was Jack.

'I warned you about all this heavy stuff,' he said, his cheerful tones at once cutting through her mood. 'And here you are, in the middle of a party, an *orgy*, for Christ's sake, feeling sorry for yourself and crying in the playpen.'

She turned and buried her face in his chest. Joan was only twenty-five and in many ways was terribly frightened of life. Jack understood that, and he acted as a real comfort to her.

'Oh Jack,' she gasped, 'have I made a fool of myself? Have I spoiled things?'

'No,' he said. 'Nobody's even noticed, except me. And I only noticed because I invited you here and feel responsible to keep an eye on you. It's just a little too much all at once,' he said, 'that's all. You are an extraordinary woman sexually, but all of us bite off more than we can chew sometimes. I mean, when you think of it, this whole thing is really outrageous, isn't it?'

And with one arm he indicated the hundred others who were building to even more frantic peaks of excitement.

She raised her head and looked around. She smiled through her tears. 'I guess so,' she stuttered, and then laughed. 'I feel so silly,' she added.

He took her hand. 'Come with me,' he said.

They stood up and Jack took her to a far corner of the room. There he lay her down, told her not to move, and brought her a drink and a cigarette. Still laughing while she wept, she blurted out, 'That's what I wanted when I was hijacked by those people in the middle of the room! I know I would have been all right if I could have just taken a break.'

Jack laughed with her. 'I know so too,' he said.

They sat side by side, smoking, watching, her head on his shoulder, sharing the private moment of calm.

Then, as though speaking from a trance, she said, 'Why do we do it, Jack? Why do we knock ourselves out this way?'

He gave her a hug and replied, 'Deep questions. Too deep for me.'

But something in her mood made him turn and look at her. Her eyes were sombre, searching. He took a drag on his cigarette, shrugged, and went on, 'I don't know. I guess it's because our lives as we live them are nothing but a tedious waiting room, a long, long line for the available space in the graveyard. We know we're going to die, and we know that nothing we do makes any difference. And we can't seem to lift ourselves out of our rut, and we no longer believe the holy men who tell us that immortal life and ecstatic light are just around the corner. so we cast about to find something, anything, that will lift us out of ourselves, to make us forget ourselves for a brief while. Some try drugs, some try booze; the rich try travel and expensive toys; and the rest of us try sex. It's the one habit we can all afford.'

She looked at him with penetrating interest. 'You know,' she said, 'I think you're right.' She stroked his back. 'You're really a very wise man.'

Jack laughed to cover the nakedness of the moment. He was suddenly aware that he was almost two decades older than the girl who sat next to him. 'Well, I didn't get to be Centaur's top salesman by being dumb.'

She impulsively put one hand on his cheek, drew his face towards hers, and kissed him softly on the lips.

'Why are you afraid to be serious?' she asked.

'Somebody's got to remain light,' he said. 'The world's too grim as it is.'

A wave of fatigue suddenly swept over her and she leaned against him again.

'Jack.'

'Hmm?'

'Will you take me home and make love to me?'

His smile froze, and then disappeared. He gazed into space for a long time, pondering the yearning, the surrender being offered. And for a moment, an ancient dream seized him again, a fantasy in which he would be able to let himself go, to flow into the heart of a woman, and be one with her, and care for her with his entire being. He looked at Joan, at Joan the beautiful young woman, at Joan with the trenchant intelligence, at Joan who could kiss him and make him remember his loneliness, at Joan who could lie under a pile of bodies at an orgy and have orgasm after orgasm like any seasoned trouper. And for a brief instant, he thought something might be possible.

And then he focused on the wider reality of his life, his weaknesses, his fears, and he shook his head.

'No, my lovely little lady,' he said, 'you would only break my heart.'

'Isn't that what you want Jack?' she implored, 'isn't that what we all want? To have our hearts break, to die once and for all with heartbreak? To destroy this prison we live in? Isn't that why we go to orgies? To burst free? And isn't love the only real key to set us free in this terrible mysterious universe?'

He put his arms around her and held her tightly. They clung to each other like children in the dark, suddenly aware that they had nothing in the world at that moment except each other, and that they were eternally strangers to each other, with nothing to offer except a mirror for solitude to see its face. They rocked back and forth, like people praying.

And all around them the sounds of the orgy grew louder, the actions grew wilder, and the roomful of bodies began to find its critical mass, moving toward a single pile of inextricable shapes, a huge organism crying its sexual challenge to the indifferent stars.

SIX

They watched darkness descend over the city. From the balcony, Lou and Margaret shared that brief illusion of omnipotence that sometimes comes from standing at the edge of a height. As the lights of New York went on, each of them could sense the giant movement that marked the end of each workday, a human tide which swept over three million people onto the tiny island of Manhattan every weekday morning, and then sent them tumbling out each evening, to the other boroughs, to Jersey, to Connecticut, to Long Island. Such was the financial magnetism of the city that there were even a few score of hardy souls who commuted the hundred and ten miles to Philadelphia.

Lou sipped at his cocktail and gazed out on the scene with half-closed lids. There was an erotic crush about the view and his relationship to it. The immense power of the city throbbed through his legs, into his loins, and made his cock tingle. Power and sex had been inextricably wound up in Lou's worldview – twin heads of a single serpent which represented the closest thing Lou would ever acknowledge as a god.

He glanced over at the woman standing next to him. Slim and cool in a sheath dress, the curves of her hips and breasts muted by the cut of the cloth, her hair in her usual bun, her face stark without makeup, Margaret presented a model of classic beauty. Her eyes contained the same crystal, penetrating focus that could be seen in Lou's eyes when he wasn't being thrown off-balance by the demands of his hectic days.

Feeling the weight of his gaze, Margaret turned to look at him, and their eyes locked. They regarded one another impassively, without tension, without expectation, without resistance. They understood each other perfectly, and they had long since given up all efforts at dissembling. Like two gunfighters who have finally come face to face, knowing that only one of them could survive, would survive, and that both might even be killed in the duel, they shared the rare camaraderie of enemies who respect one another's strength.

'I spoke to Al this morning,' he said at last.

Margaret raised her eyebrows, giving her a mask of amusement which showed only the slightest trace of apprehension. Al was the common enemy in their habitual lexicon, the one whose name could serve to rouse them to a sense of unity. But now his appearance signified something else.

As head of Zenith Distributors, he handled everything from hard-core pornography to the most elegant art magazines, from moronic comic books to intellectual journals, and a good deal of everything in between – the bulk of middle-America's reading diet. To him, Centaur was a minor entry in his ledgers, one of many he had acquired by getting greater and greater stock percentages in lieu of payment on debts the publishers had incurred with the distributor. To Al it was of no concern whether Centaur succeeded or failed, except insofar as he was able to use either eventuality to assist the empire at large. On the rare occasions he had visited the office, he treated everyone with aggressive indifference.

Margaret had decided to approach him and had set up an appointment. On the phone he had commented, 'Decided to go over Lou's head, eh?' and she had wondered at her own audacity.

The scene at his office was a different matter. After having her admitted, he studied her for a full minute, with a frank sexual appraisal that almost had her squirming, slowly smoking his cigar, flicking the ashes into a huge onyx ashtray which, except for a phone, was the only thing on his desk, a single slab of teak supported by one curved steel pillar in the center.

'Speak,' he said. 'And skip any preliminaries. If you have business, come to the point.'

She had taken a deep breath, compressed her lips, crossed her legs, and then blurted out, 'I want Lou's job. I want control of Centaur.'

Al made a bland face. 'I figured as much,' he said.

'It's been a dead loss for months now,' she went on. 'And Lou doesn't have the foggiest notion of how to change the situation.'

'And you do?' Al replied, his voice edged with sarcasm.

'I think I can start a new trend in pornography, I think I can give the whole field a new face.'

'But can you make a profit?' he asked, openly twitting her, enjoying the role.

'If I succeed, I can make a fortune,' she said.

'And if you fail?' he said.

'Then you're no worse off than you are now, are you?'

He gazed at her for a while through half-closed eyes. 'And you don't feel bad coming here behind Lou's back, doing him in?'

Margaret shook her head. 'I worried about it a long time, and then I realized that Lou has had his day. It's sad to state it so baldly, but it's a fact. He's a tired man, he's already had a couple of heart attacks. And he doesn't understand that the country's attitudes toward sex are changing radically. So what's the point of his hanging on to a business that has outgrown him? What's he got to look forward to there, dying behind his desk? I think I'm doing him a favor by pushing him out. He's been talking about retiring to Puerto Rico for a long time now.'

'You have it all figured out, haven't you?' he asked.

She lowered her eyes and her glance fell on his feet; he was wearing ankle-length desert boots. She reached down to her bag and pulled out a sheath of papers. 'Do you want to look at my ideas?' she asked.

'I'd rather see your cunt,' he told her.

The words exploded like a fragmentation bomb in the room. The reverberations bounced off their minds for a long moment. And then Al leaned forward, putting his elbows on his desk.

'I don't want to see all that stuff you've written down. You wouldn't come here with an offer like this if you didn't have the whole thing figured out. You're a smart woman, and you've been learning from Lou, so I can trust that you know what you're doing. But I try not to bother myself with details. I go by my intuition. I give all the business facts to the accountants, and they figure out financial considerations.' He squinted into her gaze as though trying to see past her eyes and into her brain. 'Sure, Lou is on the way out. We've all known that for a while, including Lou. But we go back a long time, him and me. So I'm not about to give him the bum's rush. But I might suggest that he step down to make room for his charming and intelligent second-in-command.'

Margaret's heart fluttered for several beats. She had come into fight for the job, but had geared herself emotionally to being turned down.

'You mean you will back me?' she asked.

He leaned back in his chair again and looked at her steadily. The expression on his face was not hard to read, and his startling exclamation of a moment earlier was still ringing in her ears.

'What do you want me to do?' she said, her voice faltering.

'Why don't you start by taking off your clothes,' he told her.

Margaret turned away from Lou now and looked back over the city again. A slight flush came to her cheeks as she remembered the rest of that afternoon, and that night. The inflection in Lou's voice told her that Al had given him his notice, in one way or another, but she had no way of knowing whether Al had told him what Margaret had done to help bring that about.

She had stood naked in front of Al, her hair flowing down over her shoulders. He was almost sixty, heavy enough almost to be considered fat, and like many people who subconsciously fear their bodies, he was always immaculate groomed, even to having clear nail polish on all his fingernails. He looked at her with all the cupidity of an avaricious tourist in the marketplace of an impoverished village.

'Is this your standard business practice?' she asked.

'I've got what you want,' he told her. 'Why shouldn't I ask a price?' And then, standing up, he said, 'On your hands and knees,' and she had gone down on the floor in front of him.

He strolled over to where she knelt in her position of humiliation and subservience. He lifted one foot and edged the tip of his boot into her cunt.He pulled it back and then pushed it between the cunt lips.

'Pull your pussy open,' he ordered, 'I want you to feel my shoe in your cunt.'

It was, from a sociological point of view, a bizarre scene. A fully-dressed, portly businessman standing over an attractive young woman, naked and kneeling, with his foot between her legs, the entire thing taking place in a plush office on the thirty-fifth floor of one of New York's most elegant buildings.

'But existentially, it's no more or less peculiar than anything else,' Margaret said to herself, rationalizing the situation neatly.

She reached behind her and pulled her cunt lips apart, revealing the still dry cavern to his unblinking eyes. He put the flat of his shoe on her ass and shoved forward, sending her sprawling on the rug. Her legs flew apart, and he stepped between them, standing near the crack between her buttocks. Then, slowly and deliberately, he began prodding her in the cunt, not hard enough to hurt her, but hard enough to impose his superiority. To her surprise, she felt her cunt begin to moisten, and in an instant she had begun to lift her ass slightly to allow the tip of his boot to touch her cunt more squarely.

'Don't like it *too* much, bitch,' he said, 'or you'll get carried away.'

Having no pretensions about compassion or decency, Al used his wealth and power to buy people to do his bidding, and through that had learned some rock-bottom truths about the reflex behavior of human beings, for he was often able to study them as dispassionately as a biologist viewing microbes through a microscope. And one of the things he had learned was that when, through one means or another, a woman's deep sexual energy is contacted, she will go wild with expression and cease to manifest the psychological states of disgust and loathing which he thrived on. Al was a connoisseur of the vile, and for his pleasure to be complete he required complete control of the situation.

He turned his ankle so that the toe of his boot slid in sideways, penetrating into the damp hair and beyond into the outer folds of her cunt. He applied a steady pressure until the toe of his shoe was embedded in her hole, and she cooperated by lifting her ass higher off the floor and spreading her legs wider, giving him not only the physical satisfaction but a strong, voyeuristic rush.

'Never seen it to fail,' he said. 'You're all sluts. The more elegant you are outside, the dirtier you are underneath.'

'We're born between piss and shit, Al,' she told him, quoting St Augustine.

Her reply, of course, angered him, and next to hatred, Al loved anger. He pulled his boot back, leaving her quivering in mid-air. He walked around in front of her, stopping by her head. He slid his boot under her face.

'Lick it,' he said.

'My God, he certainly is one for stereotypes,' Margaret said to herself, attempting to rescue the situation with a flourish of mental superiority. But the brute reality of the moment intervened heavily. She could not escape from the fact that she was lying naked on her belly in front of a despicable man, licking her cunt juices off his boot.

He stepped back. 'Roll over,' he said. She rolled onto her back.

'Get your hand in your cunt,' he said, 'I want to see you cum. And please, don't fake it. I won't accept anything that isn't authentic.'

She blacked out his presence from her mind and began to masturbate, doing it as she did when she was alone, beginning slowly around the inner thighs, stroking the space around her cunt, then rubbing the cunt lips themselves, touching her clitoris from time to time, and then more frequently, slipping her finger into her cunt, wetting it, rubbing her clitoris again, sliding her palm up and down over her whole cunt.

'Put your other hand under your ass,' he told her. 'Put a finger in your asshole.'

She did as she was told, and now was starting to pump her pelvis back and forth, her ass contracting and releasing, her right hand working at her cunt, her left hand fingering her anus. She rolled from side to side and a sharp moan escaped her lips. She had succeeded in forgetting Al's presence, but he reminded her by putting his boot on her face. She knew what he wanted without his asking, and she began to lick the bottom of his boot, lapping it with her tongue, wetting it with long, thick strokes. He pushed down harder, squashing her face under his foot.

And as he stepped on her, she put all her attention on her cunt, urging the sensations on, working them up, until the first tremors began and her thighs began to shake and tremble, and her legs clamped tight, and her hand slid up and down more furiously over her clitoris, and with a sob and a shudder she flexed into a brief tantalizing orgasm which, under less austere circumstances, would have been only the prelude to a series of climaxes that would have had her screaming with release.

Al knew that, too, and as his boot bruised her lips he said, 'That's just the beginning. I know you can cum better than that.'

He stepped back from her and, to her dismay, he began to undress, revealing the corpulence he had learned to revel in. 'And while you're having a good time fucking yourself with your finger,' he went on, 'I'm going to have you lick every square inch of my body.'

Then, grotesquely, he smiled. 'But now, you don't have to do this, you know. You can leave at any time. This is only if you want the key to Lou's private bathroom and his big office.'

She looked back up at him coolly. 'I'll do what you want,' she said, 'and even get a perverse pleasure out of it, and know that that's your kick, watching me get off on your sick game. But I'll tell you one thing. If you double-cross me, if you put me through this and then back out of the deal, I'll get you. I don't know how, but I'll get you. And when I do I'll cut your balls off with a rusty razor blade and make you eat them. You understand me, you rotten son of a bitch?'

Al chuckled. 'You're really very beautiful when you get angry,' he said.

Now Margaret turned back away from Lou to look out over the balcony again. She waited a long while before asking, 'Oh? And what did Al say?'

Lou let out a sound halfway between a laugh and a grunt. 'You certainly know how to act naive,' he said. 'You know perfectly well what he told me.'

'You'd better spell it out for me, Lou. A lot happened when I saw Al.'

Lou smiled. 'Oh yes, he told me all about that part of it too. But by the time he started to tell me about what happened when he brought you to that orgy club, I turned down the volume on the set.' He shook his head. 'You must want Centaur pretty bad.'

'It's not Centaur I want,' she told him. 'I just want a chance to work out my idea. I've been telling you that for a year and a half now. But you've been so fucking bullheaded you wouldn't listen to me. And I couldn't go on with the editorial stranglehold you have on the place. So I had to go over your head. I had to push you out of the way. And you can't say I didn't warn you.'

'I knew what you were up to,' he told her. 'I have my people who tell me things. I even knew the day you were going to see him, four days before you went.'

'And you didn't try to stop me?' she asked.

He shrugged. 'Maybe I'm tired. Maybe I wanted to get pushed aside.'

She felt the premonition of her victory before Lou put it into words. 'And what else did Al say this morning?'

she asked, 'Aside from telling you how I served as a sponge for all the degenerates in his private club?'

Lou blew out a cloud of smoke, watching it dissipate in the clear night air. 'Al and I have known each other a long time,' he said. 'We don't have to use too many words.' He paused; turned to her, and with a disquietingly cheerful smile he added, 'The place is yours in a month.'

The words, spoken so simply, crowning as they did such a long period of preparation, made her eyes sting with tears of surprise. She found she had trouble catching her breath, and she simply stood there, not speaking. Finally, she found her composure, and then her voice.

'I'm really sorry I had to get it this way,' she said.

'Balls,' he told her. 'It's the same way I got it. It's the same way you get anything in this world. You always have to take it away from somebody else.'

The thoughts rushed through her mind with the force of a cataract. She started at once to formulate her plans, to look over her materials, her staff, to mentally list the writers she wanted to contact, the people she wanted to fire and hire. And in the middle of it, she thought of Joan.

'And Joan,' she said to herself. 'Joan will be with me from the first.'

Lou drank another swig from his glass, took a deep breath and exhaled loudly. He had intuitively known from the first day he hired Margaret that she would take over from him, and he had watched her grow in her work, become clearer, surer, until she was champing at the bit to run the whole show herself. His preparations for leaving had long since been made, and he was ready to enter a long, rich retirement.

'What will you do now?' she asked. 'I mean, you won't have anything more to do with Centaur, will you?'

'Al offered me a deal with his men's magazines, but I have plans for a house right on the beach in Puerto Rico that interests me a hell of a lot more. I intend to devote myself to my hobbies. And to have a place for you to escape to when it's your turn to put your head on the block.'

'Do you feel betrayed?' she asked.

'No,' he told her. 'But a bit disappointed. I was hoping you could win Al over without becoming his whore.'

She tossed her chin in the air in a gesture of humorous contention. 'Lou, with your hiring practices, how can you say such a thing with a straight face?'

But his response was brittle and caught her up short, sending a momentary fright down her spine. 'You're not getting any good deal with him,' he said harshly. 'If you think working under me was a pain in the ass, wait until you have to deal with Al directly. Oh, in the beginning he'll make you think he's giving you what you want, that he really doesn't care what you do so long as your books show more black than red. But after a bit, some of his people will be dropping by, and they will make suggestions, and explain how such and such can't be done because of market changes. And you'll compromise a little here, and a little there, because he holds the purse-strings and you have no choice and it doesn't seem too much at first. And one day you will wake up and find out that you have become me. That after all the twisting and turning, you are just another puppet in a long line of mannequins who dance to someone else's tune. Just the way Al does to the people above him.'

Margaret blinked, the sudden bleakness of his vision taking away the rush of euphoria. Lou was deadly serious, his voice bitter. She had never seen him so strong in his expression.

'Maybe during the next month, as I'm showing you the ropes of what it means to be boss, I'll tell you some of what you won't find in any official accounts. You're a very smart woman, and ambitious, and you want to accomplish something, but you may be in for a few surprises. You may learn that what you sucked Al's cock to get is an empty promise.'

She sucked her breath in. 'But why would he do that?' she asked. 'He's a businessman. If he puts me in charge, he'd be a fool to interfere with what I want to do. Are you telling me he lied?'

'No,' said Lou. 'The funny thing is that Al believes what he says when he says it. He himself doesn't understand, or doesn't like to admit to himself, that he's nothing but an instrument of the machine too, and he doesn't have the power to make promises like that. He's got lawyers who tell him when to squat, and accountants who tell him when to shit, and dark men with silk suits and sunglasses who pay visits from time to time and when they show up he acts like their shoe-shine boy.' He shook his head. 'You'll call me a male chauvinist, but I think women shouldn't get mixed up in big business. You don't have the vaguest idea what's involved. You don't understand that the basic support of any financial empire is the gun.'

Lou fell silent and they stood side by side, watching

the dance of car lights many stories beneath them. Margaret shivered as the chill night air began to raise bumps on her skin.

'Can we go inside?' she said.

'Sure,' Lou replied, and he took her elbow and led her into the huge living room, closed the glass sliding door behind them and led her to a chair in front of the fireplace.

'How about another drink?' he asked. 'Maybe a hot toddy?'

She smiled weakly, and while he went into the next room to fix the drink, she stared into the flames, sunk in her own thoughts. She could still remember how she gagged when Al plugged her throat with the crown of his cock and spilled his sperm into her gullet. she shivered with the memory of revulsion, and the memory of the pleasure she took in that revulsion. She had been reckless, certain that if she came on strong with her mind and hot with her body, she would get what she wanted. And she did. But as with Pandora's box, the imagined treasures inside might all be monstrous afflictions.

'No,' she told herself, 'I mustn't let myself feel defeated before I even begin. Lou's an old man on the way out. He's describing his trip. It's up to me to make my own.'

Lou returned and put the glass of hot brew on the table next to her. 'I have something I want to show you,' he said in a semi-conspiratorial tone.

She looked up at him, his balding crown, his suit which was never pressed, and she smiled. 'Lou, you're incorrigible,' she said.

'Well, sometimes it's good to relax and enjoy this stuff we make a living out of,' he told her. 'Otherwise there's no pleasure at all anywhere in life.' He flicked a switch and the lights dimmed; another switch and the screen slid down over the far wall; a third switch and the projector began to roll.

On the square of canvas, five figures jumped into life. Two men were standing over a trio of women who knelt in front of them, their heads covered with black masks which left only their mouths exposed. They seemed young, and the sight of their firm bodies with naked breasts and tight asses, the triple triangle of pubic bushes, contrasted against the implied bondage of the masks, with their mouths open and moist, not knowing what was to be done with them, was a blend of what Lou considered aesthetic content with erotic appeal. The men wore black chaps cut away at the crotch, showing their big, dangling cocks and their rough, muscular buttocks. They were bare-chested, and their hairy pectoral muscles bulged with the evidence of weight-lifting.

'Oh Lou, this is all old stuff,' she said.

'Give them a chance,' he replied, 'they haven't even begun yet.'

'But what's the point?' she persisted. 'The girls are anonymous, the men are standard types. Of what conceivable interest can their activities be to anyone, much less me? What are they going to do, whippings and group games? That's all regressive acting-out.'

Lou frowned. 'That analyst you're seeing is going to rob you of your capacity for sexual enjoyment,' he said. 'You keep labelling perfectly lovely activities with those negative terms, and before you know it you'll start thinking that sex is beneath your dignity.'

'That kind of sex *is* beneath my dignity,' she said.

'Oh really,' he intoned drily. 'I have a few films in my archives that suggest quite the opposite.'

'I didn't say I was against doing it,' she retorted. 'I just don't find any particular point in watching it. Not unless I can find something in the people I'm watching that I can sympathize with. As it is, those people aren't actually people for me, they're just fleshy robots.'

As they spoke, the quintet on the screen was rearranging itself. One of the girls had been made to lie down, the second started licking her cunt, while the third sat on her face. One of the men put his cock in the mouth of the girl who was sitting on the first girl's face, while the second man fucked the ass of the girl who was eating the first girl's cunt. The five of them moved with slow awkward rhythms, testing the viability of the configuration before letting themselves swing more freely. There was little sound. Only a few moans and the barely audible swish of skin against skin.

'You have good microphones,' Margaret commented.

'The trouble with you,' Lou said to her, not taking his eyes off the screen, 'is that you're still in the romantic era. Pornography is in an abstract phase right now. Those people up there aren't to be probed or dissected for their life histories. They are bodies, beautiful bodies in suggestive costumes and interesting poses. And they are doing something quite splendid with their hands and mouths and cocks and cunts and asses. They are giving themselves up to a shared experience. We are witnessing a delicate and charming communion. And there is nothing to identify with except the thing itself. I mean, of what possible concern can it be to anyone that that man now sliding his fingers into that girl's cunt is a motorcycle mechanic, or that the girl who is accepting his offering works as a clerk at a McDonald's hamburger stand? What do you want to know, their opinions about the war? Or what religion they were raised in?'

Margaret, her eyes also watching the screen, listened to the slightly caustic edge in Lou's voice, and heard the validity of his argument. But she was not ready to let it lie there. 'The act itself is lovely, Lou,' she said after a few moments. 'I don't argue with that. But it's cold, alienated. I agree that sociology and history are dull, but psychology isn't. This is the century of psychology, and that's where the true art is being formed. What about these people's motives, their thoughts, their fears, their loathings, their passions?

'Wait,' Lou urged. 'Wait until they get warmed up. Then you'll see it all. You'll see it on their faces, hear it in their voices, discern it in every gesture and movement of their bodies.'

'But they aren't real.' Margaret protested.

'Well, what the fuck *is* real?' Lou asked. He pointed at the screen with his eyes. 'Look at that girl in the middle. Think of what she's experiencing. that huge cock reaming her ass alone is enough to send her into spasms of self-forgetfulness. Look at it sliding in and out between her cheeks. See her hands pulling her ass apart? She wants it to go on endlessly. She is at the point of fulfillment, and inside her she is living out all her dramas. And that's only the one orifice. That's just what most women settle for, if they can get even that much – women who need to put sex in the context of daily life, of what is called "relationship" . . . as though everything in life weren't already a relationship. This woman has left all that tedium behind. She is, to use your terms, "alienated, unreal". And yet listen to her as she begs for that cock to split her wider, to dig into her more deeply. And that's only the first cock. The second one is jammed into her cunt. The man under her is catching all her movements on his rod as she rolls her ass around to fuck the cock that's plowing her from behind. If you look closely you can see her pussy juices running down the shaft and onto his balls. In a minute she'll switch her attention from her ass to her cunt and start to cum. And then, as she cums, she will bunch her ass and feel that first cock even more sharply, and go crazy switching back and forth, until the crack between her legs is on fire, and she almost disjoints herself trying to impale herself more and more fully on those two engines of fulfillment. Well? What sort of context would you want to put that into? She doesn't even know the names of the men who are fucking her. She's just an ordinary girl, twenty-two, wanting to explore her body. And I gave her the opportunity – the set, the actors, the script, the audience. And what do you think would happen if a prospective husband saw this film a year from now? He would grow purple with jealousy and green with rage. Why? Because he sees her as a "person", and that idiotic bit of sentimentality would prevent that beautiful female animal from touching such heights and depths of experience that she would cease flowing with life and become another automaton, able only to read about what she isn't doing herself.

'And that's only two out of four who are working on her. Look at what the women are doing. One very expertly licking and sucking her nipples, sending maddening sensations throughout her entire body, feeding her frenzy. And the other woman is covering her mouth with her pungent cunt, smothering the girl in juice and aroma and vibration. What an extraordinary treat! To be filled and covered with all that flesh and warmth. And as the lucky girl humps herself wild on two cocks, thrashes about under the ministrations of a tongue on her nipples, she is curling her own tongue into a juicy cunt, sucking it greedily, exhausting herself in a crescendo of lust.'

On the screen, the girl was now lying on her back, the men fucking her mouth. They took turns filling her lips with their cocks. She took first one prick and then the other, alternating more and more frequently, until both cocks were lodged in her mouth at once. She stretched her lips to their breaking point to accommodate the two huge rods of flesh, and her tongue worked furiously to lick the space where they touched. The men pulled on their cocks, working toward climax. The second girl was still nibbling at her tits, while the third was sliding a sculpted dildo in and out of her pussy. The girl's legs were bent at the hips and knees, spread wide, so that her cunt was completely open for the giant tool to ram her twat.

The men jerked their cocks more vigorously, until they had timed themselves to have simultaneous orgasms. The girl beneath them curled her tongue out and licked the two cocks at once, lapping the red crowns vigorously. She started to whimper, begging them to cum all over her. The men shuddered, cried out, and each sent copious jets of marble-white sperm into her mouth. It splashed on her tongue, and slid down into her throat. Their discharges were phenomenally large, and filled her mouth to the brim until some of the sticky jism spilled out over her lips and down her cheeks. The dildo in her pussy whipped in and out with greater and greater speed and force, while the girl sucking her tits worked her clitoris with one hand. The girl who was at the center of it all convulsed with a sigh, her pelvis trembling with a long fluttery orgasm as she swallowed the mouthful of thick sperm, her throat working seven or eight times to get the whole tangy, pungent load down into her belly.

The screen went black.

Lou reached over, flicked a switch, and the lights in the living room went back on.

He sat back in his chair, and looked over at Margaret. She smiled at him sheepishly. 'Disgusting,' she said. But her cheeks were flushed, her breasts rose and fell with heavy breathing, and her thighs had fallen apart and were stretching the fabric of her dress, causing thin parallel wrinkles to stand out over the space which led to her cunt. Beneath her dress, her panties were gooey with secretion.

'So?' he said. 'Point made? Smut is its own context.'

She shook her head. 'I can't help but think how much more powerful that would be if it were real.'

'Real!' he exclaimed. 'That was a real situation. Those are real people. What more do you want?' He lit a cigarette and crossed one leg over the other, mashing the remains of the erection that had accompanied his watching the film. 'It was well done, it got you excited, it didn't offend your aesthetic sensibilities. What more can pornography do?'

'It can show feeling,' she replied, lighting her own cigarette, and draining her glass of the rest of its toddy, now merely warm. 'Yes, this is a minor masterpiece, I'll admit it. I've always liked your stuff. But it still looks like a bunch of sex machines choreographed for a specific program. There's no spontaneity, there's no gut reactions. And worst of all, there's no thought.'

Lou sighed, reached over, and took her hand. They had had this argument a hundred times, but this was the first time he wasn't speaking as her boss, and so he was softer in how he spoke. Also, this was the first time she hadn't been afraid to pursue the point to its very end. She was on an equal footing with Lou now, and could hold her own entirely.

'Maggie,' he said, 'do you know the root meaning of the word pornography? Originally it designated a description of prostitution. *Porne* means prostitute in Greek, and *graphy* is, of course, from the word meaning writing. Now, there are many kinds of prostitution, and so there are many kinds of pornography. Sexual pornography gets all the press, but it's only one of many. There's a pornography of the emotions: soap operas, true romances, a whole genre of novels; there's a pornography of power, a pornography of violence; the latter is as big as sex in the country right now; advertising is pornography; and there is intellectual pornography, and religious pornography. Pornography is just another name for what gets people off. And the only reason sexual porn has been given so much prominence is that we have always been such an incredibly repressed civilization. I mean, our inhibitions are at least six thousand years old.'

He poured another drink from his cocktail shaker, took a sip, and went on, 'Intrinsically there's no difference between reading Einstein and having a cerebral orgasm, and reading Tor Kung and creaming in your pants. And getting a heart-throb reading devotional literature is no more noble than getting a cunt-throb reading raunchy smut. People who erect hierarchies of nobility concerning what gets them off are the most tedious kind of snobs, pretending that the fineness of a feeling is contingent upon the social judgment of the stimulus which causes the feeling. Now, I'm a very democratic person. I think that everyone should be allowed to get it on in whatever way he or she can. If pictures of saints do it for you, fine; if you grow ecstatic over differential calculus, also fine; and if you are made most happy by watching movies which show women sucking cocks, I raise my glass to you too.

'My adult life has been little more than a study in sexual pornography. And in almost thirty years, I learned one principle which, no matter what else you do, must be followed. And I give it to you free. And it's just this: 'The name of the game is fantasy.' People want to see and read about people doing things they don't do themselves. They want to watch their private dreams acted out. And if you make the characters too dimensional, people can't project onto them. In pornography, it is the act of sex that is wanted, not the justifications, motivations, results, and extenuating circumstances of the act.'

Margaret shook her head. 'It's not a matter of projection,' she said, 'but of identification. I mean, there are probably two basic kinds of reader for erotic books. The first kind enjoys someone else doing it and pretends he or she is superior to anyone who would allow oneself to be exhibited in such a way. These people despise the actors and actresses on the screen, while secretly admiring them, and think of erotic writers as hack jerk-offs.'

'A lot of them are,' said Lou.

'There are hack jerk-offs in every field, and probably constitute the majority of any given profession, from garbage collecting to psychiatry. And for that kind of human being, the pornography you have been producing is fine. But what about the second category of reader, or viewer? People who are sophisticated enough to realize that they have all possible desires within them, who have understood that a part of them wants to be whipped, to be humiliated, to be possessed? These people want a pornography which examines the sexual core of the human condition in all its ramifications.'

'Sounds very fancy,' Lou interjected.

'Not really. It's a train of thought that began when I first read Gorky's ideas on socialist realism.'

'Socialist realism?' Lou repeated. 'In pornography?'

'Just so,' Margaret told him. 'And if you think about it a minute, you'll see that a socialist realist pornography will have to be the highest and most powerful literary art form of the century.'

'My God,' Lou said with exaggerated emphasis, 'Centaur Publications is being taken over by a Commie.'

She smiled, and then bumped back into seriousness, expressing ideas she had been formulating but had never articulated with such consistency.

'Do you realize that there are probably a hundred pornographic novels written in the twentieth century alone that stand alongside of any other important literature that has been produced in the same time? And they aren't on any college curriculum's reading list, and they aren't in bookstores, and hardly anyone but a handful of aficionados knows about them.'

'Well, the writers are as much to blame as anyone. They all use pseudonyms, and if an author is not proud enough of his or her work to sign it, then how can you expect anyone else to take it seriously?'

Margaret nodded. 'There are only a handful who use their real names,' she said. 'Barry Malzberg, Diane di Prima, Marco Vassi.'

'Marco Vassi,' Lou said suddenly. 'Isn't he the one who's writing this book?'

'Why yes,' Margaret told him. 'He's creating us at this very instant.'

Lou drew himself up to his full height and puffed his chest out a bit, as though he were trying on a new jacket and looking into a mirror. 'Well, I hope he draws me in my full complexity,' he said.

'It's unlikely,' Margaret responded. 'He's not being paid very much and the book won't get very wide distribution, so he's not likely to do more than two drafts. And I'm afraid you might emerge as something of a caricature.' She smiled to herself as she spoke.

'A caricature!' Lou exploded.

'This makes my point better than anything else I might say,' she went on. 'If porn became a recognized genre, then serious writers could expect substantial advances and produce work with some dimension to it.' She paused, looking out over the balcony. 'One of my first policy decisions is that writers use their real names on anything we publish.'

Lou leaned back in his chair and sighed. He was filled with that vague sense of defeat which comes as a corollary to realizing that one's life style has passed, inexorably, into the dustbin of history. It was not a question of who was right and who was wrong in the discussion, but of who was on the way in and who was on the way out. Subtly, he began to understand the deeper significance of the notion of resignation.

Then, with a gesture of good-natured comeback, he slapped one arm of the chair with an open palm, looked up at Margaret, smiled, and said, 'Well, I just hope you don't get so caught up with the big picture that you forget where your own money comes from to even do what you want to do.'

'And where is that?' she asked.

'From people who have a much less exalted concept of pornography, and who define a different purpose for smut.'

'Which is?'

Lou pointed with an exaggerated gesture to his cock. 'It's to get that thing hard,' he said, and then, pointing to her cunt, added, 'And to get that thing wet.' He downed the rest of the drink that was in his glass, and poured another.

'Want some more?' he asked.

'Why not?' she replied. And he poured a large cocktail into the glass which had just held her toddy.

'What do you want Lou?' Margaret asked wryly. 'Do you want me to give you head? That can't be the case. How many blowjobs have you had in your life?'

Although she had asked the question rhetorically, Lou answered her. 'I was thinking about that just last week as a matter of fact, and I tried to figure it out. As near as I can reckon, I've had my cock sucked more than four thousand times. Which doesn't sound like too much until you consider that about two thousand of those were by different women.' He paused. 'Can you imagine? I've had more than two thousand different pairs of lips on my cock, and two thousand lovely tongues lick my prick until I came, and two thousand young and open throats gulping my sperm down.' He leaned forward, slightly aroused now. 'I'll tell you something,' he went on. 'I've grown tired of individual women, but I've never gotten bored with the experience. If it's a woman I've never had before, getting blown by her is as exciting as my first time.'

'Well then,' she drawled, 'you couldn't want me. I've eaten you . . . what is it now . . . must be all of six or seven times. Why, I can't imagine your wanting this old mouth again.'

'Ah, what a fine cockteaser you are, Maggie,' he said expansively.

She looked at him a long time. 'You know, Lou, I'm much more lonely than I am horny. I've done just about everything that we've ever published. And I don't know how many cocks have been inside me, up my ass, in my cunt, down my throat. My body has been and is as hungry for sensation as anyone else's. And I've done the whole route with women too, and found that I dig it more, everything being equal. If I were stranded on that desert island and had a choice of sharing it with a man or a woman, I wouldn't hesitate to pick one of my own kind. But when all the cocks have cum and all the cunts have throbbed, it just seems like a lot of empty experience shot off into the night. Because deep inside, I'm as empty as I ever was. And sometimes I think I'd rather have a warm talk with someone who is dear to me than the ultimate orgasm who is only interested in sexual dramatics.'

Made slightly sentimental by the drinking and the emotionality of having learned that she was now the titular publisher of Centaur books, she began to speak words that revealed more of her soul than she might have been comfortable to expose had she been more self-conscious. The frailty, uncertainty, and tenderness were still intact inside her, protected by the wall of defensive armor that we all learn very early in life to construct against the harshness of the human world.

'I mean,' she continued, 'I don't care if people are homosexual or bisexual or omnisexual or transsexual. I don't care how many there are or how they want to get it on. I've been whipped and stuck with pins and tried every other attempt to go past myself that's listed in any of the books on perversion. But all of that is meaningless. Those things are hangups only for cowards. The real point is that even after you get over all the inhibitions and have worked out the entire glossary in Krafft-Ebing, there's still that ache inside, that awful void that nothing seems to fill. And if I'm going to publish books about sex, *that's* what I want my writers to address themselves to, because that's what is important to me. They can have their characters arrange their bodies any way they like, but they must go inside, into the feelings and thoughts, into the unending emptiness that gnaws at a woman's belly and won't be assuaged, not by a cock, not by a baby, not by anything. And even if they write fantasy, it has to be someone's fantasy, and that someone has to bleed and cry out in the night and at least be trying to care for one other person or one other thing in the world. There must be the totality of life in their work, and if there is that, the sex will take care of itself.'

Her speech had lifted her to her feet and propelled her to the middle of the room, where she stood swaying and declaiming like an actress in a film from the late forties. After she finished, the echoes of her voice hummed softly against the walls, and she rocked back and forth for a moment, almost embarrassed at having grown so passionate in her declamation. But Lou was looking at her with open admiration, which for him meant lust. His eyes shone like those of a proud father watching his teenage daughter graduate with honors, contemplating the virgin body beneath the scholastic gown. He smiled into her confusion.

'The idealist,' he said, mocking gently.

She sniffed and walked over to the cocktail shaker and poured another drink. 'I'm going to get smashed,' she said.

'Charming,' he replied.

'And you'll have my drunken body and my feverish mind completely at your mercy.' She nudged him in the ribs as he sat. 'Hey,' she yelled. 'You'll like that, won't you? You can strip this dress off, and reveal my helpless form. You can fuck me while I'm half asleep. You can whisper things in my ear and get me to perform all kinds of degrading acts. The new publisher of Centaur, the chic sophisticated Margaret Hayes, being drooled on by the ex-champion, the former pornographer to the empire. How's that, Lou? Does that get your cock hard? Do you think that will satisfy your imaginary readers?'

Lou only smiled.

She picked up the tumbler and downed the drink in a gulp, then turned and walked away from him to look out through the glass door onto the terrace and over the city beyond. Lou watched the way her buttocks stretched the cloth as she moved, and his cock did get hard as he pictured what would happen before the evening was over. He would have his fingers in her cunt, and then he would have her lick them dry of her own secretions. He would shove his cock slowly the entire length into her ass, feeling the hot tight hole widen and receive him, and then clutch his cock, and her buttocks would arch as she silently begged him to fuck her. Then her words would disappear and her mind would be empty, and he would be able to take unimpeded pleasure with her, the way he liked it, the way she too, despite all her protestations, liked it also.

She turned to face him. Her face was a mask of questioning. 'I love sex,' she said. 'I love writing about sex and reading about sex. I think pornography is the most beautiful of all the arts. Why can't it be understood for what it is? Why don't people see that it's not only as good as any other art form, but *better?* Why can't we have novels as profound as *The Brothers Karamazov* that make your cock hard and your cunt wet as well? Why this separation? Great literature on one side; great erotic writing on the other? As though sex and life weren't the same thing. As though life didn't come from sex, and sex didn't come from life. Why, Lou?'

He stood up, walked up to her, and put his hands on her shoulders. Although he didn't perceive it as such, something in him realized that Margaret was feeling her first waves of insecurity. Now she no longer had the excuse of impotence to keep her from attempting to realize her dream, which meant that she had to articulate it, and then make it real. And there would be no Lou to lean on. For, despite all his obtuseness in many areas, he was a thorough professional who knew how to run a business, how to deal with the crises and personalities and complexities. Now all this was hers, a heavy burden for her shoulders. And she was just beginning to wonder whether she would really be able to manage it.

'Maggie,' he said in a low voice, 'out there, in the city, in the world, it's a dormitory. Those people are all asleep in their shoes. You and me, we're no great minds, but we at least are honest about a few things that most everyone else pretends doesn't exist.' He put his hand under her chin. 'Do you know that the President of the United States doesn't have a cock?' he asked.

She smiled, half unwilling to be pulled from her mood.

'It's true,' he said. 'Do you think the people of this great nation would let into the highest office a man who had such a nasty thing as a cock hanging between his legs?' He stepped back a few paces, fished for a cigarette, lit it, and continued, 'The machine is taking over. People are turning themselves into machines. They are trying to pretend they don't secrete. They hate the fact that they fuck. They want to kill fucking. They are the ones who keep pornography where it is. They want it to stay dirty. That way they can suppress it, and point to it and say, "See how dirty sex is". And I learned all this before you were born. And I've made my peace with it. I published the way I was forced to, and I thought, "It's all right. Somewhere people read these things and they remember that sex is our most extraordinary gift, even if they can only have it in their fantasies." And I tell you, if you think you can make it otherwise, they will fight you and step on you. Beginning with your new patron, Mr Albert Leeds.'

'God, I hope you're wrong,' she said.

'Look inside yourself. You'll know whether I'm wrong. No, the only question is, are you going to get hurt too badly in the process of trying, that's all.'

He stepped forward and put one arm around her and drew her to him. Like a kindly uncle, he kissed her on the forehead. 'You're a nice lady, Maggie,' he said. 'I hope you don't get your ass kicked too hard.'

Abruptly, he stepped back. His mood fell away instantly. He had said what he wanted to and expressed what he needed to, and now she was on her own. He would never have presumed to intrude into her emotional state any further than the concern he had already exhibited. He had made the decision a long time ago that each human being was alone in the world, and that there was no point in getting sticky about it.

'So,' he said, his tone light and brisk, 'you want to have a farewell party for me?'

She looked at him quizzically.

He smiled, a kind of teasing leer. 'I'll invite a few people over, and we'll drink some more, and smoke a little bit, and . . . well, you know, we'll have a party.'

She narrowed her eyes and tried to pierce through his sudden ebullience.

'Why can't we just have it by ourselves?' she said. 'I can't go through with it if it's that impersonal.'

'These will be people you know,' he protested.

'What's the matter, Lou, are you afraid to be alone with me? Are you afraid we might actually look at each other while we're fucking, and maybe make love to each other?'

'Sure I'm afraid,' he said gruffly. 'And I'm not

ashamed that I'm afraid. I know my limits.' He paused, and then added, 'And you're still looking for yours.'

She stood there for a long minute with her eyes closed. She was tired, and she didn't want to do anything but lie down. The refrain, 'I want to lie in my lie,' went through her head again and again. She couldn't fight or resist. It was easier to be swallowed by another debauch.

'Sure, Lou,' she said. 'Invite them over. And we'll have a party.'

SEVEN

Joan saw him standing on the corner as she spun through the revolving door and out onto the street just five minutes past five o'clock. She was in a rush to get home, for she had only three hours to shower, wash her hair, and nap, before going to see Margaret.

Margaret had not arrived until after lunch that afternoon and had called Joan into her office. She looked haggard and worn, but her eyes glowed with an irrepressible excitement. After locking the door behind them, she took Joan's hands in her own.

'It's happened,' she had said quietly.

Joan had smiled. 'What's happened?' she asked.

'Centaur Publications is mine,' Margaret told her. 'Lou told me last night. By this time next month, the whole place will be in my hands.'

Joan's mouth had dropped open and Margaret took the opportunity to plant a light kiss on her lips. 'Yes, I know,' she said, 'it kind of takes your breath away, doesn't it?'

'But how . . .?' Joan had begun to inquire.

'I can't tell you now,' Margaret said. 'It's too long a story, and this isn't the place to talk about it.' She pulled Joan toward her, embracing her tightly, and ran her hands up and down her back, her fingers tracing the space between her buttocks, her thighs pressing into her own, and then stepped back and walked briskly behind her desk. She paused dramatically for a moment and then announced, 'This will be your office when I move into Lou's.'

Joan shook her head in astonishment. It was all coming very fast.

'I have a thousand plans,' Margaret went on, 'and you figure in all of them. I want you to be my secretary, but you'll really be more than that. You'll be an extension of myself, you'll help me run the whole show.'

Joan let out a sharp exhalation of breath, 'Wow,' she said. 'I don't known what to say.'

Margaret sat down in the wide leather swivel chair. 'Are you free tonight?' she asked.

'Why, yes,' Joan replied.

'Why don't you come to my place for dinner?' she said. 'Say about eight o'clock. And we can discuss the whole thing. And have champagne to celebrate. And then celebrate some more.' The implications of sex were barely hidden, and for a second Joan flared with anger that the other woman should assume physical intimacy so easily, and tie it in so neatly with the offer of a new job and a raise in salary.

But Joan had agreed, if for no other reason than that she was unbearably curious as to how Margaret had pulled off the coup, and what it would mean in terms of changes at the office, and whether there would be a means for her to take a new position without being put in a situation she would find restrictive. At worst she would have an interesting evening of gossip and a night of extraordinary sex.

'Don't say a word to anyone,' Margaret had cautioned.

Joan had worked the rest of the day, barely able to sit in her seat. She found herself squirming a lot, going to the water cooler often, and running to the ladies' room a number of times, until Bill, the art director, had called out, 'For Christ's sake, Joan, you're going to deplete the city's water supply in one day, drinking it in and flushing it down like that.' But it didn't bother her, for that was the sort of remark that was always being made in pornographic publishing houses.

At five sharp she left, and was hurrying out of the building when she caught his eye. Leaning against a truck, looking dark and serious, Manuel was scanning the three doors that opened onto the street from the building. It was obvious that he was looking for her, for when he saw her, he pushed himself upright and took a step in her direction.

She was seized with a blind unreasoning impulse to flee. It took practically the entire weight of her inhibitions against acting peculiarly on the street to keep her from gasping with alarm and running as fast as she could in the opposite direction. She was not afraid of anything specific, but could not completely suppress the anxiety that was manifest by the sudden rapid beating of her heart. She had a fleeting, insane image of Manuel's leaping on her, tearing her clothes off, and fucking her violently on the concrete, while the passersby, in typical New York fashion, would walk on past without noticing.

There was nothing for it. She waited until he came up to her.

'I have to talk to you,' he said.

'I'm in a hurry,' she told him. They stood for a few

seconds, neither abie to say a word nor to break contact. The awkwardness mounted, and she added, 'I hear you've been sick. You haven't been in for almost a week.'

'I haven't been sick,' he said. 'You know why I haven't come in.' And then he looked sharply over his shoulder, as though expecting to catch someone watching him, and added, 'Although I guess you don't know the whole story.' He pulled her aside, away from the stream of people pouring out of the door.

'I'm quitting,' he said. 'And I'm going back to Puerto Rico. I came to see you to say goodbye.'

Joan relaxed. And at the same time felt a pang of disappointment. She was relieved to hear that he was leaving, for she didn't know whether she could manage to keep working in the same space with him if he continued to smolder over her. But at the same time she remembered poignantly that she had, not more than a few days earlier, been spread apart in front of his eyes, and had covered his cock with her ass, imploring him with her actions to fuck her. And that he had not fucked her, and that somewhere inside her she was still curious, and hungry for his cock. No, for more than his cock. What she wanted was to be overpowered by the brute masculinity of the man, to surrender herself to his strength.

'Goodbye?' she repeated.

His eyes were liquid and filled with what looked like pain. He seemed to have trouble in continuing what he wanted to say. Joan felt a pang of sympathy, mingled with a low lustful vibration, for she saw in him what had always captivated Alma, the mixture of the lost boy with the powerful man. She had the sense of wanting to simultaneously suckle him and have him fuck her.

She relented in her resolve to push him away at once. She made a few calculations and reasoned she could forego her few hours of refreshing herself before going to see Margaret.

'But this is so sudden,' she said, 'isn't it?'

He rubbed his chin with one hand, and hung his head, not looking at her as he spoke. 'No,' he said, 'I've been planning to go back for a long time, saving money to buy land. And now, well, I met an old friend who wants to do the same thing, and we're going back together. Probably next month. And I wanted to see you once more before I left.' He swallowed, as though something were caught in his throat. 'You know, I really liked you,' he added. 'I mean, I thought maybe you and me . . .' He paused, and laughed to himself, and then lifted his head and stared into her eyes. 'But that was crazy, wasn't it? I mean, we live in different worlds.'

Joan was suddenly aware of people passing, some of whom were from the office. without thinking out all the implications, she said suddenly, 'I have to go home and change, Manuel. I have a date at eight. But maybe you want to come with me, and we can talk a little, while I'm getting ready. I think I have some wine, or maybe I can make you some coffee.'

He appraised her for a long instant. He knew at once that her invitation was both innocent and seductive, that she was offering him simple hospitality, and a chance for them to be in private, and that she was putting them both in a situation where their latent passion could spring forth. He was torn in two, for he boiled at the mere thought of being able to fuck her, and yet he knew what a danger that was. He understood that his emotions would drown him once more, and also, it would mean being unfaithful to Alma, and while such a consideration would not faze him if all that were involved were a casual lay, he realized that fucking Joan would create a split in him, a split he would have to pay the dues for later.

But he looked at her eyes, which held a plea she herself wasn't fully aware of, and her mouth, which he suddenly saw wrapped tightly around his cock, and without hesitation he brushed aside all scruples and said, 'Sure. I think that would be fine.'

They rode over in a taxi, the vehicle lurching slowly through the rush-hour traffic. They did not speak, for they were both becoming increasingly aware of the bare bones of the situation. As in many social contexts, the verbal message was a mask for the real transaction. And while their conversation had been carried in such a way that it would pose no challenge even to a censor for a family television serial, its esoteric content had been something else again. For if they had spoken their subliminal intentions, their dialogue might have gone like this:

Manuel: I'm leaving soon, and I've wanted you for almost a year. Before I go I want to find out what your pussy tastes like.

Joan: After you rubbed your cock against my ass. I was so hot I couldn't sleep, even after I masturbated three times. I want to feel you between my legs.

Manuel: I'm going back to Puerto Rico and I won't see you again, and I want to have more to remember than dry-humping you over your desk. I want to shove my cock in your mouth and watch you lick my balls and swallow my cum.

Joan: I don't want to get involved with you, so I'm glad you're leaving, but I want to feel your manhood again, have you on top of me, pressing me down, making me moan, making me crazy to give myself to you, making my hole hot to have you.

Manuel: I want to feel your hands all over my body, pulling my cock.

Joan: I want your fingers in my cunt.

And so on. But such a conversation could not be held, given the people, the circumstances, and the nature of the civilization they shared. And so they were suspended between the spoken and the unspoken, caught in a space which was exciting because of what was implied, but frustrating because of what was repressed. And in the small space of the cab, with the driver sitting less than two feet away, they could make no small talk at all.

At her building they entered hurriedly. In her neighborhood, the presence of a Puerto Rican dressed in jeans and an army jacket was often cause for thoughts of calling the police. Joan, despite her liberality, was riddled with the same prejudice as the people in her neighborhood; indeed, that's why she lived in the neighborhood, although she never would have admitted that truth to herself. Manuel, having been in many such situations, when middle-class white girls had taken him home from some bar, understood perfectly, and was willing to play the game according to those rules. After all, he didn't want the police to be called either. They went quickly up the two flights of stairs, Joan leading, and Manuel watching her ass as she climbed, holding off an impulse to slip his hand under her dress and feel the shifting of her buttocks and cunt lips as she moved.

When they stepped in to her apartment and she closed the door behind them, they both felt as though they had crossed the border into Switzerland.

'Well,' she said brightly, 'can I get you something cold to drink?' She bustled off towards the kitchen and waved him into the living room. 'Why don't you take off your jacket and have a seat, and I'll get you a beer.'

Manuel walked inside like a cat in a new space, tentatively, gingerly, looking about sharply, almost smelling the air. He had the feeling of *déjà vu.* The succeeding three hours appeared to him in a compressed flash, then disappeared, and he returned to ordinary reality. Joan entered with a bottle of Heineken and a tall glass.

'Make yourself comfortable,' she said cheerfully, her voice slightly higher than usual. 'I need to get out of these office clothes.'

He looked at her suddenly, and the hidden import of her words hummed between them. It was an odd instant, in which all their subconscious desires were strung out like beads before their eyes, and yet their bodies continued to play out the scenario of polite encounter. She backed away from the eerie quality of the ambience of the room. Manuel was indistinct to her, a hulking dark shape that loomed over her consciousness. She had already lost her sense of center and was incapable of coherent thought.

'I guess he'll fuck me,' was all she was able to communicate to herself.

Manuel saw the look in her eyes and smiled to himself. He felt enormously strong and self-confident. The mystique of Joan's hold over him was losing the last shred of its power. After having her in her office, he had dispelled his sense of impotence before her. and after being reunited with Alma, he had regained his sense of what it was to have a real woman make love to him. And now he was seeing Joan in a perspective that put her on a par with a million other young white office workers in the city, pathetic creatures without a real home, without a man, pretending to be sophisticated, but hungry to be had. And he was going to have her. He was going to fuck her until she was weak, and then he was going to leave. For an instant a voice inside him tweaked at his conscience, condemning him for treating this woman as an object.

'Let her alone,' it said. 'Go back to your woman and leave this creature in peace.'

But his cock was already tingling, and its dictates, as usual, were given supremacy over any other aspect of his being. It short-circuited the hard-won knowledge, that in the battle between men and women there was no final victor. And if he was now able to take a position of strength and superiority in relation to Joan, he would pay for that, one way or the other. Either while they were fucking, or afterwards, when he might discover that once again a woman had slipped in while he was being distracted by her cunt, and copped his soul.

Joan smiled, a brittle nervous smile. 'I'll be out in a few minutes,' she said.

She whirled away from him and went off into the bedroom, leaving him to contemplate the odd assemblage of furniture that represented a compromise between Joan's taste and her salary. She shut the door behind her and leaned against it for a moment, breathing hard. Her mind was awash with conflicting images.

'Why did I invite him up?' she said to herself. She pictured the tongue-tied mail-room worker in the next room, and admitted that despite his physique and the magnetism that vibrated around him, he was not someone she could relate to as an equal. 'Maybe I am frightened,' she thought. 'But I just can't find anything to talk to him about.' She frowned, pursed her lips, and resolved that she would talk politely to him for a half hour and then send him on his way, wishing him well in his plans. But even as she did so she began to take off her clothes, shedding the dress and brassiere and stockings and panties and shoes that served as her cover at work, and went to the closet where she picked out a nylon dressing gown, one which was neither transparent nor translucent, but which clearly indicated that the body underneath it had nothing on. For as she moved, her breasts could be seen swaying, and the thin fabric caught between her legs and outlined the crack of her ass. She stood naked for a moment, her decision indicating one course of action, and her choice of dress indicating another, thus delineating with perfect clarity the split between thought and deed which is indicative of the human condition.

She rubbed cold cream on her face and wiped it off expertly, leaving her skin smooth and clean. And then, taking the rubber band off her pony tail, she let her hair hang down, and still floating on the cloud of her self-delusion, her thinking that what she had in her head would be more pertinent to what happened than what she did with her body, she went back into the living room.

Manuel had found the stereo, put on an early Stones'

album, with a rough raw heat that left nothing to the imagination. He was standing next to the large window, the beer bottle in one hand, his other hand hooked into his belt. His strong legs bulged against his tight jeans, the thick roll of his cock hanging unashamedly down his left thigh. He had taken off his jacket, and his shirt was open down to his chest, showing the black hair and the broad muscles that caused more than one woman's cunt to twitch in anticipation. He was looking at her with a steady, almost malevolent glare.

Her heart sank and she almost stumbled on the spot, able to do little more than to fall to the floor and bleat with surrender. But it was not to him she would surrender, for he looked not a little ridiculous, something like a stud posing in a homosexual magazine. No, it was to the experience that she would give herself, to the blinding anonymous release of a cunt that cared for nothing except the penetration that supplied it with all the eternity it would ever hope for.

'He's going to fuck me,' she said to herself again, and took a strange pleasure in realizing that after he spread her legs and thrust his cock inside her, a few hours later Margaret would be licking her bruised cunt lips.

'Maybe I should let his sperm stay inside me, and let Margaret suck it out,' she thought, and wondered at her wicked delight in the ramifications of her situation. 'Life does get interesting at times,' she concluded, and sat down on the couch, partially because she was too shaky to stand and partially because she wouldn't do anything on her own initiative, but would let him carry the entire scene. 'If he wants me, let him take me,' she thought. 'I've already made it easy enough for him.'

He observed her stratagem. At this point, they were only abstract representatives of types to one another. In the exigencies of their condition, they had to play more inner roles than the social structure could comfortably accommodate. And the result was that they lost the ease and spontaneity which alone would have given them what they so desperately needed: a sense of their own humanity. He looked down at her as she lit a cigarette. She was making his balls ache with lust, and yet he despised her for being at once so accessible and so distant. She was both giving him permission to fuck her, and putting him in his place at the same time. His desire was laced with anger, and he sensed that the only really dignified thing to do was to leave.

'Where are you going to in Puerto Rico?' she asked in her best cocktail-party tones.

That she should continue the pretense of polite conversation at this juncture was both admirable and enraging in his eyes. His mouth was too dry to even speak, and he took a swig of the beer. He felt foolish, and as a man often does in such situations, he could see no way out of his predicament except through direct action. He put the bottle down and walked over to the couch. Abruptly, he put his hands on her shoulders and drew her face forcefully into his crotch.

She let out a grunt of surprise. She had provoked him to an action too precipitous to allow her to give herself to it, and she would now rebuff him. She felt vindicated, and her pride seemed stronger than whatever lust she might have felt. She pulled back and shook his hands off.

'What do you think you're doing?' she said in her iciest

tones. 'I thought you wanted to say goodbye. I didn't imagine you would behave like this.'

He couldn't believe his ears. He knew he had moved awkwardly and without proper preparation, but he hadn't expected to be pushed away with so much coldness. Her words shrivelled his cock, as they were meant to do.

'I mean, if you want to sit down and talk, I'm perfectly willing,' she went on, 'but don't think that gives you the right. . .'

But she never finished the sentence. For as he stared at her, naked beneath her gown, her hair a halo of light around her face, her entire activity since he had met her in front of the building a continuous seduction, and hearing her prattle in her inane way, a bolt of anger struck him through the brain, and without thinking he raised his right arm and hit her backhanded across the mouth.

She was hurled across the couch. A trickle of blood came from her upper lip and her eyes were dazed. She lay motionless for a second, then shook her head and sat up slowly. Her expression went from surprise to fear to rage to retaliation. She sprang to her feet.

'You dirty motherfucker,' she spat out at him. 'How dare you put your filthy hands on me? You think that just because you have that big cock between your legs you can do anything you want with me?' Her fists were clenched, her shoulders raised and her arms stiff at her sides. 'I let you have your chance and you blew it. Too bad. That's all the chance you get. Now get the fuck out of here you greasy little spic!'

The words were the final trigger on his reserve. In an oddly lucid way, he realized that he didn't even really want to fuck her. That his lust was more in his head than in his cock. And now, he felt no desire at all for the trembling girl who stood in front of him. He just wanted to conquer her, to make her bend to his will.

'Come on,' he said, forcing her off the couch, 'into the next room.'

He pushed her ahead of him and she half fell, half walked into the bedroom. The entire thing, which had begun with the atmosphere of a dream, was transforming itself into a nightmare.

'Manuel, please don't hurt me,' she sobbed.

Manuel had no intention of harming her, but he would not let her know that. He would hit her if he had to, but not so it would damage her seriously. What he wanted was to vanquish her, not to kill her. He let go of her suddenly and stepped back. She swayed and fell forward, landing on her knees. He took the back of her dressing gown and yanked, pulling the entire thing off her body in a single motion. She was naked on her knees in front of him.

'Crawl up on the bed,' he told her, 'and stay on your belly.'

She hesitated for a moment, and he smacked her square between the buttocks. She cried out and he reached down and clamped his hand over her mouth. Holding her by the head, he lifted her off the floor and flung her forward onto the bed, her legs sprawling behind her, her ass bouncing, her cunt black and hairy below it. He looked around him wildly and then found what he wanted. The sash around the window curtain. He strode over, pulled it down, and went back to the bed where Joan was lying still. He tied her wrists together and then tied them to one of the bedposts, so that her arms stretched out over her head. He ripped off a piece of the dressing gown, and wrapped it over her mouth as a gag. And then he stepped back, watching her, tied and unable to make any sound louder than a stifled groan.

To his amazement he found that he was trembling violently from head to toe and drenched in sweat. The enormity of what he was doing was just beginning to dawn on him. But he put all thoughts out of his mind, knowing that if he stopped for even a few seconds to consider, he would back out.

He opened his fly and let his cock fall out. Joan still did not move. 'Open your legs,' he said. She remained as she was. 'All right,' he told her. He slipped his belt out from its hooks around his waist, walked to the bed, raised his arm and brought the leather strap down on her plump ass. It whistled as it fell, hit with a loud thwack, and caused Joan to attempt to scream, a sound that only partially made it past the gag.

'I don't want to hurt you,' he said, 'but you better do what I tell you.'

Out of some deep unwillingness to lose in this absurd struggle, she kept her legs closed, and clenched the cheeks of her ass.

'If that's the way you want it,' he said, and hit her with the belt once more.'

Resigned, she rolled over, exposing the tender buttocks once more, and spread her legs apart.

Manuel threw down the belt and sat on the bed next to her. He was beginning to feel bad about the whole thing. And for a long time he did not move, but stared down at her, as her chest heaved with weeping, and her legs rolled about in sympathetic movement. He watched her ass roll around unselfconsciously, and her cunt shift as she writhed. There were no thoughts in his mind. Only the sight of her body was impressed on his brain.

Then, almost idly, he brought one hand up and laid it on her ass. She flinched, thinking he was about to hit her again, and then relaxed. He moved his hand slowly over the red welts where the belt had struck, and then ran it between the cheeks, down the crack, jamming it at last between her thighs, covering her asshole and her cunt with the curve that extended from the tip of his forefinger to the tip of his thumb. Her crotch was like an egg being held by a parabolic eggholder, and it was as gently as that that he embraced her.

Again, without any intent or conscious thought, he leaned forward and began to lick the angry belt marks with his tongue, soothing them, wetting them, removing the real and symbolic pain with the gesture of solace. He turned around so that he was facing in the same direction she was, and brought his other hand to meet his first, so that they were palm to palm between her thighs. With his hands in an attitude of prayer holding her cunt and ass, he came completely forward and gave himself totally to licking the stinging cheeks, going over the round white flesh again and again until Joan began to feel the first flush of pleasure creeping in past the tingling of pain. She turned her head from lying on her right cheek to her left, relieving the tension that had accumulated in her neck and jaw.

Manuel pulled his hands apart, gently forcing her thighs open as he did so. and with that, his mouth dipped down into the dark curve between her buttocks. His tongue found its groove and he started to lick it with total concentration. For Joan, it was more than she could keep from responding to. Tied up, gagged, beaten, she wanted to yield nothing to Manuel, but there was no way to hold back her tiny movements of pleasure as his tongue swept up and down the crack of her ass, curling from time to time to insert the tip into the puckered opening. She found herself spreading her legs wider without any urging from him.

As he felt her response, Manuel relaxed. He shuffled his body forward until he was on his knees between her legs, and with his fingers he pressed back, indicating that he wanted her to raise her hips. She slid her knees forward until her ass was off the bed, rounded, thrust backward, spread apart. Manuel dipped his head lower and then let himself go totally.

This was his hello and goodbye to Joan, to the girl of his dreams, to the prim white representative from a world he briefly aspired to. As he burrowed into the wet pungent crack, sucking at her ass, licking her cunt, lapping her juices and setting her wriggling with caresses on her clitoris, he relived the eleven months he had known her, remembering all the times he had watched her sit down, and had envied the chair she lowered herself onto. It was extraordinary to consider there was a time when he was paralyzed with lust at the mere thought of smelling her panties, and here he was with his tongue deep inside her crevices, with her beginning to rotate her hips, to push her cunt into his mouth to allow him the fullest penetration.

Joan now with the familiar vibrations of sex flooding through her, knowing that he was feeling the same thing, knew that all physical danger was past. And with that, she could start to enjoy the situation for its sensual content.

Manuel removed his mouth and sat back to look for a moment. He would never see this again, and he wanted to impress it in his memory. Joan was a single double-edged curve of flesh; underneath she was cunt and belly and tits rising from the bed, and above she was ass and spine and hair falling to her arms, which were still tied to the post. She was in a classic posture of bondage, and the picture was powerfully erotic. Manuel viewed it as he might a photograph in a pornographic magazine. Working where he did, he had accumulated, by judicious thievery, a vast collection of erotic literature and photography, and superimposed on Joan's actual body before him was a collage of bodies that he had spent many many hours looking at in his books. The one difference was that this was Joan, the editor he used to watch every day, and imagine what it was like to have sprawled naked on a bed for his pleasure. And now she was not a picture, but a real entity.

He brought his right hand up and slipped four fingers into her cunt. She flexed her pelvis and gasped. He twirled the fingers around inside her and then turned his hand sideways so that her cunt had to stretch over their width. In a few seconds he was sliding his hand in and out of her pussy, watching it grow slicker and slicker as her cunt juices became more copious.

His cock, still poking out of his pants, grew rock hard. Abruptly, tired of the foreplay, he moved up close to her, walking on his knees. He grabbed her cheeks with both hands, and pulled them apart, splitting them like an orange. Her asshole spread wide, her cunt gaping, she raised her backside higher, rotating her hips to tilt it up. Manuel watched as she clenched the sphincter and vaginal muscles, making her holes contract and open, open and contract. He positioned his cock at the opening of her cunt, and leaned forward.

They both froze. For what happened then was outside of anything they could expect to happen from the seemingly bizarre trappings of their situation. What happened then was that the entirety of the social and personal drama fell away, and they entered a space of utter privacy and silence, the true space of sex. If there is such a thing as a man and a woman being made for one another, then we must consider that there is such a thing as a cock and cunt being made for one another. And such was the case with Manuel's cock and Joan's cunt. For after all the waiting, and the rubbing, and the struggling to keep them from meeting, at the moment they touched a kind of perfection was attained.

At once they felt the sensation, which had nothing to do with friction. It was a deep, deep warmth, so sweet, so full, so penetrating, that they both collapsed under its impact. Joan slid onto the bed, lying full length on her stomach, and Manuel fell on top of her, his body covering hers, his cock having slipped out from its preliminary entrance.

After a few moments, as though he couldn't believe what had happened, Manuel came up on his elbows, adjusted the angle of his pelvis, and slid his cock up between her thighs and once more into her waiting cunt. He got no farther than the penetration by the head of his cock before it began again, an indescribable sweetness that filled his loins and seeped into his belly, and began to ooze through his entire body.

Joan, at one with him in the feeling, moaned. Her legs parted slightly, and her cunt became, almost at once, a hot dripping hole. Manuel's cock not so much entered her as was taken into her. It slid slowly forward and up, filling the tiny opening with its bulging presence, its soft bulk, until he was lodged as far as he could be in their present position. Her ass was nestled in his groin, her cunt was the undisputed home for his cock, and her heart was bursting with the feeling that she had been dimly aware was at the root of all desire for sex, but had never felt before.

Manuel cursed inwardly, for he was unarguably caught in the result of his own machinations.

She attempted to speak. He pulled the gag from her lips, and then slid his hands down her body to cup her breasts. They nestled on his palms and in his curved fingers perfectly, the nipples wrinkled, the skin smooth and intimate against his.

'Do you feel it?' she asked.

His cock throbbed in response, for he would not trust himself to words at such a moment. Her cunt tightened around the pole that split it apart, and while the bodies were still outwardly, inwardly there was a continual pulsation, as his cock vibrated with a steady beat and her cunt clasped it again and again, growing hotter and wetter with each moment. He pressed her breasts hard to her body with his hands, and then wrapped his arms tightly around her, crushing her to his chest. She stretched out full, her arms extended, her legs in full point down to her toes and revelled in the luxury of the sensations and feelings that washed over and through her. Manuel's body was a delicious weight, bearing her down, and his cock a thick rod thrust hotly into her center. She experienced a form of true bliss.

She began to move, rolling her ass around. There was not a thing she could do which didn't seem perfect. There was no posing, as there had been with Lou; there was no frenzy, as there had been with Margaret; there was no rush to climax, as there had been with almost everyone she had ever slept with. There was nothing but the moment, and the moment went on endlessly. She was in the spirit of fucking itself, and as such, she was immortal. There could be no room for the past or the future. She had, temporarily and accidently, stumbled into eternity by the most venerable of all the spiritual vehicles, the pleasure of the body.

Manuel held himself against her and then lifted his body away from hers. She curved her spine, rolled her hips, and lifted her ass to follow the movement of his cock. She chased his cock with her cunt, grappling it tightly, and when he had come to rest, hovering a foot over the bed, on his knees and elbows, her cunt fluttered all over the sturdy cock, kissing it with butterfly kisses, sucking it with wet slurping sounds, engulfing it with sudden thrusts, and soaking it with heat as it was taken deep into the deepest part of the ecstatic hole.

Manuel tried to resist, for he felt himself being swamped by a force that threatened to drown his entire rational mind. He saw a rich life with Alma, the land and house by the beach on his native island, all dissolving in the smoke of the sexual flames that would engulf him if he gave himself totally to the woman who was driving him mad with her dancing cunt, the cunt that caressed his cock with all the sureness and intimacy and playfulness of a friend from a past life.

'Oh baby,' she whispered. 'Don't hold back, baby. Let it go. Give me the whole thing.' She begged him with her words and with her movements to bury himself inside her and let himself go wild, to hold nothing back, to lose himself with her in the realm of fucking, into a wordless realization of the resplendent voidness of all existence.

He pulled back even farther. 'No,' he hissed. 'You must be crazy. I'm just the spic mail boy, remember? You ain't going to have anything to do with me. After I give you what you want, you going to spit on me again. And I'm not going to get anything, except to get all torn up inside.' He pulled his cock out violently. 'You're a witch, and you're trying to steal my soul. And I ain't going to give it to you.'

Joan turned over quickly so that she lay facing him, her arms still tied over her head, the gag now under her chin. She looked at him with an expression that could not be catalogued. Her body moved with its own volition, thrusting blindly up at him, calling him back to itself. And her mind reeled from the impact of his words. For he spoke from a context of time and place, and that jarred heavily with her state of timelessness and infinite dimension. She could not find a handle to grab onto to answer him at his level.

Her legs rose into the air and circled his waist. They pulled him down. His cock screamed to enter her, drowning all his other voices. His tension slipped from him and he sank into her again. Only this time it was not as impersonal, for he was looking deeply into Joan's eyes, and her breasts were warm and soft against his chest, and her cunt was receiving him from in front. He thrust into her forcefully and slid the head of his cock up, up against her cervix, hitting the entrance to her womb. Her legs opened wider and wider until her tendons were stretched to their capacity. Her cunt and ass were a single hot gash, and she lost all distinction between them. He was inside her, probing between her legs, and once again nothing else in the universe needed to be considered.

Manuel buried his face in her throat and pumped his cock slowly into her, drawing out to the lips of her cunt and then gliding down into the hole of her hole, the pit of her pussy. Each time he slid out, she let out a long sustaining sigh, and when he slid back in, she uttered a deep crackling groan.

'Oh my God,' she moaned at last. And turned her face to rub her cheek against his forehead, urging his face up, until he was even with her, and looking into her eyes. There, in the mirrors of his soul, she saw the heart of the man who gave her all she had ever dreamed of sexually. She saw that he was a strong beautiful spirit, and that she could love him. She raised her head up and brought her mouth to his. His lips hesitated, then pressed down, and in an instant their communion was complete, his cock and her cunt in total embrace, their mouths sealed in a fiery kiss of yearning.

Manuel's hands moved down and cupped her buttocks. He drew her even closer to him. Joan strained to push herself yet closer, to get his cock so far inside her that it would never come out. She taxed every muscle in her body to give him as much cunt as she could, to swallow his cock as fully as possible. She was at a point where there was no thought of orgasm, for what was happening involved her at a level too complex for the relatively simple phenomenon of having a climax.

And while all of Manuel's being tumbled faster and faster down the slide of surrender, he kept one thought in his mind. 'Alma, Alma,' he said over and over, remembering that no matter what passion he experienced with the woman now in his arms, they could never accept one another as equals, and thus would eventually come to despise each other.

And like any man who is forced to give himself to a woman he cannot let himself feel love for, he took refuge in reducing her to an image of herself. And he did not fuck the real Joan, the woman who for the first time in her life knew what it was to let herself be naked in a man's arms, that is, to admit to herself what she was doing and feeling, the woman who had at last broken through the unconscious attitude that sex was something nasty, and that its thrills came from violating taboos; he ignored the real flesh-and-blood female who called out his name and threw away, with each thrust of her cunt into his cock, another layer of shame and repression; he would have nothing to do with the actual hair and fingers and eyes and feelings of the creature who at last had the first intimation of what it was to give pleasure to another, and not be the receptacle for someone else, taking her pleasure selfishly, and giving it routinely. No, Manuel retreated to the realm of fantasies he had stocked for over a year, and watched the Joan of a month earlier, of eight months earlier, watched her bend over a filing cabinet, watched her scratch her cunt when she thought no one was looking, watched her lick her lips when drinking coffee and imagined a cock in her mouth.

The images and the reality raced toward a collision, and when he could no longer stand the tension, he forced himself to pull completely out of her, leaving her gasping like a fish just landed. And with a swift sudden movement, he pulled himself over her chest and then knelt by her head. She looked up at him, her eyes dazed and filled with loving desire. She had forgotten everything about him except that he was the man who had brought her to herself. And as women are wont to do, she had unconsciously relegated him to a position of being her possession, a thing that would always make her feel as she was feeling now. There was no way for her to dimly suspect what was going on in his mind. All she was aware of was the roughness between her thighs where his jeans had chafed her skin, and the fullness of his muscular buttocks, and the darkness of his face, and the joyous singing throbbing of her cunt, and the tingling of her ass where his belt had hit her. And oh, how she would be glad to let him whip her again.

She swooned as his cock plunged into her mouth. He thrust it into her throat, and she gagged and tried to pull away. But her arms were still tied, and he held her head. He pulled his cock out, letting her breathe, and then thrust in again. She gagged once more.

'Oh, just let me suck it, Manuel,' she said.

And he knelt there while she wrapped her lips around his cock, massaged it with her tongue, and sucked it gently until the juices boiled deep inside him, and with a sense that he was finally coming to the end of the spell she had cast on him, he let himself go, and shot the thick sperm onto her tongue, letting the spasms take him, letting the pleasure throb up his spine as his jism filled her mouth.

She let out a deep humming moan as she felt the underbelly of his cock contract, and then begin to pulsate as his sperm shot out of his cock and into her mouth. It was like nectar, and although she had experienced it many times, never had she wanted to taste and swallow it so badly. She let it slide down her tongue, waiting until he had finished cumming, and then she sucked the tube, drawing out the last drops from his highly sensitized cock. And when she knew there was no more to be had, she rolled the mouthful of sperm about on her tongue, and opened her mouth to let him look down on her, her face ecstatic with joy, her hair tangled all about her, her wrists tied to the bed, her body naked and open. she let him watch as she let his sperm run into her cheeks and over her lips, and then, gazing into his eyes, she swallowed once, and took the entire load down her throat.

She closed her eyes and lay there for a long while. Manuel rocked back and forth, his mind laid waste by the entire experience, not only the sensations and feelings, but the fierce conflicting thoughts in his head.

He wanted to put his cock in his pants, put on his belt, and leave, to return to Alma, who was ready to offer him a full and satisfying life. And yet, he could not move. For what had happened had rocked him to his very foundations. And he knew that the sight of the last few minutes, of Joan's sucking his cum into her, of the indescribable contrast between the implied degradation of the act and the beauty of her face and body, had imprinted an indelible image in his brain. She had done what she had done out of surrender to her finest instincts, and had, with that, presented him with the gift of seeing a deep-rooted fantasy come to life before his eyes.

Thus, with a woman who loved him, waiting to start an idyllic existence with him, and the woman who was his perfect sexual complement lying naked under him after having fucked him with everything she had and then having joyfully swallowed his cum, Manuel was paradoxically quite unhappy.

And at that point, the phone began to ring. It was Margaret, wanting to know why Joan had not yet arrived at her apartment.

EIGHT

Jack waited for Margaret to speak. She had called an hour earlier, distraught, needing to see him. They had been lovers, briefly, almost two years earlier, and had let their passion fall away in light of their mutual realization that neither wanted to pursue the relationship into anything like permanency. And like lovers who part as friends, they maintained a bond that was not contingent upon frequency of contact for its strength.

Margaret had made Jack privy to her plans for Centaur a month before she went to see Al Leeds. She wanted his opinion, as a salesman, about the possible success or failure of a new line such as she had in mind. His response had been both heartening and disillusioning.

'I can sell shit,' he said, 'if it's wrapped in the proper package.' And then had patted her rump and continued, 'I hate to lay this on you, Maggie, but the kind of stuff you have in mind won't be appreciated by more than a couple of thousand people. The rest will read anything if it has enough fucks and cunts and cums, and if the cover of the book turns them on, or if they've been told it's chic. And that's not just in pornography; the same is true in the so-called literary field. Real quality is rare; people to appreciate it are even rarer. So your line will sell as well as anything Lou has put out, and you probably won't go under financially; but I don't know if your dream of raising the pornographic consciousness of the nation will ever be anything but a fantasy.'

She had dismissed his gloom and accepted his economic optimism. To her surprise, she caught him looking at her in a way she hadn't seen for a long time. And she made a mental note to think about whether she should fuck him again. It would certainly be pleasant, and it would definitely be good politics.

Now she sprawled in the large stuffed chair that dominated one corner of his Chelsea Hotel apartment. She wore sandals, stretch pants, and her inimitable knit turtleneck. He cast her an appraising glance. Not only her generous breasts with their splashy nipples, not just her full cunt that now bulged from between her thighs against the clinging fabric, but her entire sense of self, her intelligence, her ambition, her ability to calculate with coldness and to several decimal points exactly what she wanted and how she would go about getting it . . . all this he found enormously appealing.

Her glass was empty and he walked across the room, picked it up and took it to the kitchenette that lay recessed against one wall, and filled it with ice and orange juice and vodka. He put it back on the table next to her, and she absentmindedly picked it up and sipped at it. Putting it down again, she lit a cigarette. The sounds of the splashing water and tinkling ice and glass being lifted and placed down, of the match against the book cover, of the inhalation and exhalation of smoke, all emerged distinct and sharp in the silent room.

Jack cracked his knuckles, adding another noise, and

then he burst out, 'Jesus Christ, Maggie, it's getting like a Pinter play in here.'

She looked up at him as though she were first being made aware of his presence. She had come less to talk than to be with him, for she couldn't stay in her apartment by herself any longer.

'I can't get my mind off her,' she said.

'You think she's gone for good?' he asked.

She blew out a blue cloud of smoke. 'I don't know. All I've been able to piece together is the little I told you. She was seen with Manuel in front of the office building at five o'clock three days ago. Her superintendent saw them leaving her apartment at ten o'clock the same night. She hasn't been back since.'

'Did she have a suitcase with her? Did he notice?'

'A small overnight bag.'

Jack made a gesture of conciliation with his hand. 'Well, you see,' he said. 'It's probably a short fling, I mean, he's been after her ass for almost a year. Everyone in the office knows that. And they finally got to make it, and the sparks flew, and . . .' He put his hands in front of him, palms up. 'Well, you know about all that. They're kids. They probably think they're in love.'

'He's probably got his tongue in her mouth right now!' she yelled, sending a shiver of sudden fright through Jack's body.

She looked at him, her eyes wide, her hands trembling. Her face was a mixture of fear and jealousy and embarrassment. She had not slept much since Joan disappeared.

Jack slumped down, sliding his back along the wall he was leaning against. He had not realized that she was so close to hysteria, and he decided that continuing to be casual was not going to be effective in reaching Margaret. He would have to find some method of getting inside her, and prying her loose from her immediate obsession.

'Are you afraid she's not coming back?' he asked again.

She looked up at him sharply. 'Don't you see, Jack, it doesn't matter. She's with him now. She's doing it with him now. He's licking her cunt and she's pressing his face into her, and urging him on, and calling him lovenames, and begging him to fuck her.'

'But, Maggie, you've seen the films Lou made. It's nothing she hasn't done before. I mean, I took her to an orgy, and she's a real trouper.'

Margaret lit another cigarette from the one she was holding, ran one hand through her hair, which had not been in its bun for over a day, and shook her head. 'I think it's different, Jack,' she said. 'The girl has had her body worked over like the rest of us, but she's never been touched inside. You know? Her heart is protected. She's never really fucked with love flowing through her. She's a virgin, Jack. Do you understand? And he's taking her, he's eating that sweet cherry, he's gorging himself on her, that no-good stinking greaseball, that dumb spic with his gorilla hands. He's feeling her all over, and she's knowing what it's like to be felt for the first time. And it should be me with her. It should be me she opens to for the first time. It should be me she knows her first sexual love with.'

She brought her glass to her mouth and took several quick gulps, as though the liquid would erase the gnawing in her belly and the ladder of images in her mind. Jack watched her with amusement and concern. Like any person not involved in the emotional crisis which is rending another, he could be objective. But he was experienced enough to understand that at such moments objectivity can be little more than the most sophisticated rationalization for insensitivity. He decided not to try to argue the details of the situation, but to go to the heart of what he considered the psychological reality.

'Maggie,' he said softly.

She did not respond. He repeated her name.

'Maggie,' he called.

She looked up.

He walked over to her, knelt down in front of her, took the glass and cigarette from her hands, put the objects down, and then cupped her hands in his. On the edge of tears, she did not want to relate to him directly, but he was gently insistent.

'Look,' he said in a low voice. 'Pretend it's next week.'

She shook her head in exasperation, but he forced her to pay attention by squeezing her hands more tightly.

'Roll the film forward,' he told her. 'You can tell what you'll be doing, you have the whole changeover to direct. Whatever goes on inside you, outside you'll be doing your job. You'll be meeting people, having conferences, going to long lunch hours. You'll stay up late scheming, thinking about how you will run things. And all of this will fade into the background.'

'It won't,' she protested. 'Not that easy.'

'Oh, I'm not saying you'll forget. But you'll be distracted. It may not even occur to you to think about it during some stray moment. And just then, you look up from your desk, and there she is! She has had her little trip with Manuel, and they have discovered that it was only a physical thing between them, and he has decided to return to Puerto Rico, and she asks, in the sweetest voice, "Do I still have a job here?" '

Margaret was looking at him out of the corner of her eyes. She knew she was being gently teased, and yet there was something so plausible in what he said that she couldn't help but accept it. As with all fairy tales, his fantasy provided a reality that was more accurate than any actuality. Jack saw the effect of his words and he smiled at her.

'And then,' he concluded, 'you rush to her and hold her in your arms and kiss her and she becomes your private secretary and your lover and you move in together and create a great pornographic kingdom and, of course, live happily ever after.'

Fighting her unwillingness to be taken out of her mood, Margaret tried bravely to supplant her dire scenario with the one Jack was providing for her. 'Do you really think it will be like that?' she asked.

'Of course,' he replied. 'I mean, if this were a novel, how else would it end?'

She leaned forward and put her face against his. 'I guess that's why I came here,' she said. 'You can always get me out of a bad trip one way or another.'

'The only thing that astonishes me,' he said, 'is that you should get so torn up over that slip of a girl.'

But that was the wrong thing to say, for no sooner was the last word out of his mouth than large tears rolled down Margaret's cheeks. She was as surprised by them as he was. Her mouth trembled as she attempted to smile through them, and her lips curved up and then down, making her face a tragicomic mask.

'Oh Jack,' she confessed, her voice keening like Stan Laurel's when he realized he'd committed some terrible blunder, 'I think I really love her.'

Jack threw up his hands and got to his feet. His attitude shifted from one of projected sympathy to one of exasperation. He had known Margaret too long and seen her in too many tough situations to accept what he now judged to be softheadedness.

'Oh please, Maggie,' he said as he walked to the sink to fix himself another drink, 'not that word, not from you, anything but that god-awful word.'

'You have a napkin?' she asked.

He gave her a paper towel, and she dried her eyes and blew her nose. A spasm of pain went through her as another blinding photograph exploded in her mind. It had Joan staring up into Manuel's face as he fucked her slowly and deliciously, her eyes filled with rapture, and her voice saying, 'Oh darling, I never knew it could be like this.'

'What's happening?' Jack asked.

'My fantasies are not only painful, but the dialogue is trite.' And for the first time in several days, she was treated to the priceless luxury of being able to laugh at herself.

'Thank you again, Jack,' she said.

'Want to get married?' he asked.

'Do you really think she'll come back?' Margaret insisted.

'Well,' he began, lighting a cigarette, and throwing himself down on the couch opposite where Margaret sat, 'they have no money, I'll bet on that; and almost nothing in common. I doubt that he can move in with her and keep his pride, and I don't see her living in a cold-water flat in the ghetto. Yeah, the chances are very good she'll be back.'

'It might be a few weeks,' she said, 'or a month. Or even a year before they burn themselves out.' She passed her hand over her forehead. 'My God,' she went on, 'listen to me. "Burn themselves out." And if I stop for just an instant to picture them making love, it's like knives in my belly.'

'A year's a long time,' he told her, 'so's a month. How long can you sustain this level of jealousy? Probably not more than a few days.'

She tightened her lips. That's what rubs the salt in the wound,' she said. 'Knowing that it will pass as quickly as it came. Knowing that it's a momentary storm. And wondering whether or not I'm still human, or whether I've become a machine like Lou, like everyone else who works in this cement city. I thought I was through with jealousy, had outgrown it. And now I realize I've just been suppressing it by closing myself off to really wanting someone else. It's been so long since I've been vulnerable, since someone could hurt me. And now that I'm having just a touch of it, I remember that it's actually the only thing in life that isn't some kind of unreality.' She looked at him searchingly. 'What is it, Jack? What have we become?'

'We're just the incidental punctuation marks of our epoch,' he said. 'Our little dramas have no more sense or import than the obscure thoughts of a blind fish in an underground lake. These emotional jags are the same as sexual jags, on a different level of experience. Nothing but a kind of drug to rouse us from our stupor from time to time.'

'And there is no love?' she asked. 'These past three days, what have I been feeling?'

'Maybe there is love. Maybe you have been feeling love. And what of it? The person who aroused this feeling is now having a cock stuffed up her anal orifice. And if she weren't, she would be having your tongue slipped into her genital orifice. And just last week I took her to an orgy where she was having just about everything piled into all her orifices. And that's what has you bugged. What's the good of love if it remains the enemy of sex? From what I understand about that much-misused notion, love means that you care only for the well-being of the loved one. So. Joan's all right. That means you relax and let her have her experience. And you just take care of business. Because you're too old and too wise to be playing children's games.'

His words and the tone in which they were delivered were like a cold compress on her neck. Margaret sobered rapidly.

'The only real sin I know is thinking that one's feelings, tender or violent, have to do with anything but oneself. I am not saying you should or shouldn't feel love. All I am telling you is not to think that your feeling is in any way involved with Joan. Because if she or anyone else tried to do to you what she and Manuel are now probably doing with each other, you'd give them the bum's rush in a minute. Let her learn from what she does with him, and when she has acquired a touch more maturity, you'll still be here, and if you have done your job, you'll be in a position where you can have her if you want her.'

Jack stood up and walked over to the window to look down on the flow of traffic on Twenty-third street. He stretched and rubbed his eyes with both his hands. He seemed suddenly weary.

'Hell,' he said, 'you know all this.'

'I know all this,' she told him, her voice warm, 'but I needed to have you remind me. I've been on a bender for a few days.'

He turned and smiled at her, his face filled again with the good humor that few people ever saw him without, 'It sounds like it was fun,' he said.

Margaret hoisted herself out of the deep chair and walked over to him. Standing next to him, she was almost a full inch taller than he was. Although a world of complexity had kept the two of them from ever forming a permanent union, he had always told her that the real thing that made their relationship impossible was the fact that she was taller than he was.

Jack looked at the slender, lovely woman who stood in front of him. She was one of the most beautiful women he had ever known, and it was only by constant dilligence that he prevented himself from becoming as emotional about her as she had been about Joan. But there were times when he just wanted to throw his arms around her and bury himself in her and pour out all the words and feelings which he had just finished telling her must remain within the individual, and not be cast upon others. He wasn't certain whether his behavior bespoke a true manliness or a neurotic defense system, and he had stopped trying to figure it out.

'What's the point?' he had reasoned. 'I'm not going to change. And if I'm just a coward, then I might as well enjoy what I can of it.'

Margaret felt like a diver who had just burst from

beneath the water, and was luxuriating in the simple fact of breathing. From the moment she learned that Joan had gone off with Manuel, she had watched herself sink deeper and deeper into the morass of negative motions. And while at first it amused her to see herself so wrought up, a moment had arrived when the critical aspect of her intelligence was tied down by the raging jealousy and anger and she had become a slave to her own weakness. All through the process, a voice well inside her reminded her that this was only a temporary eruption, but it, too, was helpless to snap her out of her convulsion. It had taken a helping hand to bring her out of the murky depths.

She looked at the man who had given her what she needed, and was taken with a feeling that mixed gratitude with honest appreciation. She saw him continuing to stand apart, knowing that his desire could be sparked in an instant, but not wanting to intrude his lust into her chaotic state. Without a word she put her arms around his neck and pressed her body to his. Her embrace said many things, that she thanked him, that she liked him, that she was ready to give him whatever he might want. But this was all implied, for in her mind there were no thoughts, no distinctions – only the warmth of friendly contact.

'You'll be all right now?' he asked, still not responding to his own desire and to her tacit invitation.

'If I stay here,' she said. 'If I go back to my apartment tonight, I know it will start all over again, and by morning I'll be a raving hysteric, and have to sedate myself to get through the day.'

He did not reply to her oblique request to spend the

night, so she added, 'It is all right for me to stay here tonight, isn't it?'

'Only if you promise not to transfer everything you think you feel for that girl onto me,' he told her. 'I don't have the energy to deal with all that emotion for more than what we've just been through.'

'Jack, you have more energy than almost anyone I know. Why do you pretend you're weak?'

She tightened her embrace and as she spoke she brought her mouth to his ear. The heat and motion of her breath sent a chill down his spine. His arms went around her waist and his hands slid over her buttocks. It was as though they had not been physically separated in all the time between their last contact. She represented his ideal form and when he held her it was like a sculptor running his hands over the statue that would always be too perfect for him to ever carve.

'If I fuck you, you get cut loose from her,' he said. 'That's what's happening, isn't it?'

'Maybe,' she said. But she knew he was right. She had called him because she needed someone she could trust to get her out of her obsession with her involvement with Joan. And Jack had helped her psychologically, and now she wanted him to complete the operation. She needed to put the experience of his body between her and Joan, so she would have perspective on her relationship with the girl on all its levels. She pressed her pelvis against his, the heat of her cunt surging through their clothes to bathe his cock.

He lowered his head and licked her throat. His hands came up and pulled her torso forward, so that her breasts flattened against his chest. The breath was forced from her lungs and she sagged slightly against him.

'Remember when it used to be that people would feel passion, and the passion would lead them to sex? Now we crank ourselves up sexually and hope that we will generate some passion. What a long way we've fallen.'

'Who are you talking about?' she asked, her hips rotating.

'You, me, the species. Everybody. Anybody.' His hands now moved with a kind of relentless momentum, skimming her spine, cupping her ass, sliding up her arms and onto her breasts. She bobbed back and forth as he played with her. They were joined at the thighs and at their genitals, while above the waist they leaned back from one another.

Jack's cock began to swell and harden even as his mind grew cold and clear. With physical energy and intellectual sharpness, he lacked only the involvement of his heart to make him complete. He looked at Margaret. Her eyes were closed and she was already sinking into the first stages of her sexual swoon. She was so superb in her simple being that Jack's knees momentarily buckled. But he stiffened his legs to support her.

'Maggie,' he said. She raised her lids half-way and looked at him through veiled eyes. Her lips were curved in a mysterious smile.

'If we could love each other, if we could just love each other. Do you know how simple all life would be? Do you know how different all existence would appear before our eyes? All these things we do? Our jobs, our sex, our intrigues . . . without love, it's all grotesque.'

Like a sliver of steel she cut into his soul with a single glance. Her voice was like wind across frozen tundra.

'Then love me,' she said. 'Love me if you can, if you will. Because I am too weak to sustain it. And it you show the way, I will follow you.'

Outside, a car screeched to a sudden halt. There was no thud, so Jack knew that the brakes had been put on in time. And the narrow escape from whatever accident had almost taken place on the street below reminded him of what was going on in his own body. The effect of Margaret's impact had taken its toll, and he was sliding into the very pit he had just dragged her out of. He laughed to himself, a mirthless sound.

'I keep forgetting my limitations,' he said.

She covered his mouth with hers. Her lips were soft and warm. Her tongue, the tip of temptation dancing behind the moment. He responded automatically. and in an instant, they were deep in a hushed embrace, blending and merging into that space which is given by the god of sex to soothe poor humanity in its painful search for love.

'Oh, fuck it,' she whispered into his mouth. 'There's this. We have this. Let's drink the wine that's in our cup and not go chasing after things that may not even exist. Sex is ours. Let's give ourselves to sex.'

They moved easily to the bed that lay, still unmade from the morning, at the far corner of the large room. They did not speak or look at one another, but walked with their arms around each other's waists toward the altar where this sacrifice would be consummated. They went slowly, as though in a ritual, a priest and priestess of pornography, having accepted that they would never know the love they desired except through the vehicle of sex. That, for them, there was no love apart from sex.

And that sex itself was no guarantee that love would flow. They could only go so far themselves. They could make themselves naked, give themselves to one another in the ultimate embrace, and let the spirit of sex take them up. And if they were honest and strong and brave, and if the unknown factor was moved to smile upon them, then a something would enter their hearts, and they would melt with the feeling that gives life its only meaning, the feeling, the experience, that some call love, and some call god, and some call truth, and some call beauty.

'Wait,' said Margaret as they stood at the edge of the bed, 'I have to pee first.'

'Mood breaker,' Jack complained as he disengaged.

'It won't take much to get back into it,' she told him as she turned and walked off toward the bathroom.

Jack let the bathrobe fall from his shoulders and, naked, flung himself on the bed, bouncing a few times on the mattress. He let out a few grunts of exuberance, letting loose the tension-energy that had been accumulating, and lay still for a few moments, collecting his attention within himself. It was so easy to be drawn out into that strange vibration which was neither his nor Margaret's, but something they concocted between them, and then be left wandering in that ghostly space, dependent on her for his own awareness. And if she were careless, she could pull away and leave him gasping for identity.

'It's called being ripped off,' he said to himself. 'And I mustn't let myself get ripped off.' Speaking to himself was his surest means of finding his balance.

Margaret undressed in the bathroom, shedding her clothes quickly. She flushed the toilet, although she had not had to urinate. She, too, needed to pull into herself for a few moments. The swings were very rapid, from heavy emotionality to stark cerebrality, from flickers of sensuality to a sense of cold isolation. She, like Jack, was caught in a process that they would both see through to completion. But it was a function of will and necessity, not a spontaneous delight.

She washed her face and hands, barely dried them and stepped out into the large room. Her body was black in front of the light behind her and cast an elongated shadow in the irregular quadrilateral of white, that was flung from the bathroom door onto the floor. The effect was highly unreal, and Jack appreciated its aesthetic qualities as he lazily stroked his cock and mentally girded himself for the ordeal of sexuality that lay ahead.

Margaret walked to the bed, slid forward, and without any other movement, covered Jack's cock with her mouth. Her hair fell down on his belly and over his thighs. He took his hand away and let her have the already erect cock. She began by swallowing it entirely, letting it slide over her tongue and into her throat. She held her breath and did not move for a very long time, the velvet tip lodged in the tiny passage, the sturdy rod stuffing her mouth, her lips lost in the curl of his pubic hair. The heat built slowly, and when it reached its peak, Jack clenched his buttocks and lifted his hips off the bed, thrusting his cock symbolically deeper into her throat. Physically, it could go no farther, for she had gulped its entire length.

She pulled back slowly, and as she did her tongue licked the underside of his cock, which had begun to throb. She continued until the purple head was at the tip of her lips, and she kissed it repeatedly, wetly, and then lapped it with broad rapid strokes of her tongue. She held it in one hand and smacked it against her mouth. And then, taking a deep breath, she swallowed it whole once more, this time going very, very slowly, so they could both feel the long, exquisite passage of his slippery cock into her beautiful mouth. He raised his head to look down at her. The light was splashed across her back, throwing her ass into high relief, the twin mounds gleaming and the deep crack between lost in dark shadow. Her legs were kicking slightly, a gentle scissors motion, as her cunt rubbed against the bed. Her face was indistinct, and he could barely make out the shape of her delicate lips as they stretched wide to encompass the base of this thick shaft. The sight of her being fucked in the face was as exciting, if not more so, than the sensations of having his cock pulsing in her throat, and when she pulled back the second time, again licking and kissing his cock as it slid out of her mouth, he almost came, and had to clutch the pillow behind him and tense his thighs to hold back the bubbling sperm which threatened to explode out of him without warning.

'Come around this way,' he said. 'I want your cunt.'

She rolled her legs over until her crotch was at his face and they were curled into one another. She took his cock once more, only halfway into her this time, and just held it there. She rested her head on the bed and let his cock throb gently on her tongue, lost in the pleasant regressive delight of drifting off into reverie with the breast-surrogate between her lips. Jack hooked his hands over her thighs and reached around and under to slip his fingers between the cheeks of her ass, the tips reaching her cunt. He applied a small bit of pressure and her legs parted. Her cunt opened to his eyes. It was already wet, and the uncanny smell assailed his nostrils. His cock warm and wet in her mouth, his body comfortable on the bed, he put his face between her thighs and slipped his tongue into her waiting pussy. She twitched once and then closed around him.

They lay like that for a long time, not moving, simply feeling. Their breathing became full and natural, and the smells and tastes of their bodies became nothing more than a part of the environment, and not something to huff and puff over. Perhaps they came close to falling asleep, but it did not matter, for they were a single closed circuit. Occasionally he would adjust his position and bring his lips forward to suck the excess juices that dripped from her cunt lips, or she would squirm and press her breasts into his thighs and curl her tongue around his cock, which now lay three-quarters hard in her mouth. They were both able to forget each other and pay full attention as they brought activity to a minimum and receptivity to a maximum.

Finally, however, the basic biology began to make its demands. Their bodies could store up only so much electricity before their separate charges had to be discharged and neutralized. They started to writhe, each pushing into the other. Jack's cock got stiff again and filled Margaret's mouth completely, and he began to lick her cunt steadily, his tongue at first covering the outer lips with broad strokes, but then covering the outer lips with broad strokes, but then curving inward, darting between, tasting the sweet mucous of the inner lips and the sharp wetness of the center. And then he was inside, his fingers pulling her hole apart as his tongue slid into the hot cavity behind. The inside of her cunt was a succulent receptacle of her body's excretions. It was odd that a man should be so powerfully drawn to a woman's fluids, yet he sucked them in vigorously, revelling in the taste and texture of the slimy secretions.

Abruptly they split apart, and he was grappling up her torso like a mountain climber scrambling for a hand-hold on a sheer rock. He grasped her breasts, and then covered one nipple with his mouth. Her huge nipples were wrinkled and looked like stretches of volcanic rock. They had the texture of petrified satin and she gasped as he sucked the sensitive violet mounds between his teeth. Her hands were at his neck, pressing him into her. Her hips rotated wildly. Her legs kicked. And Jack burrowed into her like a scorpion disappearing into hot sand.

Remembering himself, remembering what happened each time he let himself go totally, Jack slowed down and stopped all activity. He let Margaret's breast fall out of his mouth, took his hands off her body, and rolled over on his side. She reached for him once, and then, understanding what was happening, lay back.

'Heavy breathing,' he said at last. 'There aren't too many women who can get me panting and humping like that.'

'Does it make you nervous?' Her voice was mocking. She could not argue with his behavior since this fuck was a favor for her, but she could not smother her frustration entirely. Margaret rolled over on her stomach and listened to her rapidly beating heart slow down. She stretched her legs and flexed her buttocks in order to get more comfortable, but Jack, whose cock had a different morality from the rest of him, saw the movement in one dimension only.

He leaned over and began to stroke the backs of her thighs while he licked her spine with his tongue. She sighed. The sex would be like this at first, in fits and starts. She let herself get lost in her thoughts as Jack fed himself on her body, rubbing it, licking it, feasting on it with his eyes. She thought of Joan, and tried to picture her with Manuel. Now that she herself was being fucked, she could bear the idea of Joan's giving herself to her new lover. And running that film over now would make it less painful when the image returned later on; this was the process of defusing jealousy. It was what Jack was helping her to do.

As Jack covered her body with his own, Margaret became Joan underneath Manuel. The slim man above her became the tall muscular Puerto Rican that Margaret had seen five days a week for almost a year and never looked twice at. She remembered Joan's cunt wrapped around her fingers, and as Jack slid his cock slowly into her asshole, she conjured up the photograph of Joan raising her buttocks to take Manuel's cock between her cheeks.

'Oh Joan,' she said to herself, 'my sweet little Joan. Yes, let him fuck you. Let him open your ass with his dark cock.'

And she could flow with that fantasy because Jack was patiently and concentratedly pushing his cock deeper and deeper into her, until it was embedded its full length into the narrow opening between her buttocks, and the pain of imagining Joan in the same position with Manuel was wiped out by the pleasure of having her own ass fucked.

Jack looked down at the woman who was letting him use her body. He knew that her thoughts were elsewhere, and that she was doing this for reasons that had nothing to do with him. But it was a favor for a friend, and he was willing to help. Also, he was slightly drunk on the sight of Margaret's body lying so relaxed under him. Her hair was spread over the pillow, her long narrow back undulated gently, and her deep lovely ass was parted around his cock, opening to it, sucking it in while her legs kicked in a slow, steady rhythm, a counterpoint to his own thrusts.

He leaned back and pulled Margaret with him, his hands grabbing the fronts of her thighs. Her ass came back and up, until she was on her knees and her buttocks were high off the bed and curved into space. Jack knelt behind her, his back straight, his fingers pulling the cheeks apart, as he stared straight down her cleft, watching his cock slide in and out of the tiny hole, which spread and shrank as he moved forward and back, his cock filling her entirely and then leaving her empty, only to fill her again. She began to clench her cheeks, trapping his cock in a grip of firm flesh, and then, just as he was struggling to push in against the wall of muscle, would let go, and he would burst rudely into her, his cock sinking into her ass up to the hilt.

He started to fuck her more rapidly and with harder strokes, until his thighs were slapping against her buttocks and his balls were swinging against her cunt. Margaret brought her hands up under her and began to rub two fingers over her clitoris, while two more fingers slid into the hole and started to twirl around.

Her mind reeling with the images of Joan and Manuel,

seeing the slim girl being split apart by the huge muscular Latin, her fair skin a startling contrast to his swarthy complexion, Margaret climbed toward climax. The rushes in her cunt were hotter and faster, fed by the friction of Jack's cock in her ass. Her breasts swung freely under her, the nipples brushing against the sheet. She ground her ass into him, impaling herself as deeply as she could on his cock.

Jack began to whine and let himself trip into orgasm. The sweet sensations in his cock had melted his reserve. His mouth was still tingling with the taste of Margaret's cunt and his mind was still munching on the delicious warmth of their lying together in a tender sixty-nine. And superimposed on that now was Margaret kneeling in front of him, her high, wide ass rolling on his cock, her fingers probing her cunt and rocketing explosive charges into her clit, the first gasps of the evening coming from her lips.

'Fuck me,' she urged. 'Oh Jack, shove it up my ass. Let me feel it. Drive everything out of my mind. Scrape me clean, baby. Wash me with your cum.'

And, generous and obliging as always, Jack let his body go, and tremble, and his fingers dug into her cheeks, and his cock soared in her ass, and the heat and tension boiled in his belly and his balls, and with a hoarse shout he let it all shoot out, pumping the fierce ejaculation into her sucking ass, as she clenched her thighs and drank his sperm and jiggled her finger frantically until her own waves of release vibrated in her womb and into her cunt and into her loins and she spent her excitement in the vacuum of her empty box.

They stayed glued to one another for a full minute, as the last pulsations surged through his cock and the final drops of jism were pressed by her tightened buttocks into her bowels. And she rubbed her clitoris gently and softly, until a second orgasm thrilled through her, lighter than the first, but taking the ragged edge off her initial climax. And only when they were completely finished did she sink to the bed, his cock sliding out of her ass and hanging wet and limp over her as she swayed back and forth on his knees.

They did not move for a few more minutes, until the tumult had died down, and when they were out of the storm and returned to their normal states, Margaret asked for a cigarette.

'They're on the couch,' he said. 'I'll get them.'

And so they smoked, wondering as people often do, what it had all been for. Margaret's fever had abated. Through her dance with Jack, Joan's departure no longer ate at her insides. She was almost ready to dismiss the girl from her mind altogether, but with her ass throbbing and her cunt tingling and her body in a sweet lassitude, Margaret was able even to be magnanimous. If Joan returned, Margaret would forgive her totally.

Jack smoked steadily. It was as he had always remembered it, those moments after sex. His soul was seared by the intense heat of what he had seen and felt, and yet he wasn't sure whether fucking were nothing more than leaning over an abyss to stare at the fearsome void which is sometimes called hell. If he had been removed and another man put there, would it have made any difference to Margaret? He doubted it, and was on the verge of resenting her when he realised that if she had been taken away and another woman slipped under him, it would not have mattered much to him either. His criteria were physical. Any woman's ass would do if that ass attained a certain aesthetic minimum.

He decided that he was thinking too much and he put one hand over her shoulders and pulled her toward him.

'I've come to a conclusion,' he said.

'What's that?' she asked him.

'That liking the person you fuck is only important before and after the fucking. While it's going on it can be anyone, so long as it's the right anyone, if you know what I mean.'

She smiled and kissed his chest. 'I know exactly what you mean, baby,' she told him. And then a spasm of excitement seized her and she sat straight up and turned to face him. 'I mean, that's the kind of thing I want to see written about. Sex is practically indescribable except in its physical manifestations, and those are limited. But all the stuff that surrounds sex, and interpenetrates it, the philosophy of sex . . .' she paused, 'you know? Not theory, but the way of life of people who live in the sexual vibrations most of the time. What they think about it, and how they feel it, and how they discuss it. That's what pornography should be. And if it were that, there wouldn't be anything so interesting to read.'

'Well, you'll have your chance soon,' he told her.

She put her hands on his shoulders and fixed his gaze with her own. 'Will you help me?' she asked.

'You publish it, I'll sell it,' he said. 'I'm happy when you get all worked up over your ideas, but that's not where I find my pleasure. As far as the office is concerned, it's a job which allows me to travel, and to live well, and to fuck beautiful women, and to go to orgies, I'm not interested in what's between the covers.'

'You're deeper than that, Jack,' she said. 'You can put on an act for people, but I know you have a soul.'

'That's my hobby,' he added. 'The cultivation of my soul.' He saw that his cigarette had burned out in the ashtray and he lit another one. He exhaled a cloud of smoke through his nostrils and went on, 'You wouldn't think it, but basically I'm a contemplative person.'

'Did you ever think of writing a book?' she asked.

'Sure,' he told her. 'Don't we all?'

'Why don't you do it?' she prompted. 'A book about contemplation and fucking.' She took his cock on one hand and held it until it began to stir. 'Does that interest you?'

'And you'll publish it?'

'And you'll sell it.'

He laughed at the conjunction of intersecting circles.

'Is Al really going to give you your head in all this?' he asked.

'I'll get head if I give him head.'

He raised his eyebrows. 'So it's like that?'

'How else could it be?'

'Poor Maggie,' he said. 'I shudder to think of all the dirty things he makes you do.'

She squeezed his cock as it grew harder in her fingers.

She chuckled. 'Dirty?' she said. 'What's dirty? I'm surprised at you, Jack. You know there's no such thing as dirty.'

'But Al thinks there is, and when you do things he thinks are dirty, then you are being his dirty little girl. And you know that's where he gets his kicks from, and that's what you enjoy. You love it, being down there while he's projecting the vilest possible images on you. It sort of tickles a jaded girl's fancy, doesn't it?'

'You really ought to write a book,' she told him, now stroking the erect cock up and down its entire length. 'You know all the little secrets.'

'Shit, Maggie, there aren't any secrets. There are just people who won't open their eyes and admit what's really going on inside them, that's all.'

'And pornography ought to open their eyes,' she told him.

'I'll think about it,' he told her. 'Writing a book, that is.' His eyes went down to where her hands were fluttering over his thighs, caressing his balls, tugging his cock. He put his hands on her shoulders and drew her to him, his mouth seeking hers. She covered his lips with hers and she moaned as the warmth of his kiss flooded her senses. She felt relaxed, content. She was at ease with a man she liked and respected. She had come out the other side of her temporary insanity over Joan, and was going to get to work on her ideas, and Jack would help her.

He pulled her forward and she came up on her knees and straddled his thighs. She leaned into him, her breasts covering his face, and he kissed her between the firm, gently sagging orbs, his hands moving to rub her nipples. She whimpered with the pleasure of surrender to her mounting excitement and brought her hands under her buttocks. She spread her cunt lips with her fingers, and slowly lowered herself onto his waiting cock. He entered her eventually, and she felt the entire slide of his cock as it was coated and engulfed by her wet cunt.

'Oh Jack, that feels so good,' she whispered.

He cupped her buttocks with his hands and began to

rock her gently. Her pelvis swung back and forth, causing her cunt to mouth his cock from a score of rapidly alternating angles. He shook his head as the sudden rush of pleasure flushed through him and started his ears ringing.

'Oh, sweet Jesus,' he exclaimed.

'Yes,' she agreed, and rolled her beautiful body around and around, dancing on his cock.

He closed his eyes and gave himself up to the experience of Margaret's delectable cunt, sucking him wildly, her breasts sliding against his chest, her mouth hungrily seeking his, her hands flying up and down his back and into his hair. He was flooded with feelings that could not be contained, and he was moved to speak. But all the words that presented themselves to him seemed inadequate to describe the wonder of the moment. He gritted his teeth in frustration.

'What's wrong, sweetheart?' Margaret asked, falling, as she had done two years earlier, into endearments, the power of which she barely recognized.

'It's too much,' he said as his hands continued to guide her movement, pumping her into him. 'I want to tell it to you, and let it out of me, but it all sounds foolish before I say it.'

'Oh, my precious lover,' she crooned, slipping utterly into a mood of verbal abandonment, and pushed him back until he lay on the bed and she stretched out full on top of him. 'Don't do anything now, don't say anything now. Just feel me. Let me give it to you. Let me fuck it to you.'

The sounds burst from his lips as she began to ooze all over him, her cunt swarming completely over his cock, her ass rising and falling, clenching and opening. He baggled and moaned and yelled and let himself go mad for a while, not caring for anything except that he was drowning in the woman who was lavishing herself upon him.

'I'm going to fuck you all night long,' she whispered in his ear.

He bucked up into her, his cock swimming in her brimming cunt.

'And then you'll write it for me,' she said, her fingers cupped under his buttocks, pulling him into her, her ass a blur of churning white flesh in the dark room. 'Then you can tell it, and reveal how beautiful it is, oh how terribly beautiful it is.' Her words were lost in the rising wave of deep noises that surged from her chest. She was fucking him frantically now, veering toward frenzy.

As often happens to a man when the woman he is with flies off into a space of solipsistic passion and becomes a boiling sea of lascivious expression, Jack was disconnected from his body. It continued to respond as it had been doing, and his cock grew stone hard as Margaret split herself upon it. But his mind was detached, as though it were somehow something outside the animal that lay there in that delirious embrace. He could look down on both of them from the ceiling, and saw Margaret writhing on top of him, her back curving, her legs kicking.

He observed calmly as the two people on the bed built toward climax. For her it was a kind of erotic vomiting, an emission of expressions that she had not let herself have for a long time. And for him it was an almost painful culmination, without any ejaculation.

'How odd this sex thing is,' he thought. 'How frantic we become at times, and yet it is empty. An exercise in futility which serves as a metaphor for our whole life. For what is life but a vain gesture by three-dimensional shadows which think themselves real?'

Margaret collapsed against him. She was covered with cold sweat. She did not know what was going on inside him, but had been taken by the chilling notion that she was fucking a corpse, and that she herself had already died, and the two of them were fucking in a crypt. To the degree that she had been overflowing with sensation and feeling, she was now devoid of any sense of contact with any object, including her body.

'Jack,' she said in a small, still voice. 'It's all cold and black. I'm holding you and I'm all alone. Your cock is inside me but I don't exist. There's a wind blowing through everything. where am I, Jack? Where am I?'

He came back from his meditation and felt the frightened woman in his arms. He blinked and opened his eyes wide and watched the light patterns on the ceiling. He had a palpable sense of the scope of the galaxy, and was, for a few moments, experientially one with the vastness and silence of the universe.

Then he stroked her head gently.

'Then he stroked her head gently,' he said.

He put his other hand on the small of her back.

'He put his other hand on the small of her back,' he said.

'You're safe in my arms, my love,' he said.

' "You're safe in my arms, my love, he said," ' he said.

Margaret let out a long vibrant sigh.

'The book,' she said. 'We are the book.'

And Jack, who was feeling the fact that he had not yet cum, rolled slowly over, holding Margaret to him, so that she finally lay under him. And when he began to probe her cunt tentativelly with his cock, her legs spread apart, and her mind resolved the split that had kept her from beginning to understand who she was.

'It's all a fiction,' she whispered as he slid the full length of his cock inside her.

'That's a fact,' he replied, as she closed her eyes again and entered the esoteric temple of sex for the third, but not the final, time that night.

NINE

Al Leeds led a complex existence. At the age of fifty-nine he was worth, were he to liquidate all his assets, somewhere in the area of five million dollars, cash. The amount he controlled was at least twenty times that. He reminded himself at least once a day that at the age of twenty-three he had been a copy boy for *The Herald Tribune*, earning seventeen dollars a week for sixty hours work.

His rise in wealth he attributed to a single factor – luck. At one point he accidentally became privy to a deal that involved a certain shuffling of securities, and he was nicely rewarded for remaining silent. As a result, he had later been approached to serve as the front man for an operation that tested his ability to remain cool under intense police pressure. He had since moved horizontally, being placed in nominal control of bigger and bigger enterprises, some legitimate, some not, advancing as his ability to take orders and channel them was more thoroughly proved at each step. He had two indispensable qualities: he was entirely self-serving, which kept him from ever playing favorites; and he was free from any taint of greed, he merely accepted and enjoyed what fell his way and did not reach for more. When things were slow, he patted his belly, lapsed into a numb trance and watched time pass.

His image of himself was at variance with the world's image of him. To others, he was fat, ugly and mean; to himself he was a man robbed by destiny of physical attractiveness but compensated by that same destiny with immense wealth and power. He was able to buy the counterfeit of any human feeling by paying people to exhaust themselves at his bidding, while he chose from their outpouring of expressions those gestures and sensations that he desired. This was inevitably done in a sexual context.

From his religious training as a child, he carried away one thing, a deep appreciation of Ecclesiastes, whose wisdom he translated into a single sentence. 'We all go to the same grave,' Al Leeds told himself, 'so it doesn't really matter what we do until we get there.' He had found nothing in his experience to contradict that insight. He held in contempt anyone infected with abstract morality, or anyone who followed a moral code because of fear of divine retribution. He had on one wall of his office two wooden plaques. The top one was inscribed with the words of Mammy Yokum: 'Good is better than evil because it's nicer.' The one under it had the words of Leo Durocher: 'Nice guys finish last.' That pretty much summed it up for Al.

He now sat in a small room which adjoined the basement in Helene Benson's Brooklyn brownstone. Helene sat next to him in a deep armchair. They were looking through the one way mirror at a woman of about twenty-five who was lying in the middle of the floor fucking herself with a huge dildo. Al smoked a cigar and watched with lidded eyes. His breathing was slow and regular, his heartbeat normal. Helene was slightly distracted. She had had an intermittent pain in one of her back teeth for over a day, and like all people who have reduced their lives to monitoring the state of their physical bodies, everything that happened outside of her was seen as a mere backdrop to the internal phenomena.

Al visited the place from time to time. He owned the building, and Helene was on his payroll. The orgies she held and the swingers' parties she organized were sponsored by an organization called *Siege*, part of a nationwide network joined by a magazine, membership cards, and word-of-mouth recognition. It was one of the off-shoots of the conglomerate of companies of which Al's distribution wing formed one portion. The people who belonged were all innocent of anything more far-reaching than their immediate gratification; they had no notion that even orgies were part of big business.

Al never took part in any of the parties himself, but often sat in the small hidden room and watched. Occasionally, if he saw someone who tickled his appetite, he would have Helene approach the woman and discretely proposition her. If the quarry showed some interest, she met Al. And usually he was able to estimate within fifty dollars exactly how much he had to offer to get the woman to do what he wanted.

'I'm very rich and I will pay you to do things which will probably disgust you,' was a line he used frequently. He enjoyed it best when there was a tension between revulsion and greed.

The girl in the next room was one such. She was now lying on her back, the dildo two-thirds inside her. It was a perfect replica of a cock in shape and detail, but it was eighteen inches long and four inches wide. She had jammed it in as far as it would go and with both hands was twisting it around violently, her legs split in a wide V. From the contortions of her torso and the expressions on her face and the deep groans that spilled from her lips, one would be certain she was experiencing profound sexual revelations.

But Al was bored. 'She's too pat,' he said.

Helene had offered the woman two hundred and fifty dollars to fuck herself for a half hour with a dildo, knowing that a man would be watching from another room, and deciding whether he wanted to use her personally. 'If he takes you,' Helene had confided, 'it means another five hundred on top of what you get for the first part. But you have to be really good and convince him that you want him to use you.' It was a cross between what's told an actress who is trying out for a part, and the bait that is given to housewives on daytime quiz shows, in which they get a chance to win extraordinary prizes if they answer one question correctly.

'I think she's sincere,' Helene told him. 'She's married, and her husband brought her to our last party. She's just starting to break loose. And if he knew she was doing this he'd have a stroke. I think she understands what it is to be dirt, and she likes the smell of money. I think you can use her.' This all delivered in the tones of an agent selling a particular model to an ad agency.

Al peered through the glass more intently. The woman was now on her knees facing away from him. He could look straight into the crack of her ass. She had grabbed the dildo from between her thighs and was ramming it into her cunt. Her cunt lips yawned obscenely around the thick bulk of the rubber shaft. She looked over her shoulder at herself in the mirror, her face distorted with dry lust, brought to a head by the knowledge that someone was looking at her, that she was being paid to exhibit herself in this way. Like so many others who act out the manifestations of the sexual *Zeitgeist* without any understanding of what forces compel them to act as they do, she had no way to explain her behavior except to tell herself that she was depraved. Technically speaking, of course, this was not so. She did not have the depth of intelligence to grasp what true depravity involved. But that she believed it was enough for Al, for it was a woman's sense of her own lowness that he most appreciated. He was incapable of enjoying sex unless it involved the degradation of the person he was doing it with. He stared with unblinking eyes at the woman who did not know that he sat behind the mirror she was using to watch her exposed ass and violated cunt.

Al leaned back after a few moments, leaving the woman to continue without the benefit of his unacknowledged attention.

'Did that other one ever come back?' he asked.

Helene raised one eyebrow. 'She works for you,' she said.

'For me?' he repeated, and for the first time that day a twinge of sensation shot through his cock.

'Well, for Lou,' Helene told him. 'That's the same as working for you, isn't it?' She lit a cigarette and when she sucked in the smoke, she pulled it over the area of her aching tooth. 'Jack invited her. You know, Lou's salesman. And she's one of the copy editors in the office.'

Al cocked his head to one side. He was in an attitude of thought but what was going on in his mind was more like a form of pre-conceptual scheming.

'So, if you want her, ask Lou. I don't think she'll be coming back here. It was just a curiosity visit.'

'She was good,' Al said. 'Still fresh. And dirty. You know what I mean? Clean outside and dirty inside. She'd do anything, and hate it, and love it. She's a smut junky. Her head is filled with pictures, and she wants to act them out. And she's so prim and luscious.' He looked over at Helene. 'Can you imagine how lovely she would look with my cock in her mouth?'

Helene stifled her retort. It did not pay to be too blunt with Al. But she could not resist letting some air out of his balloon. 'I sat on her face,' Helene said, 'and her mouth didn't feel any different from any other mouth.'

'That's because you're only interested in the physical,' he told her. 'You don't understand about the imagination.'

In the next room the woman had pulled the dildo from her cunt and was licking it clean of her own secretions. She had shoved it into her throat and gagged violently. She was picturing herself, naked, open, a vile rubber cock in her mouth, being watched by she didn't know who or how many. And she intruded into her own imagery by asking herself why she was doing what she was doing. When Helene had put the proposition to her, an unmistakable twinge of forbidden pleasure had spanned her thighs. The whole notion of exhibiting herself and prostituting herself touched a vital chord inside her. And the fact that her husband wouldn't know, that this would be her secret, pushed her over the edge. She was a strikingly attractive woman, with red hair, breasts exactly the size of her cupped hands, deep thighs, sparse pubic hair, a large spongy cunt, and buttocks that curved a full hundred and eighty degrees. When she had married Jim, she had no idea of how sexy she was, and he had brought her out, little by little, and finally introduced her to swinging.

'Baby, you don't know how much it would turn me on to see another man's cock in your mouth,' he had told her.

And then he brought her to the orgy, where she had almost gone berserk at the glimpse of the seemingly infinite sexual panorama that opened before her. Of course, Al had spotted that. It was an old story. And he had pointed her out as the one for Helene to ask. In a rush of enthusiasm, the woman had said yes.

If anything troubled her now it was not that she was debasing herself too much, but that it wasn't enough. In the four days since the invitation, she had lived in a sea of fantasies. Her imagination became sore with attempting to picture what would be done to her, what she would be made to do. And she carried on a silent conversation with her husband in her mind. 'Want to see me with another cock in my mouth? Wait until you see me with three men in me at once. Wait until you see me with my tongue up another man's ass.'

But after arriving at Helene's, getting undressed, and performing for her hidden fan, she was becoming anxious. For there is just so much juice that can be derived from any sexual structure, and even lying spread-eagle with a giant dildo up one's cunt before the eyes of an anonymous lecher had its limitations as a source of excitement. Her worst fear was beginning to be realized – that she would let herself go to the farthest extremes of excess, and that nothing would happen.

'Her time's almost up,' Helene said. 'Do you want her?'

'I suppose I'll take her,' Al said.

Helene shook her head. 'Well for God's sake, Al, what do you want? The poor bitch is practically tearing her tendons as it is.'

'No,' he said in a voice, that for him, was loud, although it barely rose above conversational strength, 'it's not the physical part. You keep misunderstanding that. It's the look in their eyes. It's when they realize they are helpless, when they know they are lost – even though they aren't tied down, and no one is forcing them – when they discover that they weren't doing it just for money, but because they like it. They like to lie at my feet and see the contempt in my face, and then wriggle up and lap at my cock. It's not the sensation. I've had every conceivable sexual sensation, at least a thousand times each. I don't care about their bodies. I want to suck their souls.'

He got up heavily, walked over to the counter at the back of the room, and poured a cup of coffee from the pot that had been steaming on a small hotplate. He put in four teaspoons of sugar, sipped it, made a face, and sat down again.

'What's her name? The one that works for Lou?'

'Joan,' Helene told him. And then added, 'By the way, I hear Lou is on his way out.'

'That's right,' Al said.

'And Margaret is taking over?' Her tone contained a balance of surprise and envy. 'She must be very good.'

Al saw no reason to expose the sexual aspect of his arrangement with Margaret, so he pretended that Helene's last remark referred only to Margaret's editorial and business abilities.

'She'll do all right,' he said. 'She still has a few fancy ideas about dirty books, but she'll adjust. And maybe even give the place some class. Lou was getting tired. He wants to cash in and go enjoy himself in the sun. I'm half tempted to do the same thing.'

'So this girl Joan is now Margaret's property,' Helene said, not bothering to hide the cattiness in her voice. 'Do you think she'll let you have her?'

'I went to see an analyst once,' Al said in a seeming non sequitur. 'I lay on his couch every day for three weeks and then I got annoyed. I asked him to tell me, as succinctly as possible, what he saw in me. He told me, "You have such an extraordinarily low self-esteem that the only way you can feel decent is to watch someone else get lower than you are." It cost me almost two thousand dollars for that sentence, but it was worth it. Now I understand why I do what I do, and a couple of grand isn't too high a price for peace of mind.' He turned to face Helene and squinted at her through the smoke rising from his coffee. 'People who work for me do what I tell them,' he said, 'or else they no longer work for me.'

Helene heard the assertion of supremacy in his voice and she realized she had pushed just a little too hard. Changing the subject quickly, she asked, 'What do you want to do with her?' and pointed to the woman in the next room who was now lying face down on the rug, not moving.

Al gazed on the inert form. He had lost count of how

many thousands of naked women he had seen, and yet, the sight was always exciting, if it was a new woman each time. He had tried to pierce to the heart of what the attraction was, for it pulled him powerfully even when he wasn't horny. He looked at the body. Two legs, nicely tapered, but nothing extraordinary. Her back and arms and hair left him cold. Then his eyes went to her ass. And that was it, that was the source. There was something in the shape of a woman's ass that contained a profound secret. Yet it seemed simplicity itself. Two globes and the space separating them. There was no way to grasp what precisely held so much fascination that each new ass seized his will, as though it were the first one he had ever looked at.

'If a man could understand the ass,' he thought, 'all the mysteries of creation would become clear to him.'

He thought of Joan again and his cock stirred. He could picture her perfectly and was taken by a momentary ache to have her young body under him, her ass wrapped around his cock, as he split the twin orbs and sank himself into its depths. He shook his head. He didn't want to get fixated on Joan or on any woman. That was the road to defeat. And yet, now that he had remembered her so vividly, her image was stuck to his mind, like a fly on sticky paper. She was there bending over in front of him; and again, sitting on his face; and again, leaning over the edge of a bed.

Al pondered the woman who awaited his word. And thinking of the contrast between her lying there and how she probably went about her usual day, he was struck once more by the split between the dull agreement which defines social reality and the full potential that people are capable of. For, of course, sex was only one of the many ways in which human beings kept themselves from total expression and feeling. And if an average housewife could be seduced into becoming the ragged, lascivious creature this woman had just shown herself to be, then the possibilities for people to realize themselves in an infinite number of ways were staggering. And yet, the species continued to stumble about in a condition of sleep and slavery.

'Send her to the equipment room,' Al said.

Helene got up to go into the next room, but Al crooked his finger and motioned her to come stand in front of him. She sighed and walked over to the chair. He made a motion with his eyes and she lifted the front of her dress, revealing bare legs and the fact that she wore nothing underneath. Al reached forward and cupped her cunt with one hand, and slipped one finger between her pussy lips. Helene showed no expression. Al brought the finger to his nostril and inhaled deeply.

'Beautiful bouquet,' he said. 'Now get her ready for me.'

Helene dropped her dress down around her knees again and went into the basement. Al stood, stretched and went out another door into the adjoining room, which looked, at first glance, like a small gymnasium. But it was not like anything anyone would find at the YMCA. What seemed like massage tables were finely sculpted fuck slabs. A person could climb on one, and the table could be split apart, tilted, and bent in several dozen ways, so that the body on it might be presented in any attitude and position desirable. The exercise pulleys along one wall were actually free-swinging racks. A person could be tied and hung in any of a dozen ways, and weights hung from his or her body to attain certain specific effects.

Al was not interested in any of that today. Rather, he undressed and stood next to a wide, raised cot in the center of the room. Above him hung an intricate halter suspended from the ceiling. It was a variation on a device he had discovered in a Hong Kong whorehouse, where it was called The Chinese Basket Fuck.

A small door opened and Helene entered, leading the other woman, who had been blindfolded. Helene pushed the woman forward and then shoved her to her knees in front of Al. She seemed to vibrate somewhere between fear and wanton anticipation.

Al grabbed her hair and yanked her face up. her mouth fell open. 'You're a little slut, aren't you?' he said. 'Your husband opened you up, but he didn't know what was underneath, did he?' He pushed her face into his crotch. 'Suck that cock,' he ordered.

Her trembling mouth closed gently over his limp prick and her lips and tongue began to work it slowly.

'Doesn't matter to you whose cock it is, does it?' he went on. 'You'll suck any cock for money, and for the thrill of it. You like being a whore, don't you?'

Helene yawned discreetly. She had heard this litany many times. It astonished her how effective it was. For, as so many times in the past, the woman had begun to whimper and was cupping Al's balls with her fingers, sucking his cock, now almost hard, with urgent slurping sounds. Al was staring down at her; watching his cock disappear between her lips, and slide out wet and glistening.

'You don't suck your husband's cock like this, do

you?' he continued. 'You don't love it when it's respectable. What you want is to be an open mouth, a cocksucker for whoever wants you.'

In the woman's mind, however, were a different range of thoughts. She hoped that no photos were being taken, and planned what she would do with the seven-hundred and fifty dollars. Al's words wove in and out of her stream of thought, and when she heard them, they sent her off on brief flurry of clutched excitation. To be naked on her knees, blindfolded, sucking a strange man's cock while Helene looked on, and then to be told that she was a bought cunt, gave her some of the thrill she had hoped would result from this adventure.

Al motioned to Helene, and his cohort grabbed the woman's hair and pulled back, until her lips were only an eighth of an inch from Al's cock. Al leaned forward and graced her mouth with the tip of his cock, and the woman tried to reach forward to take it on her tongue. But Helene kept the pressure steady. They did that several times and then Al rasped, 'Reach for it, bitch, reach for it with your tongue.'

The game was then clear. She was to yearn for his cock, openmouthed and tongue curling, while Helene pulled her head back, and Al kept himself just out of range. Like any demonstration of the James-Lange hypothesis, the behavior gave rise to the concomitant feeling. And within a minute, the woman was actually straining to take the cock in her mouth, having been worked up into a somatic belief that she had to have it. She started to bleat, begging him to put his cock in her mouth.

A tired smile of satisfaction played across Al's mouth. He had vindicated himself again, and reduced a woman to her most basic responses. His feeling was not unlike that of a rat psychologist who has finally trained an animal to leap when a certain color is flashed. He pushed his pelvis forward, and his cock jumped into the woman's mouth. She gulped it voraciously, swallowed its entire length, spewed it out, swallowed it again, let it slide halfway out, and then kissed and sucked it with smacking sounds. Al let her suck his cock for several minutes, and then he made another gesture to Helene.

Helene pulled the woman away. Dragged back from the cock that was filling her, the woman protested, but Helene was too strong.

'You can have her for a while,' Al said.

Helene pushed the woman onto her back, and with a single motion squatted over her, tenting her torso and head with her dress. Under her dress, her cunt came down onto the woman's mouth. The woman gasped, but Helene only pressed down harder. Her pelvis rocking, Helene fucked the woman's mouth with her cunt, until she could feel the warmth beginning and the juices flowing. The woman started to lick the demanding pussy, and to suck its center. Helene rode her dispassionately until she felt her climax approach, and then closing her eyes, took her brief, small, neat orgasm, and let all the tension flow out of her legs. She stood up again.

'Put her in the straps,' Al said.

Helene guided the woman up and helped her climb into the halter that was hanging down from the ceiling. It was so constructed that the woman had to half lie in it, something like sinking into a hammock. Except that there was no bottom, and when she folded in the middle, her arms and legs extended, her buttocks hung down, exposed. Helene strapped her in tightly so that she was held in that position.

'Grease her up,' Al said.

Helene fetched a jar of Vaseline and, using two fingers, covered the crack between her buttocks and then inserted them into her vulnerable asshole. The woman, who had been told on her way to the room that she must not speak at all or not get paid, squirmed slightly. There was a kind of voluptuous pleasure which came from hanging down in such an inviting position, and then to have Helene's fingers penetrate her anus and thrash about gave the first real sensual glow she had had all day.

Al pressed a button next to the cot and the woman rose several feet in the air. Then Al lay on the cot beneath her, moved about until he had the proper position, and then pressed another button, lowering the woman down onto him. Her body descended until it was less than a foot away from Al's, and then he stopped its fall with the appropriate button. Helene came over and put her head between Al's thighs. She covered his cock with her mouth and sucked it slowly from its semi-erect state into hardness. When it had attained the necessary rigidity, Al pushed her head away, pressed the button, and watched the woman's ass come down on his cock. He took his cock with one hand until he had positioned it right at her asshole, and when the halter descended its full course, the woman was impaled, her ass split on Al's upright rod.

She let out a sigh of surprised delight. This was something utterly unique in her experience. She had been fucked in the ass before, but never like this, with the combined sensations of helplessness and weightlessness. She wished she could look in a mirror and see herself, suspended and sagging, covering her strange benefactor's cock with her hanging ass.

Al pressed yet another button a double motion began. The halter began to spin and to rise at a slow rate, an eighth of an inch for each revolution. The woman gasped audibly and Al let out a grunt of pleasure. She spun about effortlessly, the rotation making her slightly dizzy and causing her to glide more deeply into her feeling of disconnectedness. The sensations in her asshole were excruciatingly erotic. As she turned she was reamed out completely, the shaft of Al's cock a steady friction in her anus, while the head hit all the surfaces of the canal inside. And as she turned, she was lowered so that at each instant a different portion of her was being fucked. It went so slowly and so steadily that she could give in to it thoroughly. It was the single most delightful experience she had ever had.

After what seemed like an eternity, she stopped and hung there, rocking gently, her ass grasping the very tip of Al's cock. And then he pressed another button, and she started moving in the opposite direction, this time coming down instead of going up, so that each revolution meant a new level of penetration. She cried out in sheer anticipation of joy.

It was outrageous, insane. It went far beyond what she had ever considered when she thought of sex. It was so mechanical, so impersonal, so manipulative, that she should be turned off by it. And yet she couldn't get enough. It was free and abstract sensation, and she was totally won over by the experience.

Al glanced at Helene, indicating that he wanted her to take the controls, while he lay back, his eyes closed, and enjoyed his end of the episode. The woman's ass got hotter and hotter, looser and looser, and each ride up and down was like a lava flow on his cock. In his relaxed state he could lie there for a half hour before cumming, and by that time the woman would be screaming. She would be taken to the outermost limits of her capacity for excitation, and then kept there for a very long time. And she would try to get loose, which would only cause her body to rock back and forth on his cock, adding one more motion to the up and down and circular activities already going on.

Al lay back and went into deep relaxation, almost dozing off, as one woman swung in graceful and pirouettes above him, and the other handled the controls and buttons with the precision of an engineer at Cape Kennedy.

'It's extraordinary what money will buy,' he thought. He conjured up an image of the woman's husband. 'Probably knocks himself out taking care of her, worries about her, tries to please her sexually, thinks he can turn her into a swinger and still have her be somehow faithful to him.' Al was filled with scorn for the entire swinging scene. 'They're all phonies,' he had remarked more than once. 'Bored with marriage and too scared to step out of their emotional and financial bondage, they run around swapping and tell themselves that it makes their marriages stronger.'

He opened his eyes and looked at the body circling above him, the arms and legs swinging wide, the ass a steady blur.

'And for a couple of hundred bucks she's ready to do anything I tell her,' he mused.

[illegible]

[illegible]

[illegible]

[illegible]

[illegible]

[illegible]

TEN

'For he's a jolly good fellow, for he's a jolly good fellow, for he's a jolly good fellow, so say all of us . . .'

The voices had that mixture of slightly drunken sincerity and raucousness which characterizes the ambience at office parties. Lou stood behind his desk, his face flushed, a champagne glass in his hand, as the twenty or so people who were in one way or another involved with Centaur Publications sang their trite toast. The announcement of his departure had been made two weeks earlier, and the celebration to see him off had been organized by Margaret, who took the opportunity to use her executive muscles for the first time on her own. She had sent around a memo giving the date of the party, and had appended a note which informed everyone that changes in personnel would be forthcoming.

Thus, the people at Lou's farewell gathering were filled with a sense of relief, cut with a sliver of apprehension about their jobs.

It was late Friday afternoon. All work had been put aside, and the workers were giving themselves to alcohol and loose behaviour, indulging in a faint unconscious imitation of an orgy, that social function which had always served as the escape valve for the repressions of civilization at large. For most of them, it was an insignificant flurry in a monotonous routine. But for some, it marked a milestone.

Lou was looking back on over thirty years as a pornographer. Through his efforts there had been born some three thousand titles, ranging from the most sleazy and badly written potboilers to astonishing masterpieces of erotic fiction which, due to the nature of the culture in which they were spawned, ended with their covers torn off, being sold for small change in decayed book shops in the unofficial red light districts of a thousand American cities and towns. He had been responsible for films, for videotapes, for photographs, for drawings. He had staged hundreds of live sex shows, and served as caterer to very expensive, very private stag parties in the most respectable circles. And now, as he looked around the room, he had the same zest for uncovering the female body that he had had since he was a teenager and had learned that, for him, sex was the only thing worth pursing as a way of life.

He had put all his affairs in the hands of his lawyer: selling his co-op apartment, storing his collection of books and records and films and tapes until he had a new house to keep them in, and liquidating his assets, the stocks and bonds and financial holdings he had amassed during his long career. Lou was going to go to Puerto Rico with a clear mind, a fat bankroll and a small suitcase. He would drift until he found the exact spot he wanted, then buy land and build a house, and settle down to enjoying the virtues of the island and its inhabitants.

His glance fell on Alma, who stood in one corner, drinking quietly, watching the others the way people do when they feel themselves outside the general space. He let out a sigh of sexual appreciation that was the closest thing Lou Morris did to praying. A smoldering sensuality oozed from her very pores and it made him wilt just to contemplate actually having her body. Under her tight dress, every curve was caught in sharp outline. Her high firm breasts and full thighs sent signals to Lou's brain that were as commanding as the scream of sirens on a fire engine.

'Dark meat,' Lou thought, and closed his eyes, flipping out into an image of himself on a hot beach, surrounded by bikini-clad girls lying from horizon to horizon.

He opened his eyes, and when he did, he saw that Manuel had come up to stand next to the exotic woman. Manuel caught his glance and returned it in such a way as to let him know that he knew Lou had been panting over Alma, and that it was all right because she was his, and the most any other man would have of her was a wish to feel her body, a wish that would not be fulfilled.

The two men had met in the men's room of the office a week earlier. Manuel had returned to empty the mail room of his personal effects, and as he stood in front of the urinal, Lou had entered and taken the stand next to his. Following the unspoken ritual of that situation, each man had stared straight ahead and ignored the presence of the other, until Manuel had finished, zippered up and was washing his hands. Then Lou spoke.

'I hear you're going to Puerto Rico,' he said.

'That's right,' Manuel told him.

'Whereabouts on the island are you settling?' he asked.

'Don't know yet,' Manuel said.

'Well, I'm retiring there next month,' Lou went on, 'and I'm up in the air about which spot to try also.' He zippered his pants and stepped back, indicating that he wanted to use the sink but that Manuel could take his time.

'Maybe we ought to get together sometime and talk about it,' Lou continued.

Manuel turned around and looked directly at the other man. Now that Lou was no longer his employer, the young man felt a surge of directness flow through him. 'Well, I don't think we got that much to talk about,' he said. 'I mean, the boss and the mailboy ain't going to get adjoining beach houses.'

Lou, unaccountably, was stung by the rebuff.

'Well, you're not the mail boy anymore, and I'm not the boss. I guess we're just two men now.'

Manuel heard the conciliatory tone in the other's voice and modified his response. 'I suppose you didn't treat me any worse than you had to,' he said.

'We should stay in touch,' Lou told him. 'I don't have any friends on the island, and I'm sure you could tell me a lot about life there.'

'And what would you do for me?' Manuel asked, drying his hands on a paper towel.

'I don't know, Manuel,' he replied. 'I have money, and I have contacts. I might be useful to you in some way.' He stepped up to the sink as Manuel moved back. 'In any case, call me Lou. And come to the party. After all, we've shared the same space for almost a year. We're really probably more intimate than we imagine.'

'You mean that we have probably fucked the same woman,' Manuel said, stripping the euphemism of its cover.

'Probably,' Lou replied, glad, in an obscure way, to

have held his own in the exchange without the weight of his status to help him. Manuel had looked at Lou with different eyes then, for if Joan had been to bed with him, there must be something about him that was worth relating to. Also, there was an overtone, however faint, of the camaraderie felt by two men who have met through a woman's cunt.

Manuel had decided that, all things being equal, it would not be a bad idea to keep an open channel to Lou. In the depths of his street wisdom, he understood that a friendly acquaintance with a wealthy man was often as valuable as money in the bank. Besides, he had wanted to bring Alma to the office, to show her the faces and places that had figured in the stories he told her.

'Which one is Joan?' Alma now asked him.

Manuel pointed across the room to where Joan was engaged in conversation with an earnest young writer who wanted to discuss the plot of his next book. She was dressed modestly, with a wide skirt that came below her knees, a thick cotton blouse with a sweater over it. Her hair was rolled in a knot at the top of her head. She wore no makeup, and looked like an elementary school teacher in a Presbyterian town.

Alma evaluated her with her eyes. Manuel had, of course, told her of his long infatuation with the other woman, and had spilled the story of what had happened in her office the night he found her masturbating. But he had not revealed the happenings of the evening he went to her apartment, nor anything of the subsequent three days. Alma intuitively knew that there had been more, but was certain that it was finished. Now she was curious to get a feel of Joan, to find out what kind of woman could have such a hold on her man's mind. And she was able to perceive at once that beneath the plain exterior, Joan was a blind pit of passion.

'It's always like that with those nice types,' she thought. 'Take off their pretty clothes and they are nothing but hot holes underneath.'

Manuel followed the arrows of Alma's stare and looked at the woman who had almost owned his soul. His thought sped back to the previous week. After the phone had stopped ringing at Joan's apartment, she had told him that she was expected at Margaret's, and that the other woman might get worried and come over there.

'What are you doing with her?' Manuel asked.

'We're lovers,' Joan told him.

Some chord in his atavistic reserve of machismo was struck, and he was both crudely excited and repelled by the notion that the woman he had just fucked was having a lesbian affair.

'You want to see her?' he asked.

'Not tonight,' she replied. 'I just want to fuck you all night long.'

'Then let's get out of here,' he said.

He took her to a dingy hotel at the end of Christopher Street, over a gay bar, and they rented a five-dollar-a-night room with a view of the Hudson River through a window that hadn't been washed since the previous spring. In the following seventy-two hours they only left once, to stock up on food and cigarettes. The rest of the time was spent naked, on the bed.

The first night they didn't speak, but exhausted themselves trying, it seemed, to strain their bodies into each other, yearning for that oneness which can only be conceptual, but never actual. Yet, in the same way that God has been defined as the search for God, so union may be understood as the attempt to merge into a single organism. When he entered her the first time, his cock did not leave her cunt for four hours. They fucked so long, so steadily, that they fell into the same euphoric state that allows long-distance runners to move indefinitely.

It wasn't until late the next morning that they talked, smoking, watching boats chug by on the polluted river.

'I have a woman I love,' he said. 'Not like I love you. It is not so explosive. But it is rich. And we can make a good life together. We are much alike, she and I. And I don't want to leave her. Because you and me don't have enough to sustain us for a long time. You are a hot cunt, and an exciting ass, and I have never fucked with anyone like I fuck with you, not even with Alma. But I don't want to get crazy about it. You understand? I want to fuck you until I'm filled with you, and then I want to leave, and never see you again.'

To his relief and disappointment, she complemented his feelings. 'You are the first person who ever really touched me all the way inside,' she told him. 'What I feel with you I've been hungry for all my life. And if you tell me to stay with you and be your whore and work for you and clean for you and be ready for you to fuck whenever you want me, I'll do it. Because I'm a slave to what you do to me. But deep inside me I understand that it's not you. It's the feeling you give me. And one day I'll have enough of that feeling, and then I'll hate you, and want to kill you.'

They spoke with that maturity often aroused by

moments of deep surrender to another. As a wise man once noted, 'Although there will always be a bell curve of distribution so far as enlightenment is concerned, with a few people who have realized themselves at one end, and a few who haven't the foggiest clue at the other, and the rest of us knocking around in the middle, we can all come to know the truth through communion; for in communion, everyone is enlightened.'

And so they talked and ate and drank beer and smoked and fucked, and the entire universe was reduced to their single room, and their brief space and time allowed. As Manuel watched Joan at the party, he could not believe that the almost prissy woman talking so seriously was the same as the wild animal who had flung herself at him with such fury. The entire experience had been a single dance without parts, and the scores of positions and changes they had been through were not so much separate actions as aspects of a single expression. He saw her again with her clothes off, back in the tiny dark room with flaking green paint and a gurgling sink. He remembered sitting at the foot of the bed, nodding out from his third orgasm in four hours. Joan lay before him, and he looked up the curves of her parted legs and into her cunt, that powerful organ of feeling which had attained an intelligence of its own, and spoken to him in languages not conceived of in any written lexicon. Her hands were gently stroking the outer lips, pulling them apart, her fingers caressing her clitoris, and occasionally down into the tiny opening itself, and half disappearing into the cave behind.

'Oh Manuel,' she was saying, 'I feel so sexy, so cunty. Everything else has fallen away, my job, my apartment, my friends, even my name. I'm just this body now, just this moment now. All my flesh is tingling with your touch. I feel your hands and tongue and chest and thighs all over me. And I feel your cock. Your gorgeous enormous cock.'

She ran her hands down between her buttocks, which pressed into the sheet, and over her hips and up the space between her thighs and her cunt, and onto her belly, and over her breasts, flattening them and rubbing her nipples with her palms.

'Your cunt has made love to my mouth and to my cunt and to my ass. Your delicious cum is like oil on my skin and honey on my tongue. I'll do anything for you now, Manuel. I am all open and flowing, my sweet. I am a flower filled with juice and you can enter me and drink deep, darling, drink deep.'

Despite his tiredness, Manuel had been roused yet another time and, with a moan, buried his head between her legs, his mouth gluing itself to her cunt, his nostrils filled with the intoxicating smell of her pussy. He licked her like a man would drink water after days in the desert. He sucked her as though the elixir of life flowed from her loins.

And she had cried out, 'Oh baby, I can't give you enough, I can't take you enough. It's too much, all too much.' And burst into loud sobs as he snaked up her body and plunged his cock once more into her hot wet center.

But they had reached the limitation they knew they would. Simple fatigue took its toll and, by the third night, they felt nothing more than the sour taste of over-exhaustion. They were caked with secretions and numb from nicotine. The rust-lined tub in the hallway outside the room mocked any notion of bathing. And at their ebb, they decided to leave, he to his place and on to Alma's, and she back to her apartment.

'This is going to hurt a lot later on,' she said. 'When the reaction has set in and passed on, and I begin to digest everything we did and felt. I'm going to ache for you and want you so badly I won't be able to stand it.'

'I'll be two thousand miles away,' he told her.

'Being consoled by Alma,' she added.

'That's what that's all about,' he said. And putting on his pants had added. 'You don't have to be at a loss for company.'

She had not moved.

'Aren't you going to get dressed?' he asked.

'You leave first,' she said.

He began to protest, for no good reason he could name, but she cut him short. 'Just go,' she said, 'or we'll start saying hateful things to each other.'

The memory had flooded his mind, and it took a few seconds before he felt the pressure of Alma's hand in his. He looked down at her.

'Can we go now?' she asked.

He looked at her for a few seconds, brought himself back to the present. The woman at his side was scintillatingly attractive, dark and hard, bright and soft, all at the same time. And with her, there were no hidden traps, no ragged edges to tear him apart. She felt him ascending from his reverie, which she knew involved Joan, and returning to her. They smiled at each other, and their connection clicked again. They could feel the warmth surging back.

After his trip with Joan, he had gone to his apartment,

slept for fourteen hours, cleaned up, and walked to Alma's place. He was apprehensive about what she would say. But, at her door, she had not known any trace of emotion.

'You disappeared,' she said.

'I had one last bit of business to clear up,' he told her.

'Are you all clear now?' she asked.

'There's just us, now,' he said.

Alma had not asked anything more of him, and that afternoon he had moved into her apartment, and they began making plans to leave the city. Now, he squeezed her hand.

'Five minutes,' he said.

'I'll meet you in the hallway,' she told him.

She went out into the foyer and through the door that led to the elevators. As she walked, more than one pair of eyes followed her. Most of the men were acting out of reflex, watching her ass as it moved the way a cat will idly stare at flickering shadows on a wall; and the women looked with more narrow gazes, their eyes reflecting something faintly akin to the kind of shrewdness they manifest when shopping for clothes, a feeling somewhere between critical intelligence and the fear born of suspicion that one is being cheated.

Joan watched also. But her images were more specific. She saw Manuel's body covering hers. 'She'll be lying under him tonight,' she thought. 'She will be kissing him and taking him inside her. And I wonder whether he will be thinking of me.'

Manuel walked up to her, stepping into her trance, supplanting her vision of him with his actual presence.

The writer who had been talking to her fell suddenly silent, for at once her attention was riveted on Manuel.

'We are leaving,' he said.

She looked into his eyes, and for a long heartbeat they plunged into each other's souls. They exchanged communications too compact, too deep, too complex, for words. They stared at each other in silence. And then, as with all true tragedies, they experienced the real horror of their situation not in the pain of separation, but in order to separate they had to pull masks over their naked faces, over the faces that throbbed with feeling, and become once more the copy editor and the mail room boy.

'I . . . hope you enjoy . . . Puerto Rico,' she said.

Another few seconds and she would begin to weep, and dislike herself for crying, since the rational part of her had convinced her emotions that it had decided what was best over the long haul and would punish her for any excess sentiment.

'Adios,' he whispered, and turned violently on his heel and strode from the room.

As he reached the door, he caught Lou's eye. They nodded briefly to each other. They had an appointment for lunch the next afternoon. An odd and totally unexpected bond was springing up between them. They would have an oblique commonality once they reached the island.

Manuel sped past, past the hollow goodbyes of people he had worked with for a year, and with each step, a sense of the curtain's closing behind him sent shivers up his spine. And when he finally reached the spot where Alma stood, he put one arm around her and hugged her to him.

She leaned into him, and sent her heat into his body, her breasts giving him tactile promise of the succor she would offer him later that day, and through many days and months and years to come. She slipped one hand into his.

'Let's go now,' she said.

The young writer who had been talking to Joan, perplexed at having witnessed something he didn't understand, stood frowning, wanting to get her attention again. But she was staring into space, unmindful of everything that went on around her. She felt as though a bandage had been rudely ripped from her heart, and while the wound was on its way to being healed, the pain of the cut and the sudden harsh exposure to the air were fierce. She was breathing rapidly and shallowly, very alert, very alive, very beautiful in her terrible desertion.

Margaret stroked her arm.

Joan turned, startled at the touch.

'Why don't you come into my office,' she said. And then amended, 'Your office, after today.'

Joan nodded and let herself be led. Margaret walked with her through the crowd, which had swelled to its noisiest and most chaotic level. She smiled and bobbed her head in purely mechanical actions that passed for social intercourse, impatient with the forced jolliness of the occasion, but knowing that nothing was to be gained by not acceding to the structure of the event. She, like everyone else there, was trapped in a social convention that none of them cared for or found meaningful in any way whatsoever.

When she shut the door behind them, the sounds diminished by half.

'Some party,' Margaret said.

Joan stood in the middle of the room looking as though she were trying to remember something both trivial and specific. Her mind had recoiled from the goodbyes with Manuel, and she was finding ways of putting distance between herself and the fact that she would probably never see him again.

Margaret went to her desk, reached into a drawer, pulled out a pint of brandy, and poured two large drinks into two paper cups that had held champagne. She took one over to Joan, put it in her hand, and then led the girl to the couch. They sat down and sipped at their drinks for a while.

'It hurts,' Margaret said, voicing what she sensed Joan was feeling.

Joan shook her head. 'I'm numb,' she said. 'And my common sense tells me it's for the best. I just need to assimilate it all.'

Margaret closed her eyes in silence. She had her own difficulties in accepting Joan's feelings, and the reason for those feelings, without jealousy. She took a long deep breath and centered herself in calm.

Joan had, as Jack had predicted, just walked into the office one day. Margaret had already begun to think she might not return, and was considering calling her, when the copy editor walked up to the desk and said, 'Do I still have a job here?' Margaret had thought for one wild moment that Jack had given her the line to say.

There had been no hesitation. The moment she saw Joan, Margaret's heart melted, and in a flash she knew that without her having even been aware of the process, she had begun to love her. The doubts, the thoughts, evaporated, and Margaret had done nothing more than to take Joan in her arms and embrace her gently.

That night they went to Margaret's apartment. Joan poured out the whole story of what had happened with Manuel. And had ended it by saying, 'I belong to him. I mean, if he wants me, ever, there is a place inside me he can reach, and hold, and I will open to him. And it goes deeper than anything I can rationalize, and has nothing to do with my other feelings for him or about him. And it has nothing to do with my loving anyone else. Can you understand that?'

Margaret, who had touched the edges of that experience with Jack a few nights earlier, understood perfectly.

'I suppose on some level, a man and a woman fit together in a way that goes beyond our control. And when the right man and woman meet, the key goes into the lock and opens it. And it's as inexorable as any other law of nature.

'And I will probably never see him again,' Joan said.

'You're getting your first big lesson in the ways of destiny a little earlier than you may have expected, that's all,' Margaret said. 'I wish I could comfort you, but I can't. I would be lying if I tried.'

'But what about us?' Joan asked.

'I think I love you,' Margaret told her. 'And that means it doesn't matter why you are who you are. I accept you.' And she quoted the lines from Poe's ultimate expression of love: 'I know not, I ask not, if guilt's in that heart; I but know that I love thee, whatever thou art.'

They had gone to bed then, and Joan was frightened to try. After what she had known with Manuel, she wasn't sure whether she could feel anything with Margaret. It would hurt the other woman if she didn't, and she couldn't pretend. Joan had returned for no good reason she could define. But the day after her final night with Manuel, her feet just took her to the office, and when she saw Margaret, she knew she wanted only to be taken in by the older woman. She could not call what she felt love or even desire; it was a kind of mute instinct that shaped her behavior beyond her immediate understanding.

As Joan now sat in her office, sipping the brandy, staring into space, Margaret thought of what it had been like to make love to her that night. The room was suffused with the soft light of candles and the flames in the fireplace. Everything was orange and yellow, and low winged piano music fell from the stereo speakers onto the charged air. They walked to the bed as though they were clouds, wafting through space, not aware of any hard surface or extraneous realities. They had gone to extremes, each in her own way with another and then with each other. They had inadvertently tested themselves and found that, without plan, they were deeply intertwined. Had they bothered to think about it at all, they might have considered that they each sought refuge from the failure of having formed a union with a man; but then, one might also think that their seeming inability to merge with a man was due to their more profound desire to remain free for each other.

But for them, there were no thoughts, merely the exaltation of their condition, making it sacred through a ritual of flesh.

Margaret took Joan to the bed and laid her down. The

girl was suffused with a beauty so piercing that Margaret had trouble catching her breath. What she had been through with Manuel had purified her, made her lean, burned the excess from her soul, and in the wake of that, her body shone with a distinct light. Joan was trembling from head to foot, a light quivering that signaled willing helplessness before the event. She felt like a virgin. The patina of sophisticated sexuality was not present, and she now remained exposed to the sweet urgings of her most tender desires . . . to be held so lightly, to be stroked so softly, to be entered so delicately.

And Margaret was not only able, but enraptured, to give her all that. She peeled the clothing from Joan's body slowly, kissing each part of her as it was exposed, licking her arms, the insides of her elbows, her shoulders. She raised Joan's skirt and unhooked it, and for a moment feasted her eyes on the girl's long legs, white and vulnerable against the bedspread, joining in a tangle of hair that was covered by the thinnest of fabrics. Margaret removed Joan's panties, pulling them down her thighs, over her knees, past her calves, off her feet, and then began to look over the places she had passed, sucking the other woman's toes, lapping the soles of her feet, gently biting her calves, running her tongue up the inside of her thighs.

Joan did not move, but let herself tingle with the mounting sense of surrender. She moaned softly and continuously, her lips pursed, and said, 'Oh, oh, oh,' again and again as wave after wave of sensual realization broke over her.

Margaret continued removing clothing, unbuttoning Joan's blouse, exposing her naked breasts. Margaret kissed the mounds unceasingly, taking the nipples between her teeth and flicking them with her tongue. She sucked the breasts into her mouth one at a time, and held each one inside her, flooding it with warmth, smothering it in sensation.

Joan did not move. Margaret was a fluttering moth on her skin. It was so different from what it had been with Manuel, utterly different. And that is how she was able to respond. For if Margaret had raised the slightest ghost of the man Joan had just been ravished by, they could not have continued. But Manuel did not even come into account, for what was happening was taking place in a totally *other* realm. Joan's trembling increased until she was shaking visibly, and she raised her arms to embrace Margaret lightly.

Margaret slid up until the two women were face to face. She had her left arm under Joan's back and with her right hand was stroking the length of her, going from her thighs, brushing her cunt, sweeping over her belly, cupping her breasts, and coming to rest on her lips. Joan kissed Margaret's fingers with breathy, curled kisses, and when Margaret's hand moved down again, Joan's mouth went on kissing the air, making her face a pool of exquisite expressions in which Margaret could see reflected her own ideal beauty.

Joan opened her eyes and woman looked at woman, soul mirrored soul, and that thing took place which was beyond what happens between man and woman, so far removed from the other that no comparison is possible. And then Joan surrendered, for she saw that there was no conflict, that what she and Margaret knew together could never be touched by what either of them did with any man, that they were safe within their mutual awareness, shielded forever from all external harm. And like all who glimpse what it is to be a lover, they understood that it would always be like this if they were faithful to their highest insight into their relationship, if they continued to honor their love by not attempting to make it into something it was not.

'Oh yes, my darling, my love,' Joan said. 'Now, I want you, now.'

Margaret kissed her again, sucking Joan's lips passionately with her mouth, and held her tightly and fingered her cunt, then took her own clothes off, and the two of them nestled into each other, mouth to cunt and cunt to mouth, and completed the circle of energy that demonstrated, more than any theoretical argument, that Woman is One. And with that, they passed into a realm that cannot be understood by anyone who has not known what they knew that night, that to blend in sexual union with one's own sex is the indispensable complement to all other sexual awareness.

In the office, Joan finished her brandy, put the cup down, and leaned back on the couch.

'Do you want to spend the weekend at my place?' Margaret said.

Joan inclined her head and looked down at the floor.

'Monday begins a whole new world here. And we might not have another chance to relax for a while.'

Joan held out one hand and Margaret took it between both of hers. It was the answer to her question. Margaret grew warm as she was struck again, as she was more and more often, that sex was only the expression of something much deeper that was going on between them.

As they sat, silent, holding on to the awareness of their feeling for each other, there was a knock at the door.

Margaret leaned forward, sitting erect on the edge of the couch.

'Come in,' she said.

The door opened and revealed Lou and Jack standing in the hallway, the salesman slightly behind the other man, and both of them diffident about entering. It was the first time either woman had seen Lou sensitive to the vibrations of anything that was happening in one of the office rooms.

Margaret raised one eyebrow as she looked at them. 'Well?' she said.

'Can I come in?' Lou asked. And as he spoke he walked into the room, Jack following behind.

'Lou came to say goodbye,' Jack said as he spied the brandy bottle on the desk and made for it.

Lou walked to the middle of the room and stood facing the two women. He had his hands clasped at his chest and he was rocking slightly on his heels. He was feeling the impact of his departure, coming to understand it as an indicator of his age, that he was truly getting older, closer to the fatigue that beckons to death, and that a new generation was filling in behind him and would obliterate all his traces. The realization made him sentimental.

'So,' he said. 'I guess it's time to get my ass out of here and leave all the headaches to you.'

Margaret stood up. She and her former boss shared a long moment within which they allowed each other to die. It was painful, but there can be no birth without pain.

'Goodbye, Lou,' she said softly.

Lou nodded, and then looked over at Joan. The copy editor was watching the scenario with slightly glazed eyes. Her face open, her body relaxed on the couch, her tumultuous feelings swarming through her expression, she seemed no older than sixteen. Lou felt a paternal pang, which, for him, was almost indistinguishable from a carnal spasm. He recalled all the times she had come to his apartment, and the things they did together, and it all seemed remote, a surreal sexuality that was the manifestation of a kind of unconsciousness, a working out of deep chaotic urges, a series of impersonal unions that was redeemed by the tenderness with which they had treated each other.

Looking at her now, so vulnerable and young, he thought, 'Can this be the woman that sucked my cock and let me fuck her in the ass?'

The room was momentarily locked into a frieze, as the four people were tripped into a psychic communion that transcended all social definition.

Joan seemed to snap out of her trance, and she got up from the couch, walked over to Lou, and kissed him on the cheek.

'Goodbye, Lou,' she said.

He put his arms around her and looked into her eyes, and then said, 'If you need me, you'll know where I am. Maybe you'll want a vacation in the sun sometime. And when you visit, I'll show you some interesting movies.'

She blinked. 'Oh, you still have those,' she said, and as she formed the words wondered how she could have forgotten about what once would have seemed so terrible, that somewhere in the world there would be pictures of her being seen by strangers, pictures which showed her in the most lewd actions possible.

'I've passed into history,' she thought.

Lou disengaged and stepped back. 'You should all come visit,' he added. And each of the three people who heard him caught the obliquely humorous implication, for they had all been captured, one way or another, by Lou's camera. There was even some footage of Jack, tied naked to a post, while a fat woman who stood more than six feet tall whipped him vigorously.

'Goodbye, Maggie,' Lou said, and Margaret walked over and embraced him. He held her slim body against his, hugged her once, and then stepped back.

'Well, what is there left to say?' he told her. 'You'll learn as you go along and you'll do the best you can.'

'I hope so, Lou,' she told him.

'And you'll be careful with Al,' he added. 'He's a cunning man. And he really has no concern about hurting anybody. I mean, he'll run over you and not even notice.' And, without changing his tone of voice, went on, 'And he'll hurt you in ways you might not even imagine. He has an instinct for people's blind spots and vulnerabilities.'

Jack stepped forward from the desk where he had been sipping brandy and watching the entire interaction.

'Stop, Lou,' he said, 'you'll scare them.'

Lou smiled. 'OK,' he replied. 'You be the hero. Make sure they don't get shit on.'

Margaret shook her head. 'For God's sake, Lou, we're not children. You think just because we're women we don't know how to take care of ourselves?'

And they were a fraction of an inch from launching

into a spirited and heated argument, a thing that had formed one of their favorite activities. They realized it at once, and both burst out laughing.

'All right, all right,' he said, 'I'll go.'

And standing a few seconds longer, awkwardly, Lou dropped his gaze to the floor, and then, quickly and surprisingly, walked out of the office.

He went straight through to the elevator, rode down, came out of the building onto the street, scraped his shoes several times on the sidewalk, a subconscious gesture which was transformed into a symbol, and set off down Madison Avenue, his walk jaunty, whistling to himself.

Jack, who had poured himself another drink, turned to the two women.

'Well, here we are,' he said.

'This is who's left,' Margaret said.

'And the ones outside?' Jack asked, pointing his head in the direction of the party.

'There are a few who are necessary. The rest can be replaced.' She walked behind the desk. 'I'll make a list over the weekend, and we can have a meeting on Monday. I'll give notices then.'

Jack nodded.

He glanced out the window and then back to Margaret. 'And what about Al?' he asked.

'What about automobile accidents?' she replied. 'Life is filled with unpleasant realities. We'll deal with him as best we can, and if he makes it impossible, we'll . . .' she caught the use of the plural pronoun, realized that she was assuming too much, and went on, 'I'll leave.'

Jack perceived the shift and supported her original

articulation. 'I don't think that Joan and I will stay on if Al forces you to leave.'

'Can't we begin our own publishing house?' Joan asked.

Her voice had regained its usual timbre. She was slowly climbing out of her state of shock, and would lapse into it from time to time, but with less frequency and severity, until the whole thing with Manuel became a distant reverie.

Jack and Margaret began to exchange amused glances, to comment on the girl's business naivete, but something arrested them, and the expression became interestingly serious.

'That actually might be possible,' Jack admitted, already thinking of whom he would see for backing.

'Well, so much for Al Leeds,' Margaret said. 'If he fucks with us, we leave him his office building and take up somewhere else.'

Jack stood silently a moment and then, putting his cup down, said, 'Well, I guess I'll get on back to my apartment.' And then, catching the eyes of both Joan and Margaret at once, added, 'Unless you two want to invite me to your place.'

Margaret and Joan looked at each other. They smiled, a brief warm exchange, a glint of excited complicity passing between them.

'Too much work to be done,' Margaret said.

'Looks more like a honeymoon to me,' he told her.

'That too,' Joan replied, and she and Margaret put their arms around each other's waists.

Jack walked over to them and put his arms around their shoulders, and the three of them snuggled in together, feeling the warmth created in the central space between their bodies.

'We'll get to it,' Margaret said.

'I know,' Jack replied.

'It really feels good in here,' Joan said, 'All of a sudden, it feels good.'

'It's your office,' Margaret told her, 'so how should you feel except right at home?'

The three of them enjoyed the first few minutes of their new working and life arrangement, having arrived, after a long string of interconnecting permutations and combinations, at a synthesis in which, for the first time, they had no hidden bits of information anywhere in the triangle. Their business interests and their life involvements were free to interpenetrate.

While, outside, the writer who had been talking to Joan had become progressively drunker, and having no one to talk to, had lapsed into a fantasy which, as it became clear he would leave the party alone, was tinged with bitterness.

'I'll bet these people never have sex,' he said to himself. 'Probably sublimate it all into their pornography.' He was disgruntled enough to accept a logic which, were it presented to him when he was feeling intellectually righteous, he would have demolished.

He poured himself another glass of champagne, consoling himself for his inability to score with Joan, whose sexual potential he was able to discern beneath the plain exterior she was affecting. And, to restore his sense of self, he began to plot a novel which would be set in a pornographic publishing house, and would feature a prim secretary who, when she took her clothes off, became a wanton slut.

'He slipped his fingers in her cunt,' he wrote in his mind as the opening line, and tripped into an orgy of images in which he took revenge on all the women in his life who would not fuck him or listen to his ideas, and paradoxically, elevated them into archetypal sex goddesses whose raw beauty and power always reduced him to tears of wonder.

And as his cock began to stir in response to the pictures flooding his brain, he put down his glass and walked unsteadily to one of the desks at the far end of the room, where there sat, gleaming with cold erotic vibrations, his truest love, the typewriter.

He sjipped hix gingers in her nunt, he wrote, drunkenly, but with thundering finality and passion.

More Erotic Fiction from Headline:

EROS IN THE FAR EAST

Anonymous

Recuperating from a dampening experience at the hands of one of London's most demanding ladies, the ever-dauntless Andy resolves to titil.ate his palate with foreign pleasures: namely a return passage to Siam. After a riotously libidinous ocean crossing, he finds himself in southern Africa, sampling a warm welcome from its delightfully unabashed natives.

Meanwhile, herself escaping an unsavoury encounter in the English lakes, his lovely cousin Sophia sets sail for Panama and thence to the intriguing islands of Hawaii – and a series of bizarrely erotic tribal initiations which challenge the limits of even her sensuous imagination!

After a string of energetically abandoned frolics, Andy and Sophia fetch up in the stately city of Singapore, a city which holds all the dangerously piquant pleasures of the mysterious East, and an adventure more outrageous than any our plucky pair have yet encountered. . .

Follow Andy and Sophia's other erotic exploits:
EROS IN THE COUNTRY EROS IN TOWN
EROS IN THE NEW WORLD EROS ON THE GRAND TOUR

FICTION/EROTICA 0 7472 3449 3

More Erotica from Headline:

Lena's Story

Anonymous

The Adventures of a Parisian Queen of the Night

Irene was once a dutiful wife. Until, forsaking the protection of her husband, she embarked on a career as a sensuous woman: Lena, the most sought-after mistress in *fin de siècle* Paris. Yet despite the luxury, the champagne and the lavish attentions of her lovers, Lena feels her life is incomplete. She still longs for the one love that can satisfy her, the erotic pinnacle of a life of unbridled pleasure . . .

FICTION/EROTICA 0 7472 3334 9